THE CIVILISATION GAME

and other stories

*Further collections edited by Francis Lyall
and published by Severn House*

Clifford D. Simak

THE MARATHON PHOTOGRAPH
BROTHER
THE CREATOR

James Blish

A WORK OF ART
A DUSK OF IDOLS

THE CIVILISATION GAME

GAME

and other stories

Clifford D. Simak
Edited by Francis Lyall

This first world edition published in Great Britain 1997 by
SEVERN HOUSE PUBLISHERS LTD of
9–15 High Street, Sutton, Surrey SM1 1DF.
This title first published in the USA 1997 by
SEVERN HOUSE PUBLISHERS INC., of
595 Madison Avenue, New York, NY 10022.

British Library Cataloguing in Publication Data

Simak, Clifford D. (Clifford Donald), 1904-1988
        The civilisation game and other stories
        1.   Short stories, American
        1.   Title II. Lyall, Francis
        813.5'4 [F]

        ISBN 0-7278-5169-1

Typeset by Palimpsest Book Production Limited,
Polmont, Stirlingshire, Scotland.
Printed and bound in Great Britain by
Creative Print and Design Ltd, Ebbw Vale, Wales.

Contents

Introduction

This is the seventh collection of Clifford Simak's stories I have edited. The choice and arrangement of previous collections worked on a variety of bases. The first, *The Marathon Photograph* (1986), was a collection of 1970s and 80s stories that had not been brought together in book form. Other collections were assembled round themes: *Brother* (1987), *Off-Planet* (1988), *The Autumn Land* (1990), *Immigrant* (1991), *The Creator* (1993). This collection has been assembled mainly to show Cliff's early use of ideas that fascinated him, and, with one exception, bring together stories which have been unavailable save to the dedicated collector of the pulps since they were published. Even the exception is not fully an exception, for 'The Big Front Yard' has not been published in a UK Simak collection.

Clifford Donald Simak was a newspaperman in Minneapolis through much of his long life (1904–1988). By origin, however, he was a country boy, growing up on a farm in south-west Wisconsin, east of Highway 18/35 on top of the bluffs, above the last three or four miles of the Wisconsin River and looking over to Prairie du Chien. The farm lies in Millville township. His mother's family had been in those parts for some years. His father was a refugee from Prague.

That rural, pleasant land became a golden place in Cliff's imagination. He knew it well. Cliff and his brother Carson would gallop cross-country to school in Patch Grove, some two/three miles south of their farm, leaving their horses in a field during school hours. The whole area is full of small valleys dropping down to the Wisconsin and Mississippi rivers, and affording astonishing vistas. These valleys contain isolated farms and houses and occasional small communities. From visits, my own abiding impression is of an old, wide, unspoiled country with fascinating pockets of human life. No wonder it struck deep in CDS's imagination. It provides the locales and basic attitudes that suffuse his fiction, setting patterns that return time and again in CDS stories. The motifs recur, but always with a freshness and an attractiveness rarely found in science fiction, either now or in CDS's heyday. In many authors the reworking of theme, place and character is jaw-breakingly boring. In CDS it is a welcome return of friends.

CDS is not wholly unique in sf in his affection for the country life, but those who tread similar paths are few. Zenna Henderson comes to mind, though on a less prolific scale, and I cannot think of a current author who similarly sets their stories in the countryside. As Isaac Asimov once pointed out to me, in general science fiction is an urban or a technological fiction, farms and landscape existing only to be passed through on the way from one city to another. CDS shows that sf themes can prosper in a rural setting, albeit that setting is idealised. Not for nothing has he been dubbed 'the pastoral poet of SF'.

In Simak, then, we are often in the countryside, and more particularly in small-township (not small-town) mid-West America. There is a gentleness, and yet a recognition of the realities of humanity here. Take 'Horrible Example'. The protagonist, Tobias, turns out to be another of CDS's intriguing line of robots that runs from Jenkins of *City* to Hezekiah and Cardinal Theodosius, of *Project Pope*. Many of the Simak robots have such dignified names, often biblical in origin. Elijah of the Moore household in 'The Civilisation Game' is another example. Indeed Pertwee of that story is one of the few exceptions to the general rule of a biblical cognomen.

No matter, in 'Horrible Example' Tobias lives in yet another Simak fictional Millville, with its Baptist Church at Third and Oak, with its Happy Hollow Tavern, and with Mrs Frobisher, President of the Ladies Aid Society, comfortable on the corner of Third and Maple. Tobias is the statutory civic bum, providing an object of scorn and concern that somehow is necessary for the moral health of community. In an upside-down way, along with his human colleague, the janitor, he is a social worker. He does the job well. But when in obedience to a higher law he has to act out of character, he is withdrawn, and, rather than demotion for failure, there is the reward of a different assignment. But what do we make of the replacement? And what of the suggestion implicit in the story that societies are, or should be manipulated, for the best of all possible reasons, of course. Such manipulation is a minor but frequent theme within CDS's works.

The point crops up again in 'The Civilisation Game'. Reading it, like Paxton, I have brief flashes of memory – in my case memories of driving round and about in the bluff country of Millville township. Sometimes I reckon I could find my way to the Moore house, 'an old and rambling affair among great clumps of trees', 'set in a swale between two hillocks'; on second thoughts, perhaps not. In any event, the last time I was there my first choice for the original of the Moore house had burned down. But then mystery swirls. What has Paxton been elected President of? What is 'Project Continuation'? And Politics? And Diplomacy? Then things become clearer.

The whole is an analogue of the modern gene-banks run by botanists or zoologists, set up to preserve certain basic human elements as the galactic civilisation changes the broad lines of human society. But the Project has become more accurate than Paxton perhaps wants, especially once the bishop arrives. And so the story continues to surprise even to its end, with its foreshadowing of modern war gaming. But more serious than our play, what is the function of war, and will we or should we be allowed to retain it as a game? Perhaps. But the real message is in the last few words of the story, which strike me with added force, writing these words in the mid-1990s, with the horrors of Rwanda, Bosnia and elsewhere. Would we better off managed by a Pertwee figure?

Other stories in this collection are older, but intrigue as containing early intimations of later concerns, and characters. They also involve aliens. Cliff was good at aliens, and here some of his seed notions are to be found. They go from the Candles

3

of 'Masquerade' to the rocking-horse-saddled dickerers of 'The Big Front Yard'.

'Hermit of Mars' was published in *Astounding Science-Fiction* in June 1939. It is part of the surge of CDS's story-telling triggered when John W. Campbell took over as editor at *Astounding*, and Cliff, having previously given up on the SF editors, decided to try SF again. 'Hermit' is unusual for its time. True, its Martian data is now largely falsified – there is no sign of life on Mars. There are no Martian beavers to be hunted, nor Eaters, nor Hounds. There is no canal system to be explored by latter-day trappers clearly modelled on the North American species who first explored Simak country in the eighteenth century and whose history Cliff knew well. Nor has our present exploring found anything precisely like the valley/cleft that is the Mad-Man's Canal although some of the features revealed by Mars photography are startling clefts and chasms. But there are other elements, true then as now – the red terrain, binding so much oxygen which some now dream of unlocking through terra-forming techniques.

The two scientists are typical characters of the time. The names are, however, unexpected. 'John Smith' is traditionally the name for archetypical anonymity (swift apologies to the John Smith who is my wife's cousin). Why should Cliff have selected such a name? And Howard Carter is an extraordinary choice, given the fame of the Egyptian archaeologist of the 1930s. No matter: these are not the worker-members of some antheap of modern science but rather the omnicompetent scientists of early SF. They design and conduct their own experiments and research. Carter is capable of piloting his personal rocketship down into the ravine. The ravine itself is reminiscent of C. S. Lewis's in *Out of the Silent Planet*. The Ghosts recall Ray Bradbury's *The Fire Balloons* in their detachment, and I would note that Bradbury has spoken with affection of Cliff's influence on him. The notion of detached superior beings is something that Cliff comes back to in other stories, particularly in the occasional Guardians and Observers that appear here and there in his novels. And the notion of Carter's going on into 'ghost-hood', if I can put it

4

like that, hints at deeper thoughts that were later to recur in more mature CDS tales.

The Candles of 'Masquerade' are an intriguing reworking of the shape-changer alien, more bitterly explored in John W. Campbell's *Who Goes There?* (1938, filmed as *The Thing*, 1951, 1983). There is a good humour about the CDS variant that pleases, although there is also an element of menace and the point that Man as an immature race could be a threat to higher beings who have bypassed many of our problems.

'Hunch' is a many-layered story. Its starting point is that modern civilisation is so complex that we do not have sufficient persons of the intellectual calibre to cope with running it. That is, of course, a real question, more pressing, perhaps, than when Cliff wrote the story 50 years ago – just look around you, and reread this story. It is a question that has worried others also: compare Cyril Kornbluth's *The Marching Morons*. Allen makes the point quite clear. Under pressure men are going catatonic. Those who break down seem to be cured at a new Sanctuary, which has been created out in the Asteroids. But what is the Sanctuary? The blind Chambers with his aide Hannibal penetrates it with the help of Kemp who has been told he is likely to succumb to the disease.

The final answer surprises, and I will not spoil it by giving it here. Note, however, the poignancy as Chambers loses his 'eyes'. Do also note the hint towards the end, that the 'hunch' is perhaps a new skill, given to some and allowing them to make the right choices among the welter of avalanching fact and rumour and the decisions that civilisation requires. That strikes true. How many stupid decisions are taken by committees where more than one member realises that the decision is an error, but, lacking anything other than a 'hunch' that it is so, keeps silent? Yet there are other ways of reading the story. For example, Sam Moskowicz tagged it as a 'highly sophisticated blow at the religious claim of a hereafter, heaven being Sanctuary, a haven for those burdened by earthly woes'. What do you think?

By contrast, 'Buckets of Diamonds' is a romp. Cliff was good at these sort of stories. Shake off dull care, and enjoy it.

Finally, 'The Big Front Yard' is quintessential Simak. Occasionally cited as a 'favourite' by contributors to Internet discussions, it won the Novelette Hugo for 1958. I am surprised it has not been previously included in a UK collection. Like many Simak heroes, Hiram Taine is a loner. He is a handyman, a general fixer of machinery, and an antique dealer. Towser is his dog. (CDS loved dogs – *City* is 'In Memory of Scootie, who was Nathaniel'.) Beasly is the local simpleton, but capable of telepathy with Towser. Henry H. Horton is the local banker, slightly pompous and yet with some heart to him. Woodman, a nearby place in this story, is the township next up the Wisconsin above Millville, where CDS grew up. The characters fit that typical Simak township. So does the outcome, that a genuine mid-west trader should be the conduit between Man and the stars, and that big city or world government should have to acknowledge that the quirky but genuine rural dickerer best represents the interests of mankind. That lingers in the memory, and balances other questions about Man that CDS poses in his stories. The genuine, humane individual is the hope of the future.

Enjoy.

Francis Lyall, Aberdeen, 1997.

Horrible Example

Tobias staggered down the street and thought how tough it was.

He hadn't any money and Joe, the barkeep, had hurled him out of Happy Hollow tavern before he'd much more than wet his whistle and now all that was left for him was the cold and lonely shack that he called a home and no one gave a damn, no matter what might happen. For, he told himself, with maudlin self-pity, he was nothing but a bum and a drunken one at that and it was a wonder the town put up with him at all.

It was getting dusk, but there still were people on the street and he could sense that they were trying, very consciously, not to look at him.

And that was all right, he told himself. If they didn't want to look, that was all right with him. They didn't have to look. If it helped them any, there was no reason they should look.

He was the town's disgrace. He was its people's social cross. He was their public shame. He was the horrible example. And he was unique, for there never was more than one of him in any little town – there simply wasn't room for more than one like him.

He reeled forlornly down the sidewalk and he saw that Elmer Clark, the village cop, was standing on the corner. Not doing anything. Just standing there and watching. But it was all right. Elmer was a good guy. Elmer knew exactly how it was.

Tobias stood for a moment to get his bearings and finally he had them; he set a dead sight for the corner where Elmer waited for him. He navigated well. He finally reached the corner.

"Tobe," said Elmer, "maybe you should let me take you home. The car's just over there."

Tobias drew himself erect with fly-blown dignity.

"Couldn't think of it," he announced, every inch a gentleman. "Cannot let you do it. Very kindly of you."

Elmer grinned. "Take it easy, then. Sure that you can make it?"

"Poshitive," said Tobias, wobbling quickly off.

He did fairly well. He managed several blocks without incident.

But on the corner of Third and Maple, disaster overtook him. He fell flat upon his face and Mrs Frobisher was standing on her porch where she could see him fall. Tomorrow, he was full aware, she would tell all the women at the Ladies Aid Society what a shameful thing it was. They all would quietly cluck among themselves, pursing up their mouths and feeling extra holy. For Mrs Frobisher was their leader; she could do nothing wrong. Her husband was the banker and her son the star of Millville's football team, which was headed for the Conference championship. And that, without a doubt, was a thing of pride and wonder. It had been years since Millville High had won the Conference crown.

Tobias got up and dusted himself off, none too quietly and rather awkwardly, then managed to make his way to the corner of Third and Oak, where he sat down on the low stone wall that ran along the front of the Baptist church. The pastor, he knew, when he came from his basement study, would be sure to see him there. And it might do the pastor, he told himself, a world of good to see him. It might buck him up no end.

The pastor, he feared, was taking it too easy lately. Everything was going just a bit too smoothly and he might be getting smug, with his wife the president of the local DAR and his leggy daughter making such good progress with her music.

Tobias was sitting there and waiting for the pastor to come out when he heard the footsteps shuffling down the walk. It was fairly dark by now and it was not until the man got closer that he saw it was Andy Donovan, the janitor at the school.

Tobias chided himself a bit. He should have recognised the shuffle.

"Good evening, Andy," he said. "How are things tonight?"

Andy stopped and looked at him. Andy brushed his drooping moustache and spat upon the sidewalk so that if anyone were looking they'd be convinced of his disgust.

"If you're waiting for Mr Halvorsen to come out," he said, "it's a dreadful waste of time. He is out of town."

"I didn't know," Tobias said, contritely.

"You've done quite enough tonight," said Andy, tartly. "You might just as well go home. Mrs Frobisher stopped me as I was going past. She said we simply have to do something firm about you."

"Mrs Frobisher," said Tobias, staggering to his feet, "is an old busybody."

"She's all of that," said Andy. "She's likewise a decent woman."

He scraped around abruptly and went shuffling down the street, moving, it seemed, a trifle more rapidly than was his usual pace.

Tobias wobbled solemnly down the street behind him, with the wobble somewhat less pronounced, and he felt the bitterness and the question grew inside of him.

For it was unfair.

Unfair that he should be as he was when he could just as well be something else entirely – when the whole conglomerate of emotion and desire that spelled the total of himself cried out for something else.

He should not, he told himself, be compelled to be the conscience of this town. He was made for better things, he assured himself, hiccuping solemnly.

The houses became more scattered and infrequent and the sidewalk ended and he went stumbling down the unpaved road, heading for his shack at the edge of town.

His shack stood on a hill set above a swamp just beyond the intersection of this road on which he walked with Highway 49 and it was a friendly place to live, he thought. Often he just sat outside and watched the cars stream past.

But there was no traffic now and the moon was coming up above a distant copse and its light was turning the countryside to a black and silver etching.

He went down the road, his feet plopping in the dust and every now and then something set a bird to twitter and there was the smell of burning autumn leaves.

It was beautiful, Tobias thought – beautiful and lonely. But what the hell, he thought, he was always lonely.

Far off he heard the sound of the car, running hard and fast, and he grumbled to himself at how some people drove.

He went stumbling down the dusty stretch and now, some distance to the east, he saw the headlights of the car, travelling rapidly.

He watched it as he walked and as it neared the intersection there was a squeal of brakes and the headlights swung toward him as the car made a sudden turn into his road.

Then the headlight beams knifed into the sky and swept across it in a rapid arc and he caught the dash of glowing tail lights as the car skidded with the scream of rubber grinding into pavement.

Slowly, almost ponderously, the car was going over, toppling as it plunged toward the ditch.

Tobias found that he was running, legs pumping desperately and no wobble in them now.

Ahead of him the car hit on its side and skidded with a shrill, harsh grinding, then nosed easily, almost deliberately down into the roadside ditch. He heard the gentle splash of water as it slid to a halt and hung there, canted on its side, with its wheels still spinning.

He leaped from the road down onto the side of the car that lay uppermost and wrenched savagely at the door, using both his hands. But the door was a stubborn thing that creaked and groaned, but still refused to stir. He braced himself as best he could and yanked; it came open by an inch or so. He bent and got his fingers hooked beneath the door edge and even as he did he smelled the acrid odour of burning insulation and he knew the time was short. He became aware as well of the trapped and frightened desperation underneath the door.

A pair of hands from inside was helping with the door and he slowly straightened, pulling with every ounce of strength he had within his body and the door came open, but protestingly.

There were sounds now from inside the car, a soft, insistent whimpering, and the smell of burning sharper, and he caught the flare of flame running underneath the hood.

Something snapped and the door came upward, then stuck tight again, but now there was room enough and Tobias reached down into the opening and found an arm and hauled. A man came out.

"She's still in there," gasped the man. "She's still —"

But already Tobias was reaching down blindly into the darkness of the car's interior and now there was smoke as well as smell and the area beneath the hood was a gushing redness.

He found something alive and soft and struggling and somehow got a hold on it and hauled. A girl came out; a limp, bedraggled thing she was and scared out of her wits.

"Get out of here," Tobias yelled and pushed the man so that he tumbled off the car and scrambled up the ditchside until he reached the road.

Tobias jumped, half-carrying, half-dragging the girl, and behind him the car went up in a gush of flame.

They staggered up the road, the three of them, driven by the heat of the burning car. Somewhere, somehow, the man got the girl out of Tobias's grasp and stood her on her feet. She seemed to be all right except for the trickle of darkness that ran out of her hairline, down across her face.

There were people running down the road now. Doors were banging far away and there was shouting back and forth, while the three of them stood in the road and waited, all of them just a little dazed.

And now, for the first time, Tobias saw the faces of those other two. The man, he saw, was Randy Frobisher, Millville's football hero, and the girl was Betty Halvorsen, the musical daughter of the Baptist minister.

Those who were running down the road were getting close by now and the pillar of flame from the burning car was dying down

11

a bit. There was no further need, Tobias told himself, for him to stick around. For it had been a great mistake, he told himself; he never should have done it.

He abruptly turned around and went humping down the road, as rapidly as he could manage short of actual running. He thought he heard one of the two standing in the road call out after him, but he paid them no attention and kept on moving, getting out of there as fast as he was able.

He reached the intersection and crossed it and left the road and went up the path to where his shack perched in all its loneliness on the hill above the swamp.

And he forgot to stagger.

But it didn't matter now, for there was no one watching.

He felt all cold and shivery and there was a sense of panic in him. For this might spoil everything; this might jeopardise his job.

There was a whiteness sticking out of the rusty, battered mail box nailed beside the door and he stared at it with wonder, for it was very seldom that he got a piece of mail.

He took the letter from the box and went inside. He found the lamp and lit it and sat down in the rickety chair beside the table in the centre of the room.

And now his time was his, he thought, to do with as he wished.

He was off the job – although, technically, that was not entirely true, for he was never off the job entirely.

He rose and took off his tattered jacket and hung it on the chair back, then opened up his shirt to reveal a hairless chest. He sought the panel in his chest and pushed against it and it slid open underneath his hand. At the sink, he took out the container and emptied the beer that he had swallowed. Then he put the container back into his chest again and slid the panel shut. He buttoned up his shirt.

He let his breathing die.

He became comfortably himself.

He sat quietly in the chair and let his brain run down, wiping out his day. Then, slowly, he started up his brain again and made it a different kind of brain – a brain oriented to this private life of his, when he no longer was a drunken bum or a village conscience or a horrible example.

But tonight the day failed to be wiped out entirely and there was bitterness again – the old and acid bitterness that he should be used to protect the humans in the village against their human viciousness.

For there could be no more than one human derelict in any single village – through some strange social law there was never room for more than one of them. Old Bill or Old Charlie or Old Tobe – the pity of the people, regarded with a mingled sentiment of tolerance and disgust. And just as surely as there could not be more than one of them, there always was that one.

But take a robot, a Class One humanoid robot that under ordinary scrutiny would pass as a human being – take that robot and make him the village bum or the village idiot and you beat that social law. And it was perfectly all right for a manlike robot to be the village bum. Because in making him the bum, you spared the village a truly human bum, you spared the human race one blot against itself, you forced that potential human bum, edged out by the robot, to be acceptable. Not too good a citizen, perhaps, but at least marginally respectable.

To be a drunken bum was terrible for a human, but it was all right for a robot. Because robots had no souls. Robots didn't count.

And the most horrible thing about it, Tobias told himself, was that you must stay in character – you must not step out of it except for that little moment, such as now, when you were absolutely sure no one could be watching.

But he'd stepped out of it this night. For a few isolated moments he'd been forced to step out of it. With two human lives at stake, there had been no choice.

Although, he told himself, there might be little harm. The two kids had been so shaken up that there was a chance they'd not known who he was. In the shock of the moment, he might have gone unrecognised.

13

But the terrible thing about it, he admitted to himself, was that he yearned for that recognition. For there was within himself a certain humanness that called for recognition, for any recognition, for anything at all that would lift him above the drunken bum.

And that was unworthy of himself, he scolded – unworthy of the tradition of the robot.

He forced himself to sit quietly in the chair, not breathing, not doing anything but thinking – being honest with himself, being what he was, not play-acting any more.

It would not be so bad, he thought, if it was all that he was good for – if, in being Millville's horrible example he was working at the limit of his talent.

That, he realised, had been true at one time. It had been true when he'd signed the contract for the job. But it was true no longer. He was ready now for a bigger job.

For he had grown, in that subtle, inexplicable, curious way that robots grew.

And it wasn't right that he should be stuck with this job when there were other, bigger jobs that he could handle easily.

But there was no remedy. There was no way out of it. There was no one he could go to. There was no way he could quit.

For in order to be effective in this job of his, it was basic that no one – no one, except a single contact, who in turn must keep the secret – knew he was a robot. He must be accepted as a human. For if it should be known that he was not a human, then the effectiveness of his work would collapse entirely. As a drunken human bum he was a shield held between the town and petty, vulgar vice; as a drunken, lousy, no-good robot he would not count at all.

So no one knew, not even the village council which paid the annual fee, grumblingly, perhaps, to the Society for the Advancement and Betterment of the Human Race, not knowing for what specific purpose it might pay the fee, but fearful not to pay it. For it was not every municipality that was offered the

14

unique and distinctive service of SABHR. Once the fee should be refused, it might be a long, long time before Millville could get on the list again.

So here he sat, he thought, with a contract to this town which would run another decade – a contract of which the town knew nothing, but binding just the same.

There was no recourse, he realised. There was no one he could go to. There was none he could explain to, for once he had explained he'd have wiped out his total sum of service. He would have cheaply tricked the town. And that was something no robot could ever bring himself to do. It would not be the proper thing.

He tried to find within himself some logic for this consuming passion to do the proper thing, for the bond of honour involved within a contract. But there was no clear-cut logic; it was just the way it was. It was the robot way, one of the many conditioning factors which went into a robot's make-up.

So there was no way out of it. He faced another decade of carrying out the contract, of getting drunk, of stumbling down the street, of acting out the besotted, ambitionless, degraded human being – and all to the end that there should be no such actual human.

And being all of this, he thought, choked with bitterness, while knowing he was fit for better things, fit under his present rating for sociological engineering at the supervisor level.

He put out his arm and leaned it on the table and heard the rustle underneath his arm.

The letter. He'd forgotten it.

He picked up the envelope and looked at it and there was no return address and he was fairly certain who it might be from.

He tore it open and took out the folded sheet of paper and he had been right. The letterhead was that of the Society for the Advancement and Betterment of the Human Race.

The letter read:

Dear Associate:
You will be glad to know that your recent rating has been analysed and that the final computation shows you to be best

15

fitted as a co-ordinator and expediter with a beginning human colony. We feel that you have a great deal to offer in this type of employment and would be able to place you immediately if there were no other consideration.

But we know that you are under a contractual obligation and perhaps do not feel free to consider other employment at the moment.

If there should be a change in this situation, please let us know at once.

The letter was signed with an undecipherable scrawl.

Carefully, he folded the sheet and stuffed it in his pocket.

He could see it now: Out to another planet that claimed another star for sun, helping to establish a human colony, working with the colonists, not as a robot – for in sociology, one never was a robot – but as another human being, a normal human being, a member of the colony.

It would be a brand-new job and a brand-new group of people and a brand-new situation.

And it would be a straight role. No more comedy, no more tragedy. No more clowning, ever.

He got up and paced the floor.

It wasn't right, he told himself. He shouldn't waste another ten years here. He owed this village nothing – nothing but his contract, a sacred obligation. Sacred to a robot.

And here he was, tied to this tiny dot upon the map, when he might go among the stars, when he might play a part in planting among those stars the roots of human culture.

It would not be a large group that would be going out. There was no longer any massive colonising being done. It had been tried in the early days and failed. Now the groups were small and closely tied together by common interests and old associations.

It was more, he told himself, like homesteading than colonising. Groups from home communities went out to try their luck, even little villages sending out their bands as in the ancient past the eastern communities had sent their wagon trains into the virgin west.

And he could be in on this great adventure if he could only break his contract, if he could walk out on the village, if he could quit this petty job.

But he couldn't. There was nothing he could do. He'd reached the bare and bitter end of ultimate frustration.

There was a knocking on the door and he stopped his pacing, stricken, for it had been years since there'd been a knock upon the door. A knock upon the door, he told himself, could mean nothing else but trouble. It could only mean that he'd been recognised back there on the road – just when he'd been beginning to believe that he'd gone unrecognised.

He went slowly to the door and opened it and there stood the four of them – the village banker, Herman Frobisher; Mrs Halvorsen, the wife of the Baptist minister; Bud Anderson, the football coach, and Chris Lambert, the editor of the weekly paper.

And he knew by the looks of them that the trouble would be big – that here was something he could not brush lightly to one side. They had a dedicated and an earnest look about them – and as well the baffled look of people who had been very wrong and had made up their minds most resolutely to do what they could about it.

Herman held out his pudgy hand with a friendly forcefulness so overdone it was ridiculous.

"Tobe," he said, "I don't know how to thank you, I don't have the words to thank you for what you did tonight."

Tobias took his hand and gave it a quick clasp, then tried to let go of it, but the banker's hand held on almost tearfully.

"And running off," shrilled Mrs Halvorsen, "without waiting to take any credit for how wonderful you were. I can't, for the life of me, know what got into you."

"Oh," Tobias said uncomfortably, "it really wasn't nothing."

The banker let go of Tobias' hand and the coach grabbed hold of it, almost as if he had been waiting for the chance to do so.

"Randy will be all right, thanks to you," he said. "I don't know

17

what we'd have done without him, Tobe, in the game tomorrow night."

"I'll want a picture of you, Tobe," said the editor. "Have you got a picture? No, I suppose you haven't. We'll take one tomorrow."

"But first," the banker said, "we'll get you out of here."

"Out of here?" asked Tobias, really frightened now. "But, Mr Frobisher, this place is my home!"

"Not any more, it isn't," shrilled Mrs Halvorsen. "We're going to see that you get the chance that you never had. We're going to talk to AA about you."

"AA?" Tobias asked in a burst of desperation.

"Alcoholics Anonymous," the pastor's wife said primly. "They will help you stop your drinking."

"But suppose," the editor suggested, "that Tobe here doesn't want to."

Mrs Halvorsen clicked her teeth, exasperated. "Of course he does," she said. "There never was a man –"

"Now, now," said Herman, "I think we may be going just a bit too fast. We'll talk to Tobe tomorrow –"

"Yeah," said Tobias, reaching for the door, "talk to me tomorrow."

"No, you don't," said Herman. "You're coming home with me. The wife's got a supper waiting, and we have a room for you and you can stay with us until we get this straightened out."

"I don't see," protested Tobias, "there's much to straighten out."

"But there is," said Mrs Halvorsen. "This town has never done a thing for you. We've all stood calmly by and watched you stagger past. And it isn't right. I'll talk to Mr Halvorsen about it."

The banker put a companionable arm around Tobias's shoulder.

"Come on, Tobe," he said. "We never can repay you, but we'll do the best we can."

He lay in bed, with a crisp white sheet beneath him and a crisp

18

white sheet on top and now he had the job, when everyone was asleep, of sneaking to the bathroom and flushing all the food they'd insisted he should eat down the toilet bowl.

And he didn't need white sheets. He didn't need a bed. He had one in his shack, but it was just for the looks of things. But here he had to lie between white sheets and Herman even had insisted that he take a bath and he had needed one, all right, but it had been quite a shock.

His whole life was all loused up, he told himself. His job was down the drain. He'd failed, he thought, and failed most miserably. And now he'd never get a chance to go on a colonising venture – even after his present job was all wrapped up and done, he'd never have a chance at a really good job. He'd just get another piddling one and he'd spend another 20 years at it and he'd maybe fail in that one too – for if you had a weakness it would seek you out.

And he had a weakness. Tonight he'd found it out.

But what should he have done, he asked himself. Should he have hurried past and leave the kids to die inside the flaming car?

He lay between the clean, white sheets and looked at the clean, white moonlight streaming through the window and asked himself the question for which there was no answer.

Although there was a hope and he thought about the hope and it became a brighter hope and he felt a good deal better.

He could beat this thing, he told himself – all he had to do was get drunk again, or pretend to get drunk again, for he was never really drunk. He could go on a binge that would be an epic in the history of the village. He could irretrievably disgrace himself. He could publicly and wilfully throw away the chance that had been offered him to become a decent citizen. He could slap the good intentions of all these worthy people right smack in the puss and he'd become, because of that, a bigger stinker than he'd ever been before.

He lay there and thought about it. It was a good idea and he would have to do it – but perhaps not right away.

It might look a little better if he waited for a while. It might have more effect if he played at being decent for a week or so.

19

Then when he fell out of grace, the shock might be the greater. Let them wallow for a while in all the holiness of feeling that they had rescued him from a vicious life, let them build up hope before he, laughing in their faces, staggered back to the shack above the swamp.

And when he did that it would be all right. He'd be back on the job again, better than before.

A week or two, perhaps. Or maybe more than that.

And suddenly he knew. He fought against the knowing, but it stood out plain and clear.

He wasn't being honest.

He didn't want to go back to the person he had been.

This was what he'd wanted, he admitted to himself. It was something he had wanted for a long time now – to live in the respect of his fellow villagers, to win some acceptance from them, to win contentment with himself.

Henry had talked after supper about a job for him – an honest, steady job. And lying there, he knew that he yearned to have that job, to become in all reality a humble, worthy citizen of Millville.

But it was impossible and he knew it was and the entire situation was worse than ever now. For he was no longer a simple fumbler, but a traitor, self-confessed.

It was ironical, he told himself, that in failure he should find his heart's desire, a fulfilment he could not consider keeping.

If he'd been a man, he'd have wept.

But he couldn't weep. He lay cold and rigid in the crisp white bed with the crisp white moonlight pouring through the window.

He needed help. For the first time in his life, he was in need of friendly help.

There was one place that he could go, one place of last resort.

Moving softly, he got into his clothes and eased out of the door and went on tiptoe down the stairs.

A block from the house he figured that it was safe to run

20

and he ran in slobbering haste, with the wild horsemen of fear running at his heels.

Tomorrow was the game – the big game that Randy Frobisher was still alive to play in – and Andy Donovan would work late tonight so that he'd have time off from his janitoring to take in the game.

He wondered what the time was and he knew it must be late. But, he told himself, Andy must still be there at his chores of janitoring – he simply must be there.

He reached the school and ran up the curving walk toward the building, looming in all its massive darkness. He wondered, with a sinking feeling, if he had come in vain, if he'd run all this way for nothing.

Then he saw the dim light shining in one of the basement windows – down in the storage room – and he knew it was all right.

The door was locked and he raised a fist and hammered on it, then waited for a while, then hammered once again.

Finally he heard the shuffling footsteps come scuffing up the stairs and a moment later saw the wavering of a shadow just beyond the door.

There was a fumbling of the keys and the snicking of the lock and the door came open.

A hand reached out and dragged him quickly in. The door sighed to behind him.

"Tobe!" cried Andy Donovan. "I am glad you came."

"Andy, I made a mess of it!"

"Yes," Andy said impatiently. "Yes, I know you did."

"I couldn't let them die. I couldn't stand there and do nothing for them. It wouldn't have been human."

"It would have been all right," said Andy. "For you aren't human."

He led the way down the stairs, clinging to the rail and shuffling warily.

And all around them, silence echoing in emptiness, Tobias sensed the eerie terror of a school waiting through the night.

They turned right at the foot of the stairs into the storage room.

The janitor sat down on an empty crate and waved the robot to another.

Tobias did not sit immediately. He had quick amends to make.

"Andy," he said, 'I've got it figured out. I'll go on the biggest drunk —"

Andy shook his head, "It would do no good," he said. "You have shown a spark of goodness, a certain sense of greatness. Remembering what you've done, they'd make excuses for you. They'd say there was some good in you, no matter what you did. You couldn't do enough, you couldn't be big enough a louse for them ever to forget."

"Then," said Tobias, and it was half a question.

"You are all washed up," said Andy. "You are useless here."

He sat silently for a moment, staring at the stricken robot.

"You've done a good job here," Andy finally said. "It's time that someone told you. You've been conscientious and unsparing of yourself. You've had a fine influence on the town. No one else could have forced himself to be so low-down and despicable and disgusting —"

"Andy," said Tobias bitterly, "don't go pinning medals on me."

"I wish," said the janitor. "you wouldn't feel like that."

Out of the bitterness, Tobias felt a snicker – a very ghastly snicker – rising in his brain.

And the snicker kept on growing – a snicker at this village if it could only know that it was being engineered by two nondescripts, by a shuffling janitor and a filthy bum.

And with him, Tobias, robot, it probably didn't matter, but the human factor would. Not the banker, nor the merchant, nor the pastor, but the janitor – the cleaner of the windows, the mopper of the floors, the tender of the fires. To him had been assigned the keeping of the secret; it was he who had been appointed the engineering contact. Of all the humans in the village, he was the most important.

But the villagers would never know, neither their debt nor

their humiliation. They'd patronise the janitor. They'd tolerate the bum – or whatever might succeed the bum.

For there'd be a bum no longer. He was all washed up. Andy Donovan had said so.

And they were not alone. He could sense they weren't.

He spun swiftly on his heel and there stood another man.

He was young and polished and most efficient-looking. His hair was black and smooth and he had an eager look about him that made one ill at ease.

"Your replacement," said Andy, chuckling just a little. "This one, let me tell you, is a really dirty trick."

"But he doesn't look —"

"Don't let his appearance fool you," Andy warned. "He is worse than you are. He's the latest gimmick. He is the dirtiest of all. They'll despise him more than they ever despised you. He'll earn an honest hatred that will raise the moral tone of Millville to a degree as yet undreamed of. They'll work so hard to be unlike him that we'll make honest men out of every one of them – even Frobisher."

"I don't understand," Tobias told him weakly.

"He'll set up an office, a very proper office for an alert young business man. Insurance and real estate and property management and anything else where he can earn a dollar. He'll skin them blind, but legal. He'll be very sanctimonious, but there's no friendship in him. He'll gyp them one by one and he'll smile most prettily and sincerely while he robs them by the letter of the law. There'll be no trick so low he'll not employ it, no subterfuge so vile that he'll hesitate to use it."

"But it's unfair," Tobias cried. "At least I was an honest bum."

"We must," Andy told him unctuously, "act for the good of all humanity. Surely it would be a shame for Millville to ever have an actual human such as he."

"All right, then," Tobias said. "I wash my hands of it. How about myself?"

23

"Why, nothing at the moment," Andy told him. "You go back to Herman's place and let nature take its course. Take the job he hunts up for you and be a decent citizen."

Tobias got cold all over. "You mean you're ditching me entirely? You mean you have no further use for me at all? I only did my best. There was nothing else I could have done tonight. You can't just throw me out!"

Andy shook his head. "There's something I should tell you. It's just a little early to be saying anything – but there's quiet talk in the village of sending out a colony."

Tobias stood stiff and straight and hope went pounding through him, then the hope died out.

"But me," he said. "Not me. Not a bum like me!"

"Worse than a bum," said Andy. "Much worse than a bum. As a bum you were a known quantity. They knew what to expect from you. They could sit down at any time and plot a behaviour curve for you. As a reformed bum, you'll be something else again. You'll be unpredictable. They'll be watching you, wondering what will happen next. You'll make them nervous and uneasy. They'll be wondering all the time if what they did was right. You'll be a burden on their conscience and a rasp across their nerves and they'll be afraid that you'll somehow prove some day that they were awfully stupid."

"Feeling that way," Tobias said, with no final shred of hope, "they'd never let me go out to the colony."

"I think you're wrong," said Andy. "I am sure that you will go. The good and nervous people of this village couldn't pass up a chance like that of getting rid of you."

The Civilisation Game

For some time, Stanley Paxton had been hearing the sound of muffled explosions from the west. But he had kept on, for there might be a man behind him, trailing him, and he could not change his course. For if he was not befuddled, the homestead of Nelson Moore lay somewhere in the hills ahead. There he would find shelter for the night and perhaps even transportation. Communication, he knew, must be ruled out for the moment; the Hunter people would be monitoring, alert for any news of him.

One Easter vacation, many years ago, he had spent a few days at the Moore homestead, and all through this afternoon he had been haunted by a sense of recognition for certain landmarks he had sighted. But his visit to these hills had been so long ago that his memory hazed and there was no certainty.

As the afternoon had lengthened toward an early evening, his fear of the trailing man began to taper off. Perhaps, he told himself, there was no one, after all. Once, atop a hill, he had crouched in a thicket for almost half an hour and had seen no sign of any follower.

Long since, of course, they would have found the wreckage of his flier but they might have arrived too late and so, consequently, have no idea in which direction he had gone.

Through the day, he'd kept close watch of the cloudy sky and was satisfied that no scouting flier had passed overhead to spot him.

Now, with the setting of the sun behind an angry cloud bank, he felt momentarily safe.

He came out of a meadow and began to climb a wooded hill.

The strange boomings and concussions seemed fairly close at hand and he could see the flashes of explosions lighting up the sky.

He reached the hilltop and stopped short, crouching down against the ground. Below him, over a square mile or more of ground, spread the rippling flashes, and in the pauses between the louder noises, he heard faint chatterings that sent shivers up his spine.

He crouched, watching the flashes ripple back and forth in zigzag patterning and occasionally a small holocaust of explosions would suddenly break out and then subside as quickly.

Slowly he stood up and wrapped his cloak about him and raised the hood to protect his neck and ears.

On the near side of the flashing area, at the bottom of the hill, was some sort of four-square structure looming darkly in the dusk. And it seemed as well that a massive, hazy bowl lay inverted above the entire area, although it was too dark to make out what it was.

Paxton grunted softly to himself and went quickly down the hill until he reached the building. It was, he saw, a sort of observation platform, solidly constructed and raised well above the ground with the top half of it made of heavy glass that ran all the way around. A ladder went up one side to the glassed-in platform.

"What's going on up there?" he shouted, but his voice could be scarcely heard above the crashing and thundering that came from out in front.

So he climbed the ladder.

When his head reached the level of the glassed-in platform area, he halted. A boy, not more than 14 years of age, stood at the front of the platform, staring out into a noisy sea of fire. A pair of binoculars was slung about his neck and to one side of him stood a massive bank of instruments.

Paxton clambered up the rest of the way and stepped inside the platform.

"Hello, young man!" he shouted.

The youngster turned around. He seemed an engaging fellow, with a cowlick down his forehead.

26

"I'm sorry, sir," he said. "I'm afraid I didn't hear you."

"What is going on here?"

"A war," said the boy. "Pertwee just launched his big attack. I'm hard-pressed to hold him off."

Paxton gasped a little. "But this is most unusual!" he protested.

The boy wrinkled up his forehead. "I don't understand."

"You are Nelson Moore's son?"

"Yes, sir, I am Graham Moore."

"I knew your father many years ago. We went to school together."

"He will be glad to see you, sir," the boy said brightly, sensing an opportunity to rid himself of this uninvited kibitzer. "You take the path just north of west. It will lead you to the house."

"Perhaps," suggested Paxton, "you could come along and show me."

"I can't leave just yet," said Graham. "I must blunt Pertwee's attack. He caught me off my balance and has been saving up his firepower and there were some manoeuvres that escaped me until it was too late. Believe me, sir, I'm in an unenviable position."

"This Pertwee?"

"He's the enemy. We've fought for two years now."

"I see," said Paxton solemnly and retreated down the ladder.

He found t‌   and followed it and found the house, set in a swa‌   ‌llocks. It was an old and rambling affair
                              trees.

                    ‌atio and a woman's voice asked: "Is

                              on the smooth stone flags and was
                              ‌iteness – a white face haloed by

                              friend of your son's."
                              some trick of acoustics in the
                              ‌d of battle, although the sky
                              ‌nal flash of heavy rockets

                              ‌ld lady said, still rocking

27

gently back and forth. "Although I do wish Nelson would come home. I don't like him wandering around after it gets dark."

"My name is Stanley Paxton. I'm with Politics."

"Why, yes," she said, "I remember now. You spent an Easter with us, 20 years ago. I'm Cornelia Moore, but you may call me Grandma, like all the rest of them."

"I remember you quite well," said Paxton. "I hope I'm not intruding."

"Heavens, no. We have few visitors. We're always glad to see one. Theodore especially will be pleased. You'd better call him Granther."

"Granther?"

"Grandfather. That's the way Graham said it when he was a tyke."

"I met Graham. He seemed to be quite busy. He said Pertwee had caught him off his balance."

"That Pertwee plays too rough," said Grandma, a little angrily.

A robot catfooted out onto the patio. "Dinner is ready, madam," it said.

"We'll wait for Nelson," Grandma told it.

"Yes, madam. He should be in quite soon. We shouldn't wait too long. Granther has already started on his second brandy."

"We have a guest, Elijah. Please show him to his room. He is a friend of Nelson's."

"Good evening, sir," Elijah said. "If you will follow me. And your luggage. Perhaps I can carry it."

"Oh, course you can," said Grandma drily. "I wish, Elijah, you'd stop putting on airs when there's company."

"I have no luggage," Paxton said, embarrassed.

He followed the robot across the patio and into the house, going down the central hall and up the very handsome winding staircase.

The room was large and filled with old-fashioned furniture. A sedate fireplace stood against one wall.

"I'll light a fire," Elijah said. "It gets chilly in the autumn once the sun goes down. And damp. It looks like rain.'

Paxton stood in the centre of the room, trying to remember.

Grandma was a painter and Nelson was a naturalist, but what about old Granther?

"The old gentleman," said the robot, stooping at the fireplace, "will send you up a drink. He'll insist on brandy, but if you wish it, I could get you something else."

"No, thank you. Brandy will be fine."

"The old gentleman's in great fettle. He'll have a lot to tell you. He's just finished his sonata, sir, after working at it for almost seven years, and he's very proud of it. There were times, I don't mind telling you, when it was going badly, that he wasn't fit to live with. If you'd just look here at my bottom, sir, you can see a dent . . ."

"So I see," said Paxton uncomfortably.

The robot rose from before the fireplace and the flames began to crackle, crawling up the wood.

"I'll go for your drink," Elijah said. "If it takes a little longer than seems necessary, do not become alarmed. The old gentleman undoubtedly will take this opportunity to lecture me about hewing to civility, now that we have a guest."

Paxton walked to the bed, took off his cloak and hung it on a bedpost. He walked back to the fire and sat down in a chair, stretching out his legs toward the warming blaze.

It had been wrong of him to come here, he thought. These people should not be involved in his problems and his dangers. Theirs was the quiet world, the easygoing, thoughtful world, while his world of Politics was all clamour and excitement and sometimes agony and fear.

He'd not tell them, he decided. And he'd stay just the night and be off before the dawn. Somehow or other he would work out a way to get in contact with his party. Somewhere else he'd find people who would help him.

There was a knock at the door. Apparently it had not taken Elijah as long as it had thought.

"Come in," Paxton called.

It was not Elijah; it was Nelson Moore.

He still wore a rough walking jacket and his boots had mud

29

upon them and there was a streak of dirt across his face where he'd brushed back his hair with a grimy hand.

"Grandma told me you were here," he said, shaking Paxton by the hand.

"I had two weeks off," said Paxton, lying like a gentleman. "We just finished with an exercise. It might interest you to know that I was elected President."

"Why, that is fine," said Nelson enthusiastically.

"Yes, I suppose it is."

"Let's sit down."

"I'm afraid I may be holding up the dinner. The robot said —"

Nelson laughed. "Elijah always rushes us to eat. He wants to get the day all done and buttoned up. We've come to expect it of him and we pay him no attention."

"I'm looking forward to meeting Anastasia," Paxton said. "I remember that you wrote of her often —"

"She's not here," said Nelson. "She – well, she left me. Almost five years ago. She missed Outside too much. None of us should marry outside Continuation."

"I'm sorry. I shouldn't have —"

"It's all right, Stan. It's all done with now. There are some who simply do not fit into the project. I've wondered many times, since Anastasia left, what kind of folks we are. I've wondered if it all is worth it."

"All of us think that way at times," said Paxton. "There have been times when I've been forced to fall back on history to find some shred of justification for what we're doing here. There's a parallel in the monks of the so-called Middle Ages. They managed to preserve at least part of the knowledge of the Hellenic world. For their own selfish reasons, of course, as Continuation has its selfish reasons, but the human race was the real beneficiary."

"I go back to history, too," said Nelson. "The one that I come up with is a Stone Age savage, hidden off in some dark corner, busily flaking arrows while the first spaceships are being launched. It all seems so useless, Stan . . ."

"On the face of it, I suppose it is. It doesn't matter in the

30

least that I was elected President in our just-finished exercise. But there may be a day when that knowledge and technique of politics may come in very handy. And when it does, all the human race will have to do is come back here to Earth and they have the living art. This campaign that I waged was a dirty one, Nelson. I'm not proud of it."

"There's a good deal of dirty things in the human culture," Nelson said, "but if we commit ourselves at all, it must be all the way – the vicious with the noble, the dirty with the splendid."

The door opened quietly and Elijah glided in. It had two glasses on a tray.

"I heard you come in," it said to Nelson, "so I brought you something, too."

"Thank you," Nelson said. "That was kind of you."

Elijah shuffled in some embarrassment. "If you don't mind, could you hurry just a little? The old gentleman has almost killed the bottle. I'm afraid of what might happen to him if I don't get him to the table."

Dinner had been finished and young Graham hustled off to bed. Granther unearthed, with great solemnity, another bottle of good brandy.

"That boy is a caution," he declared. "I don't know what's to become of him. Imagine him out there all day long, fighting those fool battles. If he was going to take up something, I should think he'd want it to be useful. There's nothing more useless than a general when there are no wars."

Grandma clacked her teeth together with impatience. "It isn't as if we hadn't tried. We gave him every chance there was. But he wasn't interested in anything until he took up warring."

"He's got guts," said Granther proudly. "That much I'll say for him. He up and asked me the other day would I write him some battle music. Me!" yelled Granther, thumping his chest. "Me write battle music!"

"He's got the seeds of destruction in him," declared Grandma righteously. "He doesn't want to build. He just wants to bust."

"Don't look at me," Nelson said to Paxton. "I gave up long ago. Granther and Grandma took him over from me right after Anastasia left. To hear them talk, you'd think they hated him. But let me lift a finger to him and the both of them –"

"We did the best we could," said Grandma. "We gave him every chance. We bought him all the testing kits. You remember?"

"Sure," said Granther, busy with the bottle. "I remember well. We bought him that ecology kit and you should have seen the planet he turned out. It was the most pitiful, down-at-heels, hungover planet you ever saw. And then we tried robotry —"

"He did right well at that," said Grandma tartly.

"Sure, he built them. He enjoyed building them. Recall the time he geared the two of them to hate each other and they fought until they were just two piles of scrap? I never saw anyone have such a splendid time as Graham during the seven days they fought."

"We could scarcely get him in to meals," said Grandma.

Granther handed out the brandy.

"But the worst of all," he decided, "was the time we tried religion. He dreamed up a cult that was positively gummy. We made short work of that . . ."

"And the hospital," said Grandma. "That was your idea, Nels . . ."

"Let's not talk about it," pleaded Nelson grimly. "I am sure Stanley isn't interested."

Paxton picked up the cue Nelson was offering him. "I was going to ask you, Grandma, what kind of painting you are doing. I don't recall that Nelson ever told me."

"Landscapes," the sweet-faced old lady said. "I've been doing some experimenting."

"And I tell her she is wrong," protested Granther. "To experiment is wrong. Our job is to maintain tradition, not to let our work go wandering off in whatever direction it might choose."

"Our job," said Grandma bitterly, "is to guard the techniques. Which is not to say we cannot strive at progress, if it still is human progress. Young man," she appealed to Paxton, "isn't that the way you see it?"

32

"Well, in part," evaded Paxton, caught between two fires. "In Politics, we allow evolvement, naturally, but we make sure by periodic tests that we are developing logically and in the human manner. And we make very sure we do not drop any of the old techniques, no matter how outmoded they may seem. And the same is true in Diplomacy. I happen to know a bit about Diplomacy, because the two sections work very close together and —"

"There!" Grandma said.

"You know what I think?" said Nelson quietly. "We are a frightened race. For the first time in our history, the human race is a minority and it scares us half to death. We are afraid of losing our identity in the great galactic matrix. We're afraid of assimilation."

"That's wrong, son," Granther disagreed. "We are not afraid, my boy. We're just awful smart, that's all. We had a great culture at one time and why should we give it up? Sure, most humans nowadays have adopted the galactic way of life, but that is not to say that it is for the best. Some day we may want to turn back to the human culture or we may find that later on we can use parts of it. And this way, if we keep it alive here in Project Continuation, it will be available, all of it or any part, any time we need it. And I'm not speaking, mind you, from the human view alone, because some facet of our culture might sometime be badly needed, not by the human race as such, but by the Galaxy itself."

"Then why keep the project secret?"

"I don't think it's really secret," Granther said. "It's just that no one pays much attention to the human race and none at all to Earth. The human race is pretty small potatoes against all the rest of them and Earth is just a worn-out planet that doesn't amount to shucks."

He asked Paxton: "You ever hear it was secret, boy?"

"Why, I guess not," said Paxton. "All I ever understood was that we didn't go around shooting off our mouths about it. I've thought of Continuation as a sort of sacred trust. We're the guardians who watch over the tribal medicine bag

33

while the rest of humanity is out among the stars getting civilised."

The old man chortled. "That's about the size of it. We're just a bunch of bushmen, but mark me well, intelligent and even dangerous bushmen."

"Dangerous?" asked Paxton.

"He means Graham," Nelson told him quietly.

"No, I don't," said Granther. "Not him especially. I mean the whole kit and caboodle of us. Because, don't you see, everybody who joins in this galactic culture that they are stewing up out there must contribute something and must likewise give up something – things that don't fit in with the new ideas. And the human race has done just like the rest of them, except we haven't given up a thing. Oh, on the surface, certainly. But everything we've given up is still back here, being kept alive by a bunch of subsidised barbarians on an old and gutted planet that a member of this fine galactic culture wouldn't give a second look."

"He's horrible," said Grandma. "Don't pay attention to him. He's got a mean and ornery soul inside that withered carcass."

"And what is Man?" yelled Granther. "He's mean and ornery, too, when he has to be. How could we have gone so far if we weren't mean and ornery?"

And there was some truth in that, thought Paxton. For what humanity was doing here was deliberate double-crossing. Although, come to think of it, he wondered, how many other races might be doing the very selfsame thing or its equivalent?

And, if you were going to do it, you had to do it right. You couldn't take the human culture and enshrine it prettily within a museum, for then it would become no more than a shiny showpiece. A fine display of arrowheads was a pretty thing to look at, but a man would never learn to chip a flint into an arrowhead by merely looking at a bunch of them laid out on a velvet-covered board. To retain the technique of chipping arrows, you'd have to keep on chipping arrows, generation after generation, long after the need of them was gone. Fail by one generation and the art was lost.

And the same necessarily must be true of other human

techniques and other human arts. And not the purely human arts alone, but the unique human flavour of other techniques which in themselves were common to many other races.

Elijah brought in an armload of wood and dumped it down upon the hearth, heaped an extra log or two upon the fire, then brushed itself off carefully.

"You're wet," said Grandma.

"It's raining, madam," said Elijah, going out the door.

And so, thought Paxton, Project Continuation kept on practising the old arts, retaining within a living body of the race the knowledge of their manipulation and their use.

So the section on politics practised politics and the section on diplomacy set up seemingly impossible problems in diplomacy and wrestled with those problems. And in the project factories, teams of industrialists carried on in the old tradition and fought a never-ending feud with the trade unionism teams. And, scattered throughout the land, quiet men and women painted and composed and wrote and sculpted so that the culture that had been wholly human would not perish in the face of the new and wonderful galactic culture that was evolving from the fusion of many intelligences out in the farther stars.

And against what day, wondered Paxton, do we carry on this work? Is it pure and simple, and perhaps even silly, pride? Is it no more than a further expression of human skepticism and human arrogance? Or does it make the solid sense that old Granther thinks it does?

"You're in Politics, you say," Granther said to Paxton. "Now that is what I'd call a worthwhile thing to save. From what I hear, this new culture doesn't pay too much attention to what we call politics. There's administration, naturally, and a sense of civic duty and all that sort of nonsense – but no real politics. Politics can be a powerful thing when you need to win a point."

"Politics is a dirty business far too often," Paxton answered. "It's a fight for power, an effort to override and overrule the principles and policies of an opposing body. In even its best phase, it brought about the fiction of the minority, with the connotation that the mere fact of being a minority carries with it the penalty of being to a large extent ignored."

"Still, it could be fun. I suppose it is exciting."

"Yes, you could call it that," said Paxton. "This last exercise we carried out was one with no holds barred. We had it planned that way. It was described somewhat delicately as a vicious battle."

"And you were elected President," said Nelson.

"That I was, but you didn't hear me say I was proud of it."

"But you should be," Grandma insisted. "In the ancient days, it was a proud thing to be elected President."

"Perhaps," Paxton admitted, "but not the way my party did it."

It would be so easy, he thought, to go ahead and tell them, for they would understand. To say: I carried it too far. I blackened my opponent's name and character beyond any urgent need. I used all the dirty tricks. I bribed and lied and compromised and traded. And I did it all so well that I even fooled the logic that was the referee, which stood in lieu of populace and voter. And now my opponent has dug up another trick and is using it on me.

For assassination was political, even as diplomacy and war were political. After all, politics was little more than the short-circuiting of violence; an election was held rather than a revolution. But at all times the partition between politics and violence was a thin and flimsy thing.

He finished off his brandy and put the glass down on the table.

Granther picked up the bottle, but Paxton shook his head.

"Thank you," he said. "If you don't mind, I shall go to bed soon. I must get an early start."

He never should have stopped here. It would be unforgivable to embroil these people in the aftermath of the exercise.

Although, he told himself, it probably was unfair to call it the aftermath – what was happening would have to be a part and parcel of the exercise itself.

The doorbell tinkled faintly and they could hear Elijah stirring in the hall.

"Sakes alive," said Grandma. "who can it be this time of night? And raining outdoors, too!"

It was a churchman.

He stood in the hall, brushing water from his cloak. He took off his broad-brimmed hat and swished it to shake off the raindrops.

He came into the room with a slow and stately tread.

All of them arose.

"Good evening, Bishop," said old Granther. "You were fortunate to find the house in this kind of weather and we're glad to have Your Worship."

The bishop beamed in fine, fast fellowship.

"Not of the church," he said. "Of the project merely. But you may use the proper terms, if you have a mind. It helps me stay in character."

Elijah, trailing in his wake, took his cloak and hat. The bishop was arrayed in rich and handsome garments.

Granther introduced them all around and found a glass and filled it from the bottle.

The bishop took it and smacked his lips. He sat down in a chair next to the fire.

"You have not dined, I take it," Grandma said. "Of course you haven't – there's no place out there to dine. Elijah, get the bishop a plate of food, and hurry."

"I thank you, madam," said the bishop. "I've had a long, hard day. I appreciate all you're doing for me. I appreciate it more than you can ever know."

"This is our day," Granther said merrily, refilling his own glass for the umpteenth time. "It is seldom that we have any guests at all and now, all of an evening, we have two of them."

"Two guests," said the bishop, looking straight at Paxton. "Now that is fine, indeed."

He smacked his lips again and emptied the glass.

In his room, Paxton closed the door and shot the bolt full home.

The fire had burned down to embers and cast a dull glow along the floor. The rain drummed faintly, half-heartedly, on the window pane.

And the question and the fear raced within his brain.

There was no question of it: The bishop was the assassin who had been set upon his trail.

No man without a purpose, and a deadly purpose, walked these hills at night, in an autumn rain. And what was more, the bishop had been scarcely wet. He'd shaken his hat and the drops had fallen off, and he'd brushed at his cloak and after that both the hat and cloak were dry.

The bishop had been brought here, more than likely, in a hovering flier and let down, as other assassins probably likewise had been let down this very night in all of half a dozen places where a fleeing man might have taken shelter.

The bishop had been taken to the room just across the hall and under other circumstances, Paxton told himself, he might have sought conclusions with him there. He walked over to the fireplace and picked up the heavy poker and weighed it in his hand. One stroke of that and it would be all over.

But he couldn't do it. Not in this house.

He put the poker back and walked over to the bed and picked up his cloak. Slowly he slid it on as he stood there, thinking, going over in his mind the happenings of the morning.

He had been at home, alone, and the phone had rung and Sullivan's face had filled the visor – a face all puffed up with fright.

"Hunter's out to get you," Sullivan had said. "He's sent men to get you."

"But he can't do that!" Paxton remembered protesting.

"Certainly he can," said Sullivan. "It comes within the framework of the exercise. Assassination has always been a possibility . . ."

"But the exercise is finished!"

"Not so far as Hunter is concerned. You went a little far. You should have stayed within the hypothesis of the problem; there was no need to go back into Hunter's personal affairs. You

38

dug up things he thought no one ever knew. How did you do it, man?"

"I have my ways," said Paxton. "And in a deal like this, everything was fair. He didn't handle me exactly as if I were innocent."

"You better get going," Sullivan advised. "They must be almost there. I can't get anyone there soon enough to help you."

And it would have been all right, Paxton thought, if the flier had only held together.

He wondered momentarily if it had been sabotaged.

But be that as it may, he had flown it down and had been able to walk away from it and now, finally, here he was.

He stood irresolutely in the centre of the room.

It went against his pride to flee for a second time, but there was nothing else to do. He couldn't let this house become involved in the tag-end rough and tumble of his exercise.

And despite the poker, he was weaponless, for weapons on this now-peaceful planet were very few indeed – no longer household items such as once had been the case.

He went to the window and opened it and saw that the rain had stopped and that a ragged moon was showing through a scud of racing clouds.

Glancing down, he saw the roof of the porch beneath the window and he let his eye follow down the roof line. Not too hard, he thought, if a man were barefoot, and once he reached the edge there'd be a drop of not much more than 7ft.

He took off his sandals and stuffed them in the pocket of his cloak and started out the window.

But, halfway out, he climbed back in again and walked to the door. Quietly he slid back the bolt. It wasn't exactly cricket to go running off and leave a room locked up.

The roof was slippery with the rain, but he managed it without any trouble, inching his way carefully down the incline. He dropped into a shrub that scratched him up a bit, but that, he told himself, was a minor matter.

He put on his sandals and straightened up and walked rapidly away. At the edge of the woods, he stopped and looked back at the house. It stood dark and silent.

Once he got back home and this affair was finished, he promised himself, he'd write Nelson a long apologetic letter and explain it all.

His feet found the path and he followed it through the sickly half-light of the cloudy moon.

"Sir," said a voice close beside him, "I see that you are out for a little stroll . . ."

Paxton jumped in fright.

"It's a nice night for it, sir," the voice went on quietly. "After a rain, everything seems so clean and cool."

"Who is there?" asked Paxton, with his hair standing quite on edge.

"Why, it's Pertwee, sir. Pertwee, the robot, sir."

Paxton laughed a little nervously. "Oh, yes, I remember now. You're Graham's enemy."

The robot stepped out of the woods into the path beside him.

"It's too much, I suppose," Pertwee said, "to imagine that you might be coming out to look at the battlefield."

"Why, no," said Paxton, grasping at a straw. "I don't know how you guessed it, but that's exactly what I'm doing. I've never heard of anything quite like it and I'm considerably intrigued."

"Sir," said the robot eagerly, "I'm entirely at your service. There is no one, I can assure you, who is better equipped to explain it to you. I've been in it from the very first with Master Graham and if you have any questions, I shall try to answer them."

"Yes, I think there is one question. What is the purpose of it all?"

"Why, at first, of course," said Pertwee, "it was simply an attempt to amuse a growing boy. But now, with your permission, sir. I would venture the opinion that it is a good deal more."

"You mean a part of Continuation?"

"Certainly, sir. I know there is a natural reluctance among humankind to admit the fact, or to even think about it, but

40

for a great part of Man's history war played an important and many-sided role. Of all the arts that Man developed, there probably was none to which he devoted so much time and thought and money as he did to war."

The path sloped down and there before them in the pale and mottled moonlight lay the battle bowl.

"That bowl," asked Paxton, "or whatever it might be that you have tipped over it? Sometimes you can just make it out and other times you miss it . . ."

"I suppose," said Pertwee, "you'd call it a force shield, sir. A couple of the older robots worked it out. As I understand it, sir, it is nothing new – just an adaptation. There's a time factor worked into it as an additional protection."

"But that sort of protection . . ."

"We use TC bombs, sir – total conversion bombs. Each side gets so many of them and uses his best judgment and . . ."

"But you couldn't use nuclear stuff in there!"

"As safe as a toy, sir," said Pertwee gaily. "They are very small, sir. Not much larger than a pea. Critical mass, as you well understand, no longer is much of a consideration. And the yield in radiation, while it is fairly high, is extremely short-lived, so that within an hour or so . . ."

"You gentlemen," said Paxton grimly, "certainly try to be entirely realistic."

"Why, yes, of course we do. Although the operators are entirely safe. We're in the same sort of position, you might say, as the general staff. And that is all right, of course, because the purpose of the entire business is to keep alive the art of waging war."

"But the art . . ." Paxton started to argue, then stopped.

What could he say? If the race persisted in its purpose of keeping the old culture workable and intact in Continuation, then it must perforce accept that culture in its entirety.

War, one must admit, was as much a part of the human culture as were all the other more or less uniquely human things that the race was conserving here as a sort of racial cushion against a future need or use.

"There is," confessed Pertwee, "a certain cruelty, but perhaps

41

a cruelty that I, as a robot, am more alive to than would be the case with a human, sir. The rate of casualties among the robot troops is unbelievable. In a restricted space and with extremely high firepower, that would be the natural consequence."

"You mean that you use troops – that you send robots in there?"

"Why, yes. Who else would operate the weapons? And it would be just a little silly, don't you think, to work out a battle and then . . ."

"But robots . . ."

"They are very small ones, sir. They would have to be, to gain an illusion of the space which is normally covered by a full-scale battle. And the weapons likewise are scaled down, and that sort of evens things out. And the troops are very single-minded, completely obedient and dedicated to victory. We turn them out in mass production in our shops and there's little chance to give them varying individualities and anyhow . . ."

"Yes, I see," said Paxton, a little stunned. "But now I think that I . . ."

"But, sir, I have only got a start at telling you and I've not shown you anything at all. There are so many considerations and there were so many problems."

They were close to the towering, fully shimmering force field now and Pertwee pointed to a stairway that led from ground level down toward its base.

"I'd like to show you, sir," said Pertwee, ducking down the stairs.

It stopped before a door.

"This," it said, "is the only entrance to the battlefield. We use it to send new troops and munitions during periods of truce, and at other times we use it to polish up the place a bit."

Its thumb stabbed out and hit a button to one side of the door and the door moved upward silently.

"After several weeks of battle," the robot explained, "the terrain is bound to become a little cluttered."

Through the door, Paxton could see the churned-up ground and the evidence of dying, and it was as if someone had pushed him in the belly. He gulped in a stricken breath and couldn't let it out and he suddenly was giddy and nearly sick. He put out a hand to hold himself upright against the trench-like wall beside him.

Pertwee pushed another button and the door slid down.

"It hits you hard the first time you see it," Pertwee apologised, "but given time, one gets used to it."

Paxton let his breath out slowly and looked around. The trench with the stairway came down to the door, and the door, he saw, was wider than the trench, so that at the foot of the steps the area had been widened into a sort of letter T, with narrow embrasures scooped out to face the door.

"You all right, sir?" asked Pertwee.

"Perfectly all right," Paxton told the robot stiffly.

"And now," said Pertwee happily, "I'll explain the fire and tactical control."

It trotted up the steps and Paxton trailed behind it.

"I'm afraid that would take too long," said Paxton.

But the robot brushed the words aside. "You must see it, sir," it pleaded plaintively. "Now that you are out here, you must not miss seeing it."

He'd have to get away somehow, Paxton told himself. He couldn't afford to waste much time. As soon as the house had settled down to sleep, the bishop would come hunting him, and by that time he must be gone.

Pertwee led the way around the curving base of the battle bowl to the observation tower which Paxton had come upon that evening.

The robot halted at the base of the ladder.

"After you," it said.

Paxton hesitated, then went swiftly up the ladder.

Maybe this wouldn't take too long, he thought, and then he could be off. It would be better, he realised, if he could get rid of Pertwee without being too abrupt about it.

The robot brushed past him in the darkness and bent above the bank of controls. There was a snick and lights came on in the panels.

"This, you see," it said, "is the groundglass – a representation of the battlefield. It is dead now, of course, because there is nothing going on, but when there is some action certain symbols are imposed upon the field so that one can see at all times just how things are going. And this is the fire control panel and this is the troop command panel and this . . ."

Pertwee went on and on with his explanations.

Finally it turned in triumph from the instruments.

"What do you think of it?" the robot asked, very clearly expecting praise.

"Why, it's wonderful," said Paxton, willing to say anything to make an end of his visit.

"If you are going to be around tomorrow," Pertwee said, "you may want to watch us."

And it was then that Paxton got his inspiration.

"As a matter of fact," Paxton said, "I'd like to try it out. In my youth, I did a bit of reading on military matters, and if you'll excuse my saying so, I have often fancied myself somewhat of an expert."

Pertwee brightened almost visibly. "You mean, sir, that you'd like to go one round with me?"

"If you'd be so kind."

"You are sure you understand how to operate the board?"

"I watched you very closely."

"Give me fifteen minutes to reach my tower," said Pertwee. "When I arrive, I'll press the ready button. After that, either of us can start hostilities any time we wish."

"Fifteen minutes?"

"It may not take me that long, sir. I'll be quick about it."

"And I'm not imposing on you?"

"Sir," Pertwee said feelingly, "it will be a pleasure. I've fought against young Master Graham until the novelty has worn off. We know one another's tactics so well that there's little chance for surprise. As you can understand, sir, that makes for a rather humdrum war."

"Yes," said Paxton, "I suppose it would."

44

He watched Pertwee go down the ladder and listened to its footsteps hurrying away.

Then he went down the ladder and stood for a moment at the foot of it.

The clouds had thinned considerably and the moonlight was bright now and it would be easier travelling, although it still would be dark in the denser forest.

He swung away from the tower and headed for the path, and, as he did so, he caught a flicker of motion in a patch of brush just off the trail.

Paxton slid into the denser shadow of a clump of trees and watched the patch of brush.

He crouched and waited. There was another cautious movement in the brush and he saw it was the bishop. Now suddenly it seemed that there was a chance to get the bishop off his neck for good – if his inspiration would only pay off.

The bishop had been let down by the flier in the dark of night, with the rain still pouring down and no moonlight at all. So it was unlikely that he knew about the battle bowl, although more than likely he must see it now, glittering faintly in the moonlight. But even if he saw it, there was a chance he'd not know what it was.

Paxton thought back along the conversation there had been after the bishop had arrived and no one, so far as he remembered, had mentioned a word of young Graham or the war project.

There was, Paxton thought, nothing lost by trying. Even if it didn't work, all he'd lose would be a little time.

He darted from the clump of trees to reach the base of the battle bowl. He crouched against the ground and watched, and the bishop came sliding out of his clump of brush and worked his way along, closing in upon him.

And that was fine, thought Paxton. It was working just the way he'd planned.

He moved a little to make absolutely sure his trailer would know exactly where he was and then he dived down the stairs that led to the door.

He reached it and thumbed the button and the door slid slowly upward without a single sound. Paxton crowded back into the embrasure and waited.

It took a little longer than he had thought it would and he was getting slightly nervous when he heard the step upon the stairs.

The bishop came down slowly, apparently very watchful, and then he reached the door and stood there for a moment, staring out into the churned-up battlefield. And in his hand he held an ugly gun.

Paxton held his breath and pressed his shoulders tight against the wall of earth, but the bishop didn't even look around. His eyes were busy taking in the ground that lay beyond the door.

Then finally he moved, quickly, like a leopard. His silken garments made a swishing noise as he stepped through the door and out into the battle area.

Paxton held himself motionless, watching the bishop advance cautiously out into the field, and when he was far enough, he reached out a finger and pressed the second button and the door came down, smoothly, silently.

Paxton leaned against the door and let out in a gasp the breath he had been holding.

It was over now, he thought.

Hunter hadn't been as clever as he had thought he was.

Paxton turned from the door and went slowly up the stairs.

Now he needn't run away. He could stay right here and Nelson would fly him, or arrange to have him flown, to some place of safety.

For Hunter wouldn't know that this particular assassin had hunted down his quarry. The bishop had had no chance to communicate and probably wouldn't have dared to even if he could.

On the top step, Paxton stubbed his toe and went down without a chance to catch himself, and there was a vast explosion that shook the universe and artillery fire was bursting in his brain.

Dazed, he got to his hands and knees and crawled painfully, hurling himself desperately down the stairs – and through the

46

crashing uproar that filled the entire world ran an urgent thought and purpose.

I've got to get him out before it is too late! I can't let him die in there! I can't kill a man!

He slipped on the stairs and slid until his body jammed in the narrowness and stuck.

And there was no artillery fire, there was no crash of shells, no wicked little chitterings. The dome glittered softly in the moonlight and was as quiet as death.

Except, he thought, a little weirdly, death's not quiet in there. It is an inferno of destruction and a maddening place of sound and brightness and the quietness doesn't come until afterward.

He'd fallen and hit his head, he knew, and all he'd seen and heard had been within his brain. But Pertwee would be opening up any minute now and the quietness would be gone and with it the opportunity to undo what he had so swiftly planned.

And somewhere in the shadow of the dome another self stood off and argued with him, jeering at his softness, quoting logic at him.

It was either he or you, said that other self. You fought for your life the best way you knew, the only way you knew, and whatever you may have done, no matter what you did, you were entirely justified.

"I can't do it!" yelled the Paxton on the stairs and yet even as he yelled he knew that he was wrong, that by logic he was wrong, that the jeering self who stood off in the shadows made more sense than he.

He staggered to his feet. Without his conscious mind made up, he went down the stairs. Driven by some as yet unrealised and undefined instinctive prompting that was past all understanding, he stumbled down the stairs, with the throb still in his head and a choking guilt and fear rising in his throat.

He reached the door and stabbed the button and the door slid up and he went out into the cluttered place of dying and stopped in horror at the awful loneliness and the vindictive desolation of this square mile of Earth that was shut off from all the other Earth as if it were a place of final judgment.

And perhaps it was, he thought – the final judgment of Man.

Of all of us, he thought, young Graham may be the only honest one; he's the true barbarian that old Granther thinks he is; he is the throwback who looks out upon Man's past and sees it as it is and lives it as it was.

Paxton took a quick look back and he saw the door was closed and out ahead of him, in the ploughed and jumbled sea of tortured, battered earth, he saw a moving figure that could be no one but the bishop.

Paxton ran forward, shouting, and the bishop turned around and stood there, waiting, with the gun half lifted.

Paxton stopped and waved his arms in frantic signalling. The bishop's gun came up and there was a stinging slash across the side of Paxton's neck and a sudden, gushing wetness. A small, blue puff of smoke hung on the muzzle of the distant gun.

Paxton flung himself aside and dived for the ground. He hit and skidded on his belly and tumbled most ingloriously into a dusty crater. He lay there, at the bottom of the crater, huddled against the fear of the bullet's impact while the rage and fury built up into white heat.

He had come here to save a man and the man had tried to kill him!

I should have left him here, he thought.

I should have let him die.

I'd kill him if I could.

And the fact of the matter now was that he had to kill the bishop. There was no choice but to kill him or be killed himself.

Not only did he have to kill the bishop, but he had to kill him soon. Pertwee's 15 minutes must be almost at an end and the bishop had to be killed and he had to be out the door before Pertwee opened fire.

Out the door, he thought – did he have a chance? If he ran low and dodged, perhaps, would he have a chance to escape the bishop's bullets?

That was it, he thought. Waste no time on killing if he didn't have to; let Pertwee do the killing. Just get out of here himself.

He put his hand up to his neck, and when he lifted it, his fingers were covered with a sticky wetness. It was funny, he thought, that it didn't hurt, although the hurt, no doubt, would come later.

He crawled up the crater's side and rolled across its lip and found himself lying in a small, massed junkyard of smashed and broken robots, sprawled grotesquely where the barrage had caught them.

And lying there in front of him, without a scratch upon it, where it had fallen from a dying robot's grasp, was a rifle that shone dully in the moonlight.

He snatched it up and rose into a crouch and as he did he saw the bishop, almost on top of him; the bishop coming in to make sure that he was finished!

There was no time to run, as he had planned to – and, curiously, no desire to run. Paxton had never known actual hate before, never had a chance to know it, but now it came and filled him full of rage and a wild and exultant will and capacity to kill without pity or remorse.

He tilted up the rifle and his finger closed upon the trigger and the weapon danced and flashed and made a deadly chatter.

But the bishop still came on, not rushing now, but plodding ahead with a deadly stride, leaning forward as if his body were absorbing the murderous rifle fire, absorbing it and keeping on by will power alone, holding off death until that moment when it might snuff out the thing that was killing it.

The bishop's gun came up and something smashed into Paxton's chest, and smashed again and yet again, and there was a flood of wetness and a spattering and the edge of Paxton's brain caught at the hint of something wrong.

For two men do not – could not – stand a dozen feet apart and pour at one another a deadly blast and both stay on their feet. No matter how poor might be their aim, it simply couldn't happen.

He rose out of his crouch and stood at his full height and let the gun hang uselessly in his hand. Six feet away, the bishop stopped as well and flung his gun away.

They stood looking at one another in the pale moonlight and

49

the anger melted and ran out of them and Paxton wished that he were almost anywhere but there.

"Paxton," asked the bishop plaintively, "who did this to us?"

And it was a funny thing to say, almost as if he'd said: "Who stopped us from killing one another?"

For a fleeting moment, it almost seemed to Paxton as though it might have been a kinder thing if they had been allowed to kill. For killing was a brave thing in the annals of the race, an art of strength and a certain proof of manhood – perhaps of humanhood.

A kinder thing to be allowed to kill. And that was it, exactly. They had not been allowed to kill.

For you couldn't kill with a popgun that shot out plastic pellets of liquid that burst on contact, with the liquid running down like blood for the sake of realism. And you couldn't kill with a gun that went most admirably through all the motions of chattering and smoking and flashing out red fire, but with nothing lethal in it.

And was this entire battle bowl no more than a toy set with robots that came apart at the right and most dramatic moments and then could be put back together at a later time? Were the artillery and the total-conversion bombs toy things as well, with a lot of flash and noise and perhaps a few well-placed items to plough up the battlefield, but without the power to really hurt a robot?

The bishop said, "Paxton, I feel like an utter fool." And he added other words which a real bishop could never bring himself to say, making very clear just what kind of obscene fool he was.

"Let's get out of here," said Paxton shortly, feeling like that same kind of fool himself.

"I wonder . . ." said the bishop.

"Forget about it," Paxton growled. "Let's just get out of here. Pertwee will be opening up . . ."

But he didn't finish what he was about to say, for he realised that even if Pertwee did open up, there'd be little danger. And there wasn't any chance that Pertwee would open up, for it would know that they were here.

Like a metal monitor watching over a group of rebellious children – rebellious because they weren't adult yet. Watching them and letting them go ahead and play so long as they were in no danger of drowning or of falling off a roof or some other reckless thing. And then interfering only just enough to save their silly necks. Perhaps even encouraging them to play so they'd work off their rebelliousness – joining in the game in the typically human tradition of let's pretend.

Like monitors watching over children, letting them develop, allowing them to express their foolish little selves, not standing in the way of whatever childish importance they could muster up, encouraging them to think they were sufficient to themselves.

Paxton started for the door, plodding along, the bishop in his bedraggled robes stumbling along behind him.

When they were a hundred feet away, the door started sliding up and Pertwee stood there, waiting for them, not looking any different than it had before, but somehow seeming to have a new measure of importance.

They reached the door and sheepishly trailed through it, not looking right or left, casually and elaborately pretending that Pertwee was not there.

"Gentlemen," said Pertwee, "don't you want to play?"

"No," Paxton said. "No, thank you. I can't speak for both of us –"

"Yes, you can, friend," the bishop put in. "Go right ahead."

"My friend and I have done all the playing we care to do," said Paxton. "It was good of you to make sure we didn't get hurt."

Pertwee managed to look puzzled. "But why should anybody be allowed to get hurt? It was only a game."

"So we've discovered. Which way is out?"

"Why," said the robot, "any way but back."

Hermit of Mars

The sun plunged over the western rim of Skeleton Canal and instantly it was night. There was no twilight. Twilight was an impossible thing in the atmosphere of Mars, and the Martian night clamped down with frigid breath, and the stars danced out in the near-black sky, twinkling, dazzling stars that jigged a weird rigadoon in space.

Despite five years in the wilderness stretches of the Red Planet, Kent Clark still was fascinated by this sudden change from day to night. One minute sunlight – next minute starlight, the stars blazing out as if they were electric lights and someone had snapped the switch. Stars that were larger and more brilliant and gave more light than the stars seen from the planet Earth. Stars that seemed to swim in the swiftly cooling atmosphere. By midnight the atmosphere would be cooled to almost its minimum temperature, and then the stars would grow still and even more brilliant, like hard diamonds shining in the blackness of the sky, but they would be picturesque, showing their own natural colours, blue and white and red.

Outside the tiny quartz igloo the night wind keened among the pinnacles and buttresses and wind-eroded formations of the canal. On the wings of the wind, almost indistinguishable from the wind's own moaning, came the mournful howling of the Hounds, the great gaunt, shaggy beasts that haunted the deep canals and preyed on all living things except the Eaters.

Charley Wallace, squatting on the floor of the igloo, was scraping the last trace of flesh from the pelt of a Martian beaver. Kent watched the deft twist of his wrist, the flashing of knife blade in the single tiny radium bulb which illuminated the igloo's interior.

Charley was an old-timer. Long ago the sudden going and comings of Martian daylight and night had ceased to hold definite wonder for him. For 20 Martian years he had followed the trail of the Martian beaver, going father and farther afield, penetrating deeper and deeper into the mazes of the even farther canals that spread like a network over the face of the planet.

His face was like old leather, wrinkled and brown above the white sweep of his long white beard. His body was pure steel and whang-hide. He knew all the turns and tricks, all the trails and paths. He was one of the old-time canal-men.

The heater grids glowed redly, utilising the power stored in the seleno cells during the hours of daylight by the great sun-mirrors set outside the igloo. The atmosphere condensers chuckled softly. The electrolysis plant, used for the manufacture of water, squatted in its corner, silent now.

Charley carefully laid the pelt across his knees, stroked the deep brown fur with a wrinkled hand.

"Six of 'em," he said. His old eyes, blue as the sheen of ice, sparkled as he looked at Kent. "We'll make a haul this time, boy," he said. "Best huntin' I've seen in five years or more."

Kent nodded. "Sure will," he agreed.

The hunting had been good. Out only a month now and they had six pelts, more than many trappers and hunters were able to get during an entire year. The pelts would bring 1,000 apiece – perhaps more – back at the Red Rock trading post. Most valuable fur in the entire Solar System, they would sell at three times that amount back in the London or New York fur marts. A wrap of them would cost a cool 100,000.

Deep, rich, heavy fur. Kent shivered as he thought about it. The fur *had* to be heavy. Otherwise the beaver would never be able to exist. At night, the temperature plunged to 40 and 50 below, Centigrade, seldom reached above 20 below at high noon. Mars was cold! Here on the equator the temperature varied little, unlike the poles, where it might rise to 20 above during the summer when, for ten long months, the Sun never set, dropped to 100 or more below in the winter, when the Sun was unseen for equally as long.

He leaned back in his chair and gazed out through the quartz walls of the igloo. Far down the slope of the canal wall he saw the flickering lights of the Ghosts, those tenuous, wraith-like forms whose origin, true nature, and purpose were still the bone of bitter scientific contention.

The starlight threw strange lights and shadows on the twisted terrain of the canal. The naturally weird surface formations became a nightmare of strange, awe-impelling shapes, like pages snatched from the portfolio of a mad artist.

A black shape crossed a lighted ravine, slunk into the shadows.

"A Hound," said Kent.

Charley cursed in his whiskers.

"If them lopers keep hangin' around," he prophesied savagely, "we'll have some of their pelts to take out to Red Rock."

"They're mighty gun-shy," declared Kent. "Can't get near one of them."

"Yeah," said Charley, "but just try goin' out without a gun and see what happens. 'Most as bad as the Eaters. Only difference is that the Hounds would just as soon eat a man, an' the Eater would rather eat a man. They sure hanker after human flesh."

Another of the black shapes, slinking low, belly close to the ground, crossed the ravine.

"Another one," said Kent.

Something else was moving in the ravine, a figure that glinted in the starlight.

Kent leaned forward, choking back a cry. Then he was on his feet.

"A man," he shouted. "There's a man out there!"

Charley's chair overturned as he leaped up and stared through the quartz.

The space-armoured figure was toiling up the slope that led to the igloo. In one hand the man carried a short blast rifle, and as they watched, the two trappers saw him halt and wheel about, the rifle leveled, ready for action, to stare back at the shadows into which the two Hounds had disappeared only a moment before.

A slight movement to the left and behind the man outside caught Kent's eye and spurred him into action.

He leaped across the igloo and jerked from its rack his quartz-treated space suit, started clambering into it.

"What's the trouble?" demanded Charley. "What the hell you doin'?"

"There's an Eater out there," shouted Kent. "I saw it just a minute ago."

He snapped down the helmet and reached for his rifle as Charley spun open the inner air-lock port. Swiftly Kent leaped through, heard the inner port being screwed shut as he swung open the outer door.

Cold bit through the suit and into his very bones as he stepped out into the Martian night. With a swift flip he turned on the chemical heat units and felt a glow of warmth sweep over him.

The man in the ravine below was trudging up the path toward the igloo.

Kent shouted at him.

"Come on! Fast as you can!"

The man halted at the shout, stared upward.

"Come on!" screamed Kent.

The spacesuit moved forward.

Kent, racing down the ravine, saw the silica-armoured brute that lurched out of the shadows and sped toward the unsuspecting visitor.

Kent's rifle came to his shoulder.

The sights lined on the ugly head of the Eater. His finger depressed the firing mechanism and the gun spat a tight column of destructive blue fire. The blast crumpled the Eater in mid-leap, flung him off his stride and to one side. But it did not kill him. His unlovely body, gleaming like a reddish mirror in the starlight, clawed upon its feet, stood swinging the gigantic head from side to side.

A shrill scream sounded in Kent's helmet phones, but he was too busy getting the sights of the weapon lined on the Eater again to pay it any attention.

Again the rifle spat and purred, the blue blast-flame impinging squarely on the silica-armoured head. Bright sparks flew from the beast's head and then suddenly the head seemed to dissolve, melting down into a gob of blackened matter that glowed redly in places. The Eater slowly toppled sidewise and skidded ponderously down the slope to come to rest against the crimson boulder.

Kent signalled to the visitor.

"Come on," he shouted. "Quick about it! There may be more!"

Swiftly the man in the space suit came up the slope toward Kent.

"Thanks," he said as he drew abreast of the trapper.

"Get going, fellow," said Kent tersely.

"It isn't safe to be out here at night."

He fell in behind the visitor as they hurried toward the open port of the airlock.

The visitor lifted the helmet and laid it on the table and in the dim light of the radium bulb Kent saw the face of a woman.

He stood silent, staring. A visit by a man to their igloo in this out-of-the way spot would have been unusual enough; that a woman should drop in on them seemed almost incredible.

"A woman," said Charley. "Dim my sights, it's a woman."

"Yes, I'm a woman," said the visitor, and her tone, while it held a hidden hint of culture, was sharp as a whip. It reminded one of the bite of the wind outside. Her eyebrows were naturally high arched, giving her an air of eternal question and now she fastened that questioning gaze on the old trapper.

"You are Charley Wallace, aren't you?" she asked.

Charley shifted from one foot to another, uncomfortable under that level stare. "That's me," he admitted, "but you have the advantage of me, ma'am."

56

She hesitated, as if uncertain what he meant and then she laughed, a laugh that seemed to come from deep in her throat, full and musical. "I'm Ann Smith," she said.

She watched them, eyes flickering from one to the other, but in them she saw no faintest hint of recognition, no start of surprise at the name.

"They told me at Red Rock I'd find you somewhere in Skeleton Canal," she explained.

"You was a-lookin' for us?" asked Charley.

She nodded. "They told me you knew every foot of this country."

Charley squared his shoulders, pawed at his beard. His eyes gleamed brightly. Here was talk he understood. "I know it as well as anyone," he admitted.

She wriggled her shoulders free of the spacesuit, let it slide, crumpling to the floor, and stepped out of it. Kent stored his own suit on the rack and, picking the girl's suit off the floor, placed it beside his own.

"Yes, ma'am," said Charley, "I've roamed these canals for over twenty Martian years and I know 'em as good as most. I wouldn't be afraid of gettin' lost."

Kent studied their visitor. She was dressed in trim sports attire, faultless in fashion, hinting of expensive shops. Her light brown, almost blond hair, was smartly coiffed.

"But why were you lookin' for us?" asked Charley.

"I was hoping you would do something for me," she told him.

"Now," Charley replied, "I'd be glad to do something for you. Anything I can do."

Kent, watching her face, thought he saw a flicker of anxiety flit across her features. But she did not hesitate. There was no faltering of words as she spoke.

"You know the way to Mad-Man's Canal?"

If she had slapped Charley across the face with her gloved hand the expression on his face could not have been more awe-struck and dumfounded.

He started to speak, stuttered, was silent.

"You can't mean," said Kent, softly, "that you want us to go into Mad-Man's Canal?"

She whirled on him and it was as if he were an enemy. Her defences were up. "That's exactly what I mean," she said and again there was that wind-like lash in her voice. "But I don't want you to go alone. I'll go with you."

She walked slowly to one of the two chairs in the igloo, dropped into it, crossed her knees, swung one booted foot impatiently.

In the silence Kent could hear the chuckling of the atmosphere condensers, the faint sputter of the heating grids.

"Ma'am," said Charley, "you sure must be jokin'. You don't really mean you want to go into Mad-Man's?"

She faced him with a level stare. "But I do," she declared. "I never was more serious in my life. There's someone there I have to see."

"Lady," protested the old trapper, "someone's been spoofin' you. There ain't nobody over in Mad-Man's. You couldn't find a canal-man in his right mind who'd go near the place."

"There is," she told him. "And probably you'll laugh at this, too, but I happen to know it to be the truth. The man I want to see is Harry, the Hermit."

Kent guffawed softly, little more than a chuckle under his breath. But she heard and came up out of the chair.

"You're laughing," she said and the words were an accusation.

"Sit down," said Kent, "and let me tell you something. Something that no canal-man could admit, but something that every one of them know is the truth."

Slowly she sat down in the chair. Kent sat easily on the edge of the table.

"There isn't any such a person as Harry, the Hermit," he said. "It's just a myth. Just one of those stories that have grown up among the canal-men. Wild tales that they think up when they sit alone in the desolation of the Martian wilderness. Just figments of imagination they concoct to pass away the time. And then, when they go out with their furs, they tell these stories over the drinks at the trading posts and those they tell them to, tell them to the others – and so the tale is started. It goes from mouth to mouth. It gains strength as it goes, and each man improves upon it just a little, until in a year or two it is a full-blown legend. Something that the canal-men almost believe themselves, but know all the time is just a wild canal-tale."

"But I know," protested Ann. "I know there is such a man. I have to see him. I know he lives in Mad-Man's Canal."

"Listen," snapped Kent and the quiet casualness was gone from his words. "Harry, the Hermit, is everywhere. Go a few hundred miles from here and men will tell you he lives here in Skeleton Canal. Or he is down in the Big Eater system or he's up north in the Icy Hills. He is just an imaginary person, I tell you. Like the Paul Bunyan of the old lumberjacks back on Earth. Like Pecos Pete of the old American south-west. Like the fairies of the old Irish stories. Some trapper thought him up one lonely night and another trapper improved on him and a fellow dealing a stud poker hand in some little town improved a little more until today he is almost a real personage. Maybe he is real – real as a symbol of a certain group of men – but for all practical purposes, he is just a story, a fabrication of imagination."

The girl, he saw, was angry. She reached into the pocket of her jacket and pulled out a flat case. Her hands trembled as she opened it and took out a cigarette. She closed the case and tapped the cigarette against her thumbnail. A pencil of metal, pulled from the case, flared into flame.

She thrust the white cylinder between her lips and Kent reached down and took it away.

"Not here," he said and smiled.

She flared at him. "Why not?" she asked.

"Atmosphere," he said. "Neither Charley nor I smoke. Can't afford to. The condensers are small. We don't have too much current to run them. Two persons is the capacity of this igloo. Everything has to be figured down to scratch in this business. We

need all the air we get, without fouling it with tobacco smoke."
He handed her the cigarette.

In silence she put it back in the case, returned the case to her
pocket. "Sorry," she said. "I didn't know."

"Sorry I had to stop you," Kent told her.

She rose. "Perhaps I had better go," she said.

Charley's jaw went slack. "Go where?" he asked.

"My canal car," she said. "I left it about a mile from here.
Went past your place before I saw the light."

"But you can't spend the night in a car," protested Kent. "I'm
afraid you'll have to stay here."

"Sure," urged Charley, "we can't let you go. Sleeping in a car
is no picnic."

"We're harmless," Kent assured her.

She flushed. "I wasn't thinking of that," she said. "But you
said two persons was the capacity of the igloo."

"It is," Kent agreed, "but we can manage. We'll cut down the
heater current a little and step up the condensers. It may get a
little chilly, but we can manage with air."

He turned to Charley. "How about a pot of coffee," he
suggested.

Charley grinned, waggled his chin whiskers like a frolicsome
billy goat. "I was just thinkin' about that myself," he said.

Ann set down the coffee cup and looked at them. "You see,"
she explained, "it's not just something I want to do myself. Not
just some foolish whim of mine. It's something I've got to do.
Something that may help someone else – someone who is very
dear to me. I won't be able to sleep or eat or live, if I fail at
least to try. You have to understand that I simply must go to
Mad-Man's Canal and try to find Harry, the Hermit."

"But there ain't no Harry, the Hermit," protested Charley. He
wiped the coffee off his beard and sighed. "Goodness knows, I
wished there was, since you're so set on findin' him."

"But even if there isn't," said Ann, "I'd at least have to go
and look. I couldn't go through life wondering if you might

have been mistaken. Wondering if I should have given up so easily. If I go and try to find him and fail – why, then I've done everything I can, everything I could have expected myself to do. But if I don't I'll always wonder . . . there'll always be that doubt to torment me."

She looked from one face to the other. "You surely understand," she pleaded.

Charley regarded her steadily, his blue eyes shining. "This thing kind of means a lot to you, don't it?" he said.

She nodded.

Kent's voice broke the spell. "You don't know what you're doing," he said. "You flew down from Landing City to Red Rock in a nice comfortable rocket ship, and now because you covered the hundred miles between here and Red Rock in a canal car, you think you're an old-timer."

He stared back at her hurt eyes.

"Well, you aren't," he declared.

"Now, lad," said Charley, "you needn't get so rough."

"Rough!" said Kent. "I'm not getting rough. I'm just telling her a few of the things she has to know. She came across the desert in the car and everything went swell. Now she thinks it's just as easy to travel the canals."

"No, I don't," she flared at him, but he went on mercilessly.

"The canal country is dangerous. There's all sorts of chances for crack-ups. There are all sorts of dangers. Every discomfort you can imagine. Crack your car against a boulder – and you peel off the quartz. Then the ozone gets in its work. It eats through the metal. Put a crack in your suit and the same thing happens. This atmosphere is poisonous to metal. So full of ozone that if you breathe much of it it starts to work on your lung tissues. Not so much danger of that up on the plateau, where the air is thinner, but down here where there's more air, there's more ozone and it works just that much faster."

She tried to stop him, but he waved her into silence and went on:

"There are the Eaters. Hundreds of them. All with an insane appetite for human bones. They love the phosphate. Everyone

61

of them figuring how to get through a car or a spacesuit and at the food inside. You've never seen more than a couple of Eaters together at a time. But Charley and I have seen them by the thousands – great herds of them on their periodic migrations up and down the canyons. They've kept us penned in our igloo for days while they milled around outside, trying to reach us. And the Hounds, too, although they aren't so dangerous. And in the deeper places you find swarms of Ghosts. Funny things, the Ghosts. No physical harm from them. Maybe they don't even exist. Nobody knows what they are. But they are apt to drive you mad. Just looking at them, knowing they are watching all the time."

Impressive silence fell.

Charley wagged his beard.

"No place for a woman," he declared. "The canal ain't."

"I don't care," said Ann. "You're trying to frighten me, and I won't be frightened. I have to go to Mad-Man's Canal."

"Listen, lady," said Charley, "pick any other place – any other place at all – and I will take you there. But don't ask me to go into Mad-Man's."

"Why not?" she cried. "Why are you so afraid of Mad-Man's?"

She tried to find the answer in their faces but there was none.

Charley spoke slowly, apparently trying to choose his words with care. "Because," he said, "Mad-Man's is the deepest canal in this whole country. Far as I know, no man has ever been to the bottom of it and come out alive. Some have gone down part way and came back – mad and frothin' at the mouth, their eyes all glazed, babblin' crazy things. That's why they call it Mad-Man's."

"Now listen to me," and Ann. "I came all this way and I'm not turning back. If you won't take me, I'll go alone. I'll make it somehow – only you could make it so much easier for me. You know all the trails. You could get me there quicker. I'm prepared to pay you for it – pay you well."

"Lady," said Charley slowly, "we ain't guides. You couldn't

give us money enough to make us go where we didn't want to go."

She pounded one small clenched fist on the table. "But I want to pay you," she said. "I'll insist on it."

Charley made a motion of his hand, as if sweeping her words. "Not one cent," he said. "You can't buy our services. But we might do it anyhow. Just because I like your spunk."

She gasped. "You would?" she asked.

Neither one of them replied.

"Just take me to Mad-Man's," she pleaded. "I won't ask you to take me down into the canal. Just point out the best way and then wait for me. I'll make it myself. All I want to know is how to get there."

Charley lifted the coffee pot, filled the cups again.

"Ma'm," he said, "I reckon we can go where you can go. I reckon we ain't allowin' you to go down into Mad-Man's all by yourself."

Dawn roared over the canal rim and flooded the land with sudden light and life. The blanket plants unfolded their broad furry leaves, spreading them in the sunshine. The traveller plants, lightly anchored to boulder and outcropping, scurried frantically for places in the Sun. The canal suddenly became a mad flurry of plant life as the travellers, true plants but forced by environment to acquire the power of locomotion, quit the eastern wall, where they had travelled during the preceding day to keep pace with the sunlight, and rushed pell-mell for the western slope.

Kent tumbled out of the canal-car, rifle gripped in his hand. He blinked at the pale Sun that hung over the canal rim. His eyes swept the castellated horizon that closed in about them, took in the old familiar terrain typical of the Martian canals.

The canal was red – blood red shading to softest pink with the purple of early-morning shadow still hugging the eastern rim. A riot of red – the rusted bones of a dead planet. Tons of oxygen locked in those ramparts of bright red stone. Oxygen enough to make Mars livable – but locked forever in red oxide or iron.

Chimney and dome formations rose in tangled confusion with weathered pyramids and slender needles. A wild scene. Wild and lonesome and forbidding.

Kent swept the western horizon with his eyes. It was 30 miles or more to the rim, but in the thin atmosphere he could see with almost telescopic clearness the details of the scarp where the plateau broke and the land swung down in wild gyrations, frozen in red rock, to the floor of the canal where he stood.

Under the eastern rim, where the purple shadows still clung, flickered the watch-fires of the Ghosts, dim shapes from that distance. He shook his fist at them. Damn the Ghosts!

The slinking form of a Hound skulked down a ravine and disappeared. A beaver scuttled along a winding trail and popped into a burrow.

Slowly the night cold was rising from the land, dissipated by the rising Sun. The temperature would rise now until mid-afternoon, when it would stand at 15 or 20 below zero, Centigrade.

From a tangled confusion of red boulders leaped a silica-armoured Eater. Like an avenging rocket it bore down on Kent. Almost wearily the trapper lifted his rifle, blasted the Eater with one fierce burst of blue energy.

Kent cursed under his breath.

"Can't waste power," he muttered. "Energy almost gone."

He tucked the rifle under his arm and glared at the tumbled Eater. The huge beast, falling in mid-leap, had ploughed a deep furrow in the hard red soil.

Kent walked around the bulk of the car, stood looking at the uptilted second car that lay wedged between the huge boulders.

Charley climbed out through the open air lock and walked toward his partner. Inside his helmet he shook his head. "No good," he said. "She'll never run again."

Kent said nothing and Charley went on: "Whole side staved in. All of the quartz knocked off. Ozone's already got in its work. Plates softening."

"I suppose the mechanism is shot, too," said Kent.

"All shot to hell," said Charley.

They stood side by side, staring mournfully at the shattered machine.

"She was a good car, too," Charley pronounced, sadly.

"This," declared Kent, "is what comes of escorting a crazy dame all over the country."

Charley dismissed the matter. "I'm going to walk down the canal a ways. See what the going is like from here on," he told Kent.

"Be careful," the younger man warned him. "There's Eaters around. I just shot one."

The old man moved rapidly down the canal floor, picking his way between the scattered boulders and jagged outcroppings. In a moment he was out of sight. Kent walked around the corner of the undamaged car, saw Ann Smith just as she stepped from the airlock.

"Good morning," she said.

He did not return the greeting. "Our car is a wreck," he said. "We'll have to use yours from here on. It'll be a little cramped."

"A wreck?" she asked.

"Sure," he said. "That crash last night. When the bank caved under the treads, it smashed the quartz, let the ozone at the plates."

She frowned. "I'm sorry about that," she said. "Of course, it's my fault. You wouldn't be here if it weren't for me."

Kent was merciless. "I hope," he sighed, "that this proves to you travel in the canals is no pleasure jaunt."

She looked about them, shivered at the desolation.

"The Ghosts are the worst," she said. "Watching, always watching –"

Before them, not more than a hundred feet away, one of the Ghosts appeared, apparently writhing up out of a pile of jumbled rocks. It twisted and reared upward, tenuous, unguessable, now one shape, now another. For a moment it seemed to be a benign old grandfather, with long sweeping beard, and then it turned

65

into something that was utterly and unnamably obscene and then, as suddenly as it had come, it disappeared.

Ann shuddered. "Always watching," she said again. "Waiting around corners. Ready to rise up and mock you."

"They get on your nerves," Kent agreed, "but there's no reason to be afraid of them. They couldn't touch you. They may be nothing more than mirage – figments of the imagination, like your Harry, the Hermit."

She swung about to face him. "How far are we from Mad-Man's?" she demanded.

Kent shrugged his shoulders. "I don't know," he said. "Maybe a few miles, maybe a hundred. We should be near, though."

From down the canal came Charley's halloo. "Mad-Man's" he shouted back to them. "Mad-Man's! Come and look at it!"

Mad-Man's Canal was a continuation of the canal the three had been travelling – but it was utterly different.

Suddenly the canal floor broke, dipped down sharply and plummeted into a deep blue pit of shadows. For miles the great depression extended, and on all sides the ground sloped steeply into the seemingly bottomless depths of the canyon.

"What is it, Charley?" asked Kent, and Charley waggled his beard behind the space-helmet.

"Can't say, lad," he declared, "but it sure is an awe-inspirin' sight. For twenty Martian years I've tramped these canals and I never seen the like of it."

"A volcanic crater?" suggested Ann.

"Maybe," agreed Charley, "but it don't look exactly like that either. Something happened here, though. Floor fell out of the bottom of the canal or somethin'."

"You can't see the bottom," said Ann. "Looks like a blue haze down there. Not exactly like shadows. More like fog or water."

"Ain't water," declared Charley. "You can bet your bottom dollar on that. If anyone ever found that much water on Mars they'd stake out a claim and make a fortune."

"Did you ever know anyone who tried to go down there, Charley?" asked Kent. "Ever talk to anyone who tried it?"

66

"No, lad, I never did. But I heard tell of some who tried. And they never were the same again. Somethin' happened to them down there. Somethin' that turned their minds."

Kent felt icy fingers on his spine. He stared down into the deep blue of Mad-Man's and strained his eyeballs, trying to pierce the veil that hid the bottom. But that was useless. If one wanted to find out what was down there, he'd have to travel down those steeply sloping walls, would have to take his courage in hand and essay what other men had tried and gone crazy for their pains.

"We can't use the car," he said suddenly and was surprised at his words.

Kent walked backward from the edge of the pit. What was happening to them? Why this calm acceptance of the fact they were going to go down into Mad-Man's? They didn't have to go. It wasn't too late yet to turn around and travel back the way they came. With only one car now, and many miles to travel, they would have to take it slow and easy, but they could make it. It was the sensible thing to do, held none of the rash foolhardiness involved in a descent into those blue depths before them.

He heard Charley's words, as if from a great distance.

"Sure, we'll have to walk. But we ought to be able to make it. Maybe we'll find air down there, air dense enough to breathe and not plumb full of ozone. Maybe there'll be some water, too."

"Charley," Kent shouted, "you don't know what you're saying! We can't —"

He stopped in mid-sentence and listened. Even as he talked, he had heard that first weird note from up the canal, a sound that he had heard many times before, the faraway rumble of running hoofs, the grating clash of stonelike body on stonelike body.

"The Eaters!" he shouted. "The Eaters are migrating."

He glanced swiftly about him. There was no way of escape. The walls of the canal had narrowed and closed in, rising sheer from the floor on either side of them, only a few miles away. There was no point of vantage where they could make a stand and hold off the horde that was thundering toward them. And

67

even if there were, they had but little power left for their guns. In the long trek down the canal they had been forced to shoot time after time to protect their lives, and their energy supply for the weapons was running low.

"Let's get back to the car!" screamed Ann. She started to run. Kent sprinted after her, grabbed her and pulled her around.

"We'd never make it," he yelled at her. "Hear those hoofs! They're stampeding! They'll be here in a minute!"

Charley was yelling at them, pointing down into Mad-Man's. Kent nodded, agreeing. It was the only way to go. The only way left open for them. There was no place to hide, no place to stand and fight. Flight was the only answer – and flight took them straight into the jaws of Mad-Man's Canal.

Charley bellowed at them, his bright blue eyes gleaming with excitement. "Maybe we got a chance. If we can reach the shadows."

They plunged down, going at a run, fighting to keep their balance. Soft, crumbly rock shifted and broke under the impact of their steel-shod feet. A shower of rubble accompanied them, chuckling and clinking down the slope. The sun blinked out and they plunged into the deep shadows, fought to reduce their speed, slowed to a walk.

Kent looked back. Above him, on the level of the canal floor, he saw a fighting mass of Eaters, indescribable confusion there on the rim of the skyline, as the great silica-armoured beasts fought against plunging into Mad–Man's. Those in front were rearing, shoving, striking savagely, battling against being shoved over the edge as those behind ploughed into them. Some of them had toppled onto the slope, were sliding and clawing, striving to regain their feet. Others were doggedly crawling back up the slope.

The three below watched the struggle above them.

"Even them cussed Eaters are afraid to go into Mad-Man's," said Charley.

They were surrounded by Ghosts. Hundreds of them, wavering

and floating, appearing and disappearing. In the blue shadows of the sunken world they seemed like wind-blown flames that rocked back and forth, flickering, glimmering, guttering. Assuming all kinds of forms, forms beautiful in their intricacy of design, forms angularly flat and ugly, gruesome and obscene and terrible.

And always there was that terrible sense of watching – of ghostly eyes watching and waiting – of hidden laughter and ghoulish design.

"Damn them," said Kent. He stubbed his toe and stumbled, righted himself.

"Damn them," he said again.

The air had become denser, with little ozone now. Half an hour before they had shut off their oxygen supply and snapped open the visors of their helmets. Still thin, pitifully by Earthly standards, the air was breathable and they needed to save what little oxygen might remain within their tanks.

Ann stumbled and fell against Kent. He steadied her until she regained her feet. He saw her shiver.

"If they only wouldn't watch us," she whispered to him. "They'll drive me mad. Watching us – no indication of friendliness or unfriendliness, no emotion at all. Just watching. If only they would go away – do something even!" Her whisper broke on a hysterical note.

Kent didn't answer. What was there to say? He felt a savage wave of anger at the Ghosts. If a man could only do something about them. You could shoot and kill the Eaters and the Hounds. But guns and hands meant nothing to these ghostly forms, these dancing, flickering things that seemed to have no being.

Charley, plodding ahead down the slope, suddenly stopped.

"There's something just ahead," he said. "I saw it move."

Kent moved up beside him and held his rifle ready. They stared into the blue shadows. "What did it look like?" Kent asked.

"Can't say, lad," Charley told him. "Just got a glimpse of it."

They waited. A rock loosened below them and they could hear it clatter down the slope.

"Funny lookin' jigger," Charley said.

Something was coming up the slope toward them, something that made a slithering sound as it came, and to their nostrils came a faint odour, a suggestion of stench that made the hair crawl on the back of Kent's neck.

The thing emerged from the gloom ahead and froze the three with horror as it came. A thing that was infinitely more horrible in form than any reptilian monster that had ever crawled through the primal ooze of the new-spawned Earth, a thing that seemed to personify all the hate and evil that had ever, through long milleniums, lived and found its being on the aged planet Mars. A grisly death-head leered at them and drooling jaws opened, displaying fangs that dripped with loathsomeness.

Kent brought his rifle up as Ann's shriek rang in his ears, but Charley reached out and wrenched the weapon from his hand.

His voice came, cool and calm.

"It's no time to be shootin', lad," he said. "There's another one over there, just to our right and I think I see a couple more out just beyond."

"Give me that gun!" yelled Kent, but as he lunged to jerk it from Charley's grasp he saw, out of the tail of his eye, a dozen more of the things squatting just within the shadows.

"We better not rile them, son," said Charley softly. "They're a hell's brood and that's for sure."

He handed the rifle back to Kent and started backing up the slope, slow step by slow step.

Together the three of them backed slowly away, guns held at ready. In front of them, between them and the squatting monstrosities, a single Ghost suddenly materialised. A Ghost that did not waver but held straight and true, like a candle flame burning in the stillness of the night. Another Ghost appeared beside the first, and suddenly there were several more. The Ghosts floated slowly down the slope toward the death-head things, and as they moved they took on a deeper colour, more substantiality, until they burned a deep and steady blue, solid columns of flame against the lighter blue of the eternal shadow.

Staring, scarcely believing, the three saw the gaping ghouls that had crept up the slope, turn and shuffle swiftly back, back into the mystery of the lower reaches of Mad-Man's.

Kent laughed nervously. "Saved by a Ghost," he said.

"Why, maybe they aren't so bad after all," said Ann and her voice was scarcely more than a whisper. "I wonder why they did it?"

"And how they did it," said Kent.

"Principally," said Charley, "why they did it. I never heard of any Ghost ever takin' any interest in a man, and I have trod these canals for twenty Martian years."

Kent expelled his breath. "And now," he said, "for Lord's sake, let's turn back. We won't find any hermit here. No man could live out a week here unless he had some specially trained Ghosts to guard him all the time. There isn't any use of going on and asking for trouble."

Charley looked at Ann. "It's your expedition, ma'am," he said.

She looked from one to the other and there was fear upon her face.

"I guess you're right," she said. "No one could live here. We won't find anyone here. I guess it must just have been a myth, after all." Her shoulders seemed to sag.

"We'll go on if you say the word," said Charley.

"Hell, yes," declared Kent, "but we're crazy to do it. I understand now why men came out of here stark crazy. A few more things like these we just seen and I'll be nuts myself."

"Look!" cried Ann. "Look at the Ghosts. They are trying to tell us something!"

It was true. The Ghosts, still flaming with their deep-blue colour, had formed into a semicircle before them. One of them floated forward. His colour flowed and changed until he took on a human form. His right hand pointed at them and then waved down the slope. They stared incredulously as the motion was repeated.

"Why," said Ann, "I do believe he's trying to tell us to go on."

"Dim my sight," shrieked Charley, "if that ain't what the critter is tryin' to tell us."

71

The other Ghosts spread out, encircled the three. The one with the manlike form floated down the slope, beckoning. The others closed in, as if to urge them forward.

"I guess," said Kent, "we go whether we want to or not."

Guarded by the circle of Ghosts they went down the slope. From outside the circle came strange and terrible noises, yammerings and hissings and other sounds that hinted at shambling obscenities, strange and terrible life forms which lived and fought and died here in the lower reaches of Mad-Man's.

The shadows deepened almost to darkness. The air became denser. The temperature rose swiftly.

They seemed to be walking on level ground.

"Maybe we've reached the bottom," suggested Kent.

The circle of Ghosts parted, spread out and the three stood by themselves. A wall of rock rose abruptly before them, and from a cave in its side streamed light, light originating in a half-dozen radium bulbs. A short distance to one side squatted a shadowy shape.

"A rocket ship!" exclaimed Kent.

The figure of a man, outlined against the light, appeared in the mouth of the cave.

"The hermit!" cried Charley. "Harry, the Hermit. Blast my hindsight, if it ain't old Harry, himself!"

Kent heard the girl's voice, beside him. "I was right! I was right! I knew he had to be here somewhere!"

The man walked toward them. He was a huge man, his shoulders square and his face was fringed in a golden-yellow beard. His jovial voice thundered a welcome to them.

At the sound of that voice Ann cried out, a cry that was half gladness, half disbelief. She took a slow step forward and then suddenly she was running toward the hermit.

She flung herself at him. "Uncle Howard!" she cried. "Uncle Howard!"

He flung his brawny arms around the space-armoured girl, lifted her off the ground and set her down.

72

Ann turned to them. "This is my uncle, Howard Carter," she said. "You've heard of him. His best friends call him Mad-Man Carter, because of the things he does. But you aren't mad, really, are you, Uncle?"

"Just at times," Carter boomed.

"He's always going off on expeditions," said the girl. "Always turning up in unexpected places. But he's a scientist for all of that, a really good scientist."

"I've heard of you, Dr Carter," said Kent, "I'm glad to find you down here."

"You might have found worse," said Carter.

"Dim my sights," said Charley. "A human being living at the bottom of Mad-Man's!"

"Come on in," invited Carter. "I'll have you a cup of hot coffee in a minute."

Kent stretched out his legs, glad to get out of his spacesuit. He glanced around the room. It was huge and appeared to be a large cave chamber. Perhaps the cliffs that rimmed in Mad-Man's were honeycombed with caves and labyrinths, an ideal place in which to set up camp.

But this was something more than a camp. The room was well furnished, but its furnishings were a mad hodge-podge. Tables and chairs and heating grids, laboratory equipment and queer-appearing machines. One machine, standing in one corner, kept up an incessant chattering and clucking. In another corner, a mighty ball hung suspended in mid-air, halfway between the ceiling and the floor, and within it glowed a blaze of incandescence which it was impossible to gaze directly upon. Piled haphazardly about the room were bales and boxes of supplies.

Kent waved his hand at a pile of boxes. "Looks like you're planning on staying here for a while, Dr Carter," he said.

The man with the fearsome yellow beard lifted a coffee pot off the stove and chuckled. His chuckle thundered in the room. "I may have to stay quite a while longer," he said, "although I doubt it. My work here is just about done." He poured steaming coffee into the cups. "Draw up your chairs," he invited.

He took his place at the end of the small table. "It's tiring work coming down into Mad-Man's. Almost five miles."

Charley lifted his cup to his mouth, drank deeply, wiped his whiskers carefully. "It's quite a little walk, I'll admit," he said. "For twenty Martian years I've trapped the canals and I never saw the like of it. What made it, Doc?"

Dr Carter looked puzzled. "Oh," he said, "you mean what made Mad–Man's."

Charley nodded.

"I really don't know," said Carter. "I've been too busy on other things since I came here to try to find out. It's a unique depression in the surface of the planet, but as to why or how it came to be, I don't know. Although I could find out for you in a minute if you want to know. Funny I never thought of finding out for myself."

He glanced around the table and his eyes came to rest on Ann. "But there's something I do want to know," he said, "and that is how this precious niece of mine ferreted me out."

"But, Uncle Howard," protested Ann, "I didn't ferret you out. I wasn't looking for you at all. I didn't even know you were anywhere around. I thought you were off on one of your crazy expeditions again."

Charley choked on a mouthful of food. "What's that?" he asked. "You weren't hunting for him?" He jerked his thumb at Dr Carter.

Ann shook her head. "No," she said. "I was looking for Harry, the Hermit."

"Cripes," exploded Charley, "I thought we had found him. I thought your uncle here was the hermit. I thought you knew all along."

Dr Howard Carter's fork clattered on his plate. "Now wait a minute," he roared. "What's all this talk about hermits?"

He eyed Ann sternly. "You didn't tell these men I was a hermit, did you."

"Hell," said Kent, "let's just admit there's no such a person as Harry, the Hermit. He's just a myth. I've told you so all along."

Ann explained. "It was this way. I was looking for Harry, the Hermit. Jim Bradley, the famous explorer, told me that if Harry, the Hermit, really existed, Mad-Man's was the place to look for him. He said Mad-Man's was the only place where a man could live for any length of time in any comfort. And he said he had reason to believe someone was living in Mad-Man's. So I started out to look."

"But," demanded her uncle, "why did you want to find this hermit? Just curiosity?"

Ann shook her head. "No, not curiosity," she said. "You see, Uncle, it's Dad. He's got into trouble again —"

"Trouble?" snapped Carter. "Some more of his fool experiments, I suppose. What is it this time? Perpetual motion?"

"Not perpetual motion," said the girl. "This time he was successful. Too successful. He built a machine that had something to do with space-time, with the interdimensions. He tried to travel to another dimension. That was a month ago."

"And he isn't back yet?" suggested Carter.

The girl glanced at him. "How did you know?" she demanded.

"Because I warned him that is what would happen if he went monkeying around with extra-dimensions."

"But what had the hermit to do with all this?" asked Kent.

"Bradley told me he thought that the Hermit really was Prof Belmont. You know, the great physicist. He disappeared a couple of years ago and has never been heard of since. Bradley thought he might be down here, conducting some sort of experiments. That might have given rise to the hermit legend."

Charley chuckled. "I heard stories about Harry, the Hermit, ten years ago," he said. "I judge, ma'am, from what you say, that they're just getting out to civilisation. Nobody gave rise to those stories, they just grew."

Carter had shoved his plate to one side. Now he leaned forward, resting his arms on the tabletop. "Belmont did come here," he said. "But he's dead. The things out there killed him."

"Killed him!" Ann's face suddenly was white. "Are you sure of that?"

Carter nodded.

75

"He was the only man who could have helped Dad," the girl said tensely. "He was the only man who could have understood –"

"The Ghosts told me," said Carter. "There's no mistake. Belmont is dead."

Charley set down his coffee cup and stared at Carter. "You been talkin' with them Ghosts, mister?" he asked.

Carter nodded.

"Dim my sights," said Charley. "Who'd've thought them things could talk."

But Carter paid no attention. "Ann," he said, "maybe I can do something for you. Perhaps not myself. But the Ghosts can."

"The Ghosts?" asked Ann.

"Certainly, the Ghosts. What would anyone come here to study if not the Ghosts? There are thousands of them in Mad-Man's. That's what Belmont came here to do. When he didn't come back, and no one was able to locate him, I came out here secretly. I thought maybe he found something he didn't want the rest of the world to know, so I didn't leave any tracks for anyone else to follow."

"But how could the Ghosts help anyone?" asked Kent. "Apparently they are an entirely different order of being. They would have nothing in common with mankind. No sympathies."

Carter's beard jutted fiercely. "The Ghosts," he said, "are beings of force. Instead of protoplasm, they are constructed of definite force fields. They live independently of everything which we know as essential to life. And yet they are life. And intelligent life, at that. They are the true, dominant being of Mars. At one time they weren't as they are now. They are a product of evolution. The Eaters evolved by taking on silica armour. The Hounds and beavers met conditions by learning to do with little food and even less water, grew heavy fur to protect them against the cold. It's all a matter of evolution.

"The Ghosts could solve many of the problems of the human race, could make the race godlike overnight. That is – if they wanted to. But they don't want to. They have no capacity for

76

pity, no yearning to become benefactors. They are just indifferent. They watch the pitiful struggle of the human race here on Mars, and if they feel anything at all, it is a smug sort of humour. They don't pity us or hate us. They just don't care."

"But you," said Ann, "you made friends with them."

"Not friends," said her uncle. "We just had an understanding, an agreement. The Ghosts lack a sense of co-operation and responsibility. They have no sense for leadership. They are true individuals, but they know that these very lacks have stood in the way of progress. Their knowledge, great as it is, has lain dormant for thousands of years. They realise that under intelligent leadership they can go ahead and increase that knowledge, become a race of purely intellectual beings, the match of anything in the System, perhaps in the galaxy."

He paused for a moment, drummed his fingers on the table.

"I'm furnishing them that leadership," he declared.

"But what about Dad?" asked Ann. "You and he never could get along, you hated one another, I know, but you can help him. You will help him, won't you?"

The scientist rose from the table, strode to the chattering, clucking machine at the other side of the room. "My communicator," he said. "A machine which enables me to talk with the Ghosts. Based on the radio, tuning in on the frequencies of the Ghosts' thought-waves. Through this machine comes every scrap of information which the Ghosts wish to relay to me. The thoughts were recorded on spools of fine wire. All I have to do to learn whatever has been transmitted over the machine is to put on a thought-translation helmet, run the spools of wire through it, and the thoughts impinge on my brain. I hear nothing, feel nothing – but I know. The thoughts of the Ghosts are impressed into my brain, become my thoughts."

Charley waggled his beard, excitement and wonder written on his features. "Then you know everything that's going on all over Mars," he said. "The Ghosts are everywhere, see everything."

"I know everything they think is important enough for me to know," Carter declared. "They can find out anything I might want to know."

77

"How do you talk to them?" asked Kent.

"Same process," said the scientist. "A helmet that broadcasts my thoughts to them."

He picked up a helmet and set it on his head. "I'm going to find out about your father," he told Ann.

"But he isn't in this space-time," objected Ann. "He's somewhere else."

Carter smiled. "The Ghosts know all about him," he said. "A few weeks ago they told me about a man lost outside of our space-time frame. It must have been your father. I didn't know."

He looked squarely at the girl. "Please believe me, Ann. If I had known who it was I would have done something."

The girl nodded, her eyes bright.

Silence fell upon the room. Finally Carter lifted the helmet from his head, set it back on the metal bench.

"Did you – did the Ghosts know anything about it?" asked the girl.

Her uncle nodded. "Ann," he said, "your father will be returned. No mortal man could get him back into his normal dimensions, but the Ghosts can. They have ways of doing things. Warping of world lines and twisting of inter-dimensional co-ordinates."

"You really mean that?" Ann asked. "This isn't just another of your practical jokes?"

The golden beard grinned broadly and then sobered. "Child," he said, "I don't joke about things like this. They are too important."

He looked about the room, as if expecting something, someone.

"Your father will be here any moment now," he declared.

"Here!" exclaimed Ann. "Here, in this room —"

Her voice broke off suddenly. The room had suddenly filled with Ghosts, and in their midst stood a man, a man with stooped shoulders and heavy-lensed glasses and lines of puzzlement upon his face. Like a puff of wind the Ghosts were gone and the man stood alone.

Ann flew at him. "Father," she cried. "You're back again, Father."

She went into his arms and the man, looking over her shoulder, suddenly saw the man with the beard.

"Yes, Ann," he said, "I am back again."

His face hardened as Carter took a step toward them.

"You here," he snapped. "I might have known. Where there's anything afoot you're always around."

Laughter gurgled in the throat of the bearded giant. "So you went adventuring in the dimensions, did you?" he asked, mockery in his voice. "You always wanted to do that, John. The great John Smith, only man to ever go outside the four dimensional continuum."

His laughter seemed to rock the room.

"I suppose you got me out," said Smith, "so you could gloat over me."

The men stood, eyes locked, and Kent sensed between them an antagonism that was almost past understanding.

"I won't thank you for it," said Smith.

"Why, John, I never expected you to," chortled Carter. "I knew you'd hate me for it. I didn't do it for you. I did it for your little girl. She came from Landing City across hundreds of miles of deserts and canals to help you. She came down into Mad-Man's. She's the one I did it for. For her and the two brave men who came with her."

For the first time, apparently, Smith noticed Kent and Charley.

"I do thank you," he said, "for whatever you have done."

"Shucks," said Charley, "it wasn't nothin'. Nothin' at all. I always wanted to see Mad-Man's. Nobody ever came down here and came out sane. Most of them came down didn't come out at all."

"If it hadn't been for my Ghosts neither would you," Carter reminded him.

"Father," pleaded Ann, "you mustn't be like this. Uncle brought

79

you back. He was the only man who could have. If it hadn't been for him, you would still be out in the extra-dimension."

"What was it like, John?" asked Carter. "Dark and nothing to see?"

"As a matter of fact," said Smith, "that is exactly what it was."

"That's what you thought," jeered Carter. "Because you had no sense of perception to see or hear or make any contacts or associations in that world. Did you actually think your pitiful little human sense would serve you in a place like that?"

"What do you know about it?" snarled Smith.

"The Ghosts," said Carter. "You must not forget. The Ghosts tell me everything."

Carter looked around the room. "And now," he said, "I fear that you must go." He looked at Ann. "I did what you wanted me to do, didn't I?"

She nodded. "You are turning us out?" she asked.

"Call it that if you wish," said Carter. "I have work to do. A great deal of work to do. One of the reasons I came to Mad-Man's was to be alone."

"Now look here, mister," said Carter bluntly. "It's a long pull up Mad-Man's. A longer pull back to our igloo. You aren't turning us out without a chance to rest, are you?"

"He's crazy," said Smith. "He's always been crazy. He's sane only half of the time. Don't pay any attention to him."

Carter paid Smith no attention. He addressed Charley. "You won't have to walk back," he said. "My rocket ship is out there. Take it." He chuckled. "You needn't bother bringing it back. I'll give it to you."

"But, uncle," cried Ann. "What about yourself?"

"Don't worry about me," Carter told her. "I won't need it. The Ghosts can take me any place I want to go upon a moment's notice. I've outgrown your silly rocket ships. I've outgrown a lot of things."

He swept his arm about the room, pointed at the globe of brilliant fire that hung suspended between floor and ceiling.

"Pure energy," he said. "In there atoms are being created.

Millions of horsepower are being generated. An efficient, continual source of power. Enclosed in a sphere of force waves, the only thing that would stand the pressure and temperature inside the sphere."

He ceased speaking, looking around.

"That's only one of the things I've learned," he said. "Only one of the things. The Ghosts are my teachers, but given time I will be their master."

There was a wild light of fanaticism in his eyes.

"Why, man," said Kent, "you will be hailed as the greatest scientist the world has ever known."

The man's eyes seemed to flame. "No, I won't," he said, "because I'm not going to tell the world. Why should I tell the world? What has mankind ever done for me?" His laughter bellowed and reverberated in the domed room. "Find out for yourselves," he shouted. "Go and find out for yourselves. It will take you a million years."

His voice calmed. "The Ghosts are almost immortal," he said. "Not quite – almost. Before I am through with this, I will be immortal. There is a way. I almost have it now. I will become a Ghost – a super-Ghost – a creature of pure force. And when that happens the Ghosts and I will forsake this worn-out world. We will go out into the void and build a new world, a perfect world. We will live through all eternity and watch and laugh at the foolish strugglings of little people. Little people like mankind."

The four of them stared at him.

"You don't mean this, Howard," protested Smith. "You can't mean it."

The wild light was gone from Carter's eyes. His voice boomed with mockery. "You don't think so, John?" he asked.

He reached into his shirt front, pulled out something that shone in the light of the radium bulbs. It was a key, attached to a string hung around his neck. He pulled the loop over his head, handed the key to Kent.

"The key to the rocket ship," he said. "The fuel tanks are nearly full. You fly her at a 30-degree angle out of here to miss the cliffs."

Kent took the key, turned it awkwardly in his hands.

Carter bowed ceremoniously to them, still with that old trace of mockery. "I hope you have a fine trip," he said.

Slowly they turned away, heading for the door.

Carter called after them.

"And you might tell anyone you see not to try to come into Mad-Man's. Tell them something unpleasant might happen."

Charley turned around. "Mister," he said, "I think you're batty as a bed-bug."

"Charley," declared Carter, "you aren't the first one to say that to me. And maybe . . . well, sometimes, I think, maybe you are right."

The sturdy rocket ship blasted its way across the red deserts. Far below, the criss-crossing of the canals, more deeply red, were etched like fiery lines.

"Lad," said Charley to Kent, "there's another story to tell the boys. Another yarn about Harry, the Hermit."

"They won't believe it," Kent declared. "They'll listen and then go out and retell it and make it a little better. And someone else will make it better yet. All we can do, Charley, is to give rise to another, an even greater, Harry, the Hermit."

Ann, sitting beside her father, smiled at them. "Just a couple of myth-makers," she said.

Charley studied the terrain beneath them, combed his beard. "You know," he said, "I still think that bird back there was off his nut. He'll try makin' himself into a Ghost – and just be an ordinary Earth kind of ghost. The kind that just ain't."

A Ghost suddenly materialised, shimmered faintly in the rocket cabin.

And for the first time known to man, perhaps for the first time in all history, the Ghost spoke, spoke with a voice they all recognised, the voice of the man back in Mad-Man's, that voice with its old mockery.

"So you think so, do you?" said the Ghost.

Then he faded from their view.

Masquerade

Old Creepy was down in the control room, sawing lustily on his screeching fiddle.

On the sun-blasted plains outside the Mercutian Power Centre, the Roman Candles, snatching their shapes from Creepy's mind, had assumed the form of Terrestrial hill-billies and were cavorting through the measure of a square dance.

In the kitchen, Rastus rolled two cubes about the table, crooning to them, feeling lonesome because no one would shoot a game of craps with him.

Inside the refrigeration room, Mathilde, the cat, stared angrily at the slabs of frozen beef above her head, felt the cold of the place and meowed softly, cursing herself for never being able to resist the temptation of sneaking in when Rastus wasn't looking.

Up in the office, at the peak of the great photocell that was the centre, Curt Craig stared angrily across the desk at Norman Page.

One hundred miles away, Knut Anderson, encased in a cumbersome photocell spacesuit, stared incredulously at what he saw inside the space warp.

The communications bank snarled warningly and Craig swung about in his chair, lifted the handset off the cradle and snapped recognition into the mouthpiece.

"This is Knut, chief," said a voice, badly blurred by radiations.

"Yes," yelled Craig. "What did you find?"

"A big one," said Knut's voice.

"Where?"

"I'll give you the location."

Craig snatched up a pencil, wrote rapidly as the voice spat and crackled at him.

"Bigger than anything on record," shrilled Knut's voice. "Space busted wide open and twisted all to hell. The instruments went nuts."

"We'll have to slap a tracer on it," said Craig, tensely. "Take a lot of power, but we've got to do it. If that thing starts to move —"

Knut's voice snapped and blurred and sputtered so Craig couldn't hear a word he said.

"You come back right away," Craig yelled. "It's dangerous out there. Get too close to that thing. Let it swing toward you and you —"

Knut interrupted, his voice wallowing in the wail of tortured beam. "There's something else, chief. Somthing funny. Damn funny —"

The voice pinched out.

Craig shrieked into the mouthpiece. "What is it, Knut? What's funny?"

He stopped, astonished, for suddenly the crackle and hissing and whistle of the communications beam was gone.

His left hand flicked out to the board and snapped a toggle. The board hummed as tremendous power surged into the call. It took power – lots of power, to maintain a tight beam on Mercury. But there was no answering hum – no indication the beam was being restored.

Something had happened out there! Something had snapped the beam.

Craig stood up, white-faced, to stare through the ray filter port to the ashy plains. Nothing to get excited about. Not yet, anyway. Wait for Knut to get back. It wouldn't take long. He had told Knut to start at once, and those puddle jumpers could travel.

But what if Knut didn't come back? What if that space warp had moved?

The biggest one on record, Knut had said. Of course, there

always were a lot of them one had to keep an eye on, but very few big enough to really worry about. Little whirlpools and eddies where the spacetime continuum was wavering around, wondering which way it ought to jump.

Not dangerous, just a bother. Had to be careful not to drive a puddle jumper into one. But a big one, if it started to move, might engulf the plant . . .

Outside, the Candles were kicking up the dust, shuffling and hopping and flapping their arms. For the moment they were mountain folk back in the hills of Earth, having them a hoe down. But there was something grotesque about them – like scarecrows set to music.

The plains of Mercury stretched away to the near horizon, rolling plains of bitter dust. The Sun was a monstrous thing of bright-blue flame in a sky of inky black, ribbons of scarlet curling out like snaky tentacles.

Mercury was its nearest to the Sun a mere 29,000,000 miles distant, and that probably explained the warp. The nearness to the Sun and the epidemic of sunspots. Although the sunspots may not have had anything to do with it. Nobody knew.

Craig had forgotten Page until the man coughed, and then he turned to the desk.

"I hope," said Page, "that you have reconsidered. This project of mine means a lot to me."

Craig was suddenly swept with anger at the man's persistence.

"I gave you my answer once," he snapped. "That is enough. When I say a thing, I mean it."

"I can't see your objection," said Page flatly. "After all, these Candles –"

"You're not capturing any Candles," said Craig. "Your idea is the most crackpot, from more than one viewpoint, that I have ever heard."

"I can't understand this strange attitude of yours," argued Page. "I was assured at Washington —"

Craig's anger flared. "I don't give a damn what Washington assured you. You're going back as soon as the oxygen ship comes in. And you're going back without a Candle."

"It would do no harm. And I'm prepared to pay well for any services you —"

Craig ignored the hinted bribe, levelled a pencil at Page.

"Let me explain it to you once again," he said. "Very carefully and in full, so you will understand.

"The Candles are natives of Mercury. They were here first. They were here when men came, and they'll probably be here long after men depart. They have let us be and we have let them be. And we have let them be for just one reason – one damn good reason. You see, we don't know what they could do if we stirred them up. We are afraid of what they might do."

Page opened his mouth to speak, but Craig waved him into silence and went on.

"They are organisms of pure energy. Things that draw their life substance directly from the Sun – just as you and I do. Only we get ours by a roundabout way. Lot more efficient than we are by that very token, for they absorb their energy direct, while we get ours by chemical processes.

"And when we've said that much – that's about all we can say. Because that's all we know about them. We've watched those Candles for five hundred years and they still are strangers to us."

"You think they are intelligent?" asked Page, and the question was a sneer.

"Why not?" snarled Craig. "You think they aren't because Man can't communicate with them. Just because they didn't break their necks to talk with men.

"Just because they haven't talked doesn't mean they aren't intelligent. Perhaps they haven't communicated with us because their thought and reasoning would have no common basis for intelligent communication with mankind. Perhaps it's because they regard Man as an inferior race – a race upon which it isn't even worth their while to waste their time."

"You're crazy," yelled Page. "They have watched us all these years. They've seen what we can do. They've seen our space ships – they've seen us build this plant – they've seen us shoot power across millions of miles to the other planet."

"Sure," agreed Craig, "they've seen all that. But would it impress them? Are you sure it would? Man, the great architect! Would you bust a gut trying to talk to a spider, or an orchard oriole, or a mud wasp? You bet your sweet life you wouldn't. And they're great architects, every one of them."

Page bounced angrily in his chair. "If they're superior to us," he roared, "where are the things they've done? Where are their cities, their machines, their civilisations?"

"Perhaps," suggested Craig, "they outlived machines and cities millennia ago. Perhaps they've reached a stage of civilisation where they don't need mechanical things."

He tapped the pencil on the desk.

"Consider this. Those Candles are immortal. They'd have to be. There'd be nothing to kill them. They apparently have no bodies – just balls of energy. That's their answer to their environment. And you have the nerve to think of capturing some of them! You, who know nothing about them, plan to take them back to Earth to use as a circus attraction, a side-show drawing card – something for fools to gape at!"

"People come out here to see them," Page countered. "Plenty of them. The tourist bureau use them in their advertising."

"That's different," roared Craig. "If the Candles want to put on a show on home territory, there's nothing we can do about it. But you can't drag them away from here and show them off. That would spell trouble and plenty of it!"

"But if they're so damned intelligent?" yelped Page, "why do they put on those shows at all? Just think of something and presto! – they're it. Greatest mimics in the Solar System. And they never get anything right. It's always cock-eyed. That's the beauty of it."

"It's cock-eyed," snapped Craig, "because man's brain never fashions a letter-perfect image. The Candles pattern themselves directly after the thoughts they pick up. When you think of something you don't give them all the details – your thoughts are sketchy. You can't blame the Candles for that. They pick up what you give them and fill in the rest as best they can. Therefore camels with flowing manes, camels with four and five humps, camels with horns, an endless parade of screwball camels, if camels are what you are thinking of."

He flung the pencil down angrily.

"And don't you kid yourself the Candles are doing it to amuse us. *More than likely they believe we are thinking up all these swell ideas just to please them.* They're having the time of their lives. Probably that's the only reason they've tolerated us here – because we have such amusing thoughts.

"When Man first came here they were pretty, coloured balls rolling around on the surface, and someone called them Roman Candles because that's what they looked like. But since that day they've been everything Man has ever thought of."

Page heaved himself out of the chair.

"I shall report your attitude to Washington, Captain Craig."

"Report and be damned," growled Craig. "Maybe you've forgotten where you are. You aren't back on Earth, where bribes and boot-licking and bulldozing will get a man almost anything he wants. You're at the power centre on the Sunward side of Mercury. This is the main source of power for all the planets. Let this power plant fail, let the transmission beams be cut off and the Solar System goes to hell!"

He pounded the desk for emphasis.

"I'm in charge here, and when I say a thing it stands for you as well as anyone. My job is to keep this plant going, keep the power pouring out to the planets. And I'm not letting some half-baked fool come out here and make me trouble. While I'm here, no one is going to stir up the Candles. We've got plenty of trouble without that."

Page edged toward the door, but Craig stopped him.

"Just a little word of warning," he said, speaking softly. "If I were you, I wouldn't try to sneak out any of the puddle jumpers, including your own. After each trip the oxygen tank is taken out and put into the charger, so it'll be at first capacity for the next trip. The charger is locked and there's just one key. And I have that."

He locked eyes with the man at the door and went on.

"There's a little oxygen left in the jumper, of course. Half an hour's supply, maybe. Possibly less. After that there isn't any more. It's not nice to be caught like that. They found a fellow who that had happened to just a day or so ago over near one of the Twilight Belt stations."

But Page was gone, slamming the door.

The Candles had stopped dancing and were rolling around, drifting bubbles of every hue. Occasionally one would essay the formation of some object, but the attempt would be half-hearted and the Candle once more would revert to its natural sphere.

Old Creepy must have put his fiddle away, Craig thought. Probably he was making an inspection round, seeing if everything was all right. Although there was little chance that anything could go wrong. The plant was automatic, designed to run with the minimum of human attention.

The control room was a wonder of clicking, chuckling, chortling, snicking gadgets. Gadgets that kept the flow of power directed to the substations on the Twilight Belt. Gadgets that kept the tight beams from the substations centred exactly on those points in space where each must go to be picked up by the substations circling the outer planets.

Let one of those gadgets fail – let that spaceward beam sway as much as a fraction of a degree . . . Curt shuddered at the thought of a beam of terrific power smashing into a planet – perhaps into a city. But the mechanism had never failed – never would. It was foolproof. A far cry from the day when the plant had charged monstrous banks of converters to be carted to the outer worlds by lumbering spaceships.

This was really free power, easy power, plentiful power. Power carried across millions of miles on Addison's tight-beam principle. Free power to develop the farms of Venus, the mines of Mars, the chemical plants and cold laboratories on Pluto.

Down there in the control room, too, were other gadgets as equally important. The atmosphere machine, for example, which kept the air mixture right, drawing on those tanks of liquid oxygen and nitrogen and other gases brought across space from Venus by the monthly oxygen ship. The refrigerating plant, the gravity machine, the water assembly.

Craig heard the crunch of Creepy's footsteps on the stairs and turned to the door as the old man shuffled into the room.

Creepy's brows were drawn down and his face looked like a thunder-cloud.

"What's the matter now?" asked Craig.

"By cracky," snapped Creepy, "you got to do something about that Rastus."

Craig grinned. "What's up this time?"

"He stole my last bottle of drinking liquor," wailed Creepy. "I was hoarding if for medical purposes, and now it's gone. He's the only one who could have taken it."

"I'll talk to Rastus," Craig promised.

"Some day," threatened Creepy, "I'm going to get my dander up and whale the everlastin' tar out of that smoke. That's the fifth bottle of liquor he's swiped off me."

The old man shook his head dolefully, whuffled his walrus-like moustache.

"Aside from Rastus, how's everything else going?" asked Craig.

"Earth just rounded the Sun," the old man said. "The Venus station took up the load."

Craig nodded. That was routine. When one planet was cut off by the Sun, the substations of the nearest planet took on an extra load, diverted part of it to the first planet's stations, carrying it until it was clear again.

He arose from the chair and walked to the port, stared out across the dusty plains. A dot was moving across the near horizon. A speedy dot, seeming to leap across the dead, grey wastes.

"Knut's coming!" he yelled to Creepy.

Creepy hobbled for the doorway. "I'll go down to meet him.

Knut and me are having a game of checkers as soon as he gets in."

Craig laughed, relieved by Knut's appearance. "How many checker games have you and Knut played?" he asked.

"Hundreds of 'em," Creepy declared proudly. "He ain't no match for me, but he thinks he is. I let him beat me regular to keep the interest up. I'm afraid he'd quit playing if I beat him as often as I could."

He started for the door and then turned back. "But this is my turn to win." The old man chuckled in his moustache. "I'm goin' to give him a first-class whippin'."

"First," said Craig, "tell him I want to see him."

"Sure," said Creepy, "and don't you go telling him about me letting him beat me. That would make him sore."

Craig tried to sleep but couldn't. He was worried. Nothing definite, for there seemed no cause to worry. The tracer placed on the big warp revealed that it was moving slowly, a few feet an hour or so, in a direction away from the centre. No other large ones had shown up in the directors. Everything, for the moment, seemed under control. Just little things. Vague suspicions and wondering – snatches here and there that failed to fall into the pattern.

Knut, for instance. There wasn't anything wrong with Knut, of course, but while he had talked to him he had sensed something. An uneasy feeling that lifted the hair on the nape of his neck, made the skin prickle along his spine. Yet nothing one could lay one's hands on.

Page, too. The damn fool probably would try to sneak out and capture some Candles and then there'd be all hell to pay.

Funny, too, how Knut's radios, both in his suit and in the jumper, had gone dead. Blasted out, as if they had been raked by a surge of energy. Knut couldn't explain it, wouldn't try. Just shrugged his shoulders. Funny things always were happening on Mercury.

Craig gave up trying to sleep, slid his feet into slippers and walked across the room to the port. With a flip of his hand he raised the shutter and stared out.

Candles were rolling around. Suddenly one of them materialised into a monstrous whisky bottle, lifted in the air, tilted, liquid pouring to the ground.

Craig chuckled. That would be either Old Creepy bemoaning the loss of that last bottle or Rastus sneaking off to where he'd hid it to take another nip.

A furtive tap came on the door, and Craig wheeled. For a tense moment he crouched, listening, as if expecting an attack. Then he laughed softly to himself. He was jumpy, and no fooling. Maybe what *he* needed was a drink.

Again the tap, more insistent, but still furtive.

"Come in," Craig called.

Old Creepy sidled into the room. "I hoped you wasn't asleep," he said.

"What is it, Creepy?" And even as he spoke, Craig felt himself going tense again. Nerves all shot to hell.

Creepy hitched forward.

"Knut," he whispered. "Knut beat me at checkers. Six times hand running! I didn't have a chance!"

Craig's laugh exploded in the room.

"But I could always beat him before," the old man insisted. "I even let him beat me every so often to keep him interested so he would play with me. And tonight I was all set to take him to a cleaning —"

Creepy's face twisted, his moustache quivering.

"And that ain't all, by cracky. I felt, somehow, that Knut had changed and —"

Craig walked close to the old man, grasped him by the shoulder. "I know," he said. "I know just how you felt." Again he was remembering how the hair had crawled upon his skull as he talked to Knut just a while ago.

Creepy nodded, pale eyes blinking, Adam's apple bobbing.

Craig spun on his heel, snatched up his shirt, started peeling off his pyjama coat.

"Creepy," he rasped, "you go down to that control room. Get

a gun and lock yourself in. Stay there until I get back. And don't let anyone come in!"

He fixed the old man with a stare. "You understand. *Don't let anyone get in!* Use your gun if you are forced to use it. *But see no one touches those controls!*"

Creepy's eyes bulged and he gulped. "Is there going to be trouble?" he quavered.

"I don't know," snapped Craig, "but I'm going to find out."

Down in the garage, Craig stared angrily at the empty stall.

Page's jumper was gone!

Grumbling with rage, Craig walked to the oxygen-tank rack. The lock was undamaged, and he inserted the key. The top snapped up and revealed the tanks – all of them, nestling in rows, still attached to the recharger lines. Almost unbelieving, Craig stood there, looking at the tanks.

All of them were there. That meant Page had started out in the jumper with insufficient oxygen. It meant the man would die out on the blistering wastes of Mercury. That he might go mad and leave his jumper and wander into the desert, a raving maniac, like the man they'd found out near the Twilight station.

Craig swung about, away from the tanks, and then stopped, thoughts spinning in his brain. There wasn't any use of hunting Page. The damn fool probably was dead by now. Sheer suicide, that was what it was. Sheer lunacy. And he had warned him, too!

And he, Craig, had work to do. Something had happened out there at the space warp. He had to lay those tantalising suspicions that rummaged through his mind. There were some things he had to be sure about. He didn't have time to go hunting a man who was already dead, a damn fool who had committed suicide. The man was nuts to start with. Anyone who thought he could capture Candles . . .

Savagely, Craig closed one of the line valves, screwed shut the tank valve, disconnected the coupling and lifted the tank out of the rack. The tank was heavy. It had to be heavy to stand a pressure of 200 atmospheres.

As he started for the jumper, Mathilde, the cat, strolled down the ramp from the floor above and walked between his legs. Craig stumbled and almost fell, recovered his balance with a mighty effort and cursed Mathilde with a fluency born of practice.

"Me-ow-ow-ow," said Mathilde conversationally.

There is something unreal about the Sunward side of Mercury, an abnormality that is sensed rather than seen.

There the Sun is nine times larger than seen from Earth, and the thermometer never registers under 650 degrees Fahrenheit. Under that terrific heat, accompanied by blasting radiations hurled out by the Sun, men must wear photocell spacesuits, must ride photocell cars and live in the power centre which in itself is little more than a mighty photocell. For electric power can be disposed of, while heat and radiation often cannot be.

There the rock and soil have been crumbled into dust under the lashing of heat and radiations. There the horizon is near, always looming just ahead, like an ever-present brink.

But it is not these things that make the planet so alien. Rather, it is the strange distortion of lines, a distortion that one sometimes thinks he can see, but is never sure. Perhaps the very root of that alien sense is the fact that the Sun's mass makes a straight line an impossibility, a stress that bends magnetic fields and stirs up the very structure of space itself.

Curt Craig felt that strangeness of Mercury as he zoomed across the dusty plain. The puddle jumper splashed through a small molten pool, spraying it out in sizzling sheets. A pool of lead, or maybe tin.

But Craig scarcely noticed. At the back of his brain pounded a thousand half-formed questions. His eyes, edged by crow's-feet, squinted through the filter shield, following the trail left by Knut's returning machine. The oxygen tank hissed softly and the atmosphere mixer chuckled. But all else was quiet.

A howl of terror and dismay shattered the quiet. Craig jerked

94

the jumper to a stop, leaped from his seat, hand streaking to his gun.

Crawling from under the metal bunk bolted at the rear of the car was Rastus, the whites of his eyes showing like bull's-eyes.

"Good Lawd," he bellowed, "Where is I?"

"You're in a jumper, sixty miles from the Centre," snapped Craig. "What I want to know is how the hell you got here."

Rastus gulped and rose to his knees. "You see, it was like this, boss," he stammered. "I was lookin' for Mathilde. Dat cat, she run me wild. She sneaks into the refrigerator all the time. I jus' can't trust her no place. So when she turned up missin' —"

He struggled to his feet, and as he did so a bottle slipped from his pocket, smashed to bits on the metal floor. Pale-amber liquor ran among the fragments.

Craig eyed the shattered glass. "So you were hunting Mathilde, eh?"

Rastus slumped on the bunk, put his head in hs hands. "Ain't no use lyin' to you, boss," he acknowledged. "Never gets away with it. I was havin' me a drink. Just a little nip. And I fell asleep."

"You hid the bottle you swiped from Creepy in the jumper," declared Craig flatly, "and you drank yourself to sleep."

"Can't seem to help it," Rastus moaned. "'Ol' debbil's got me. Can't keep my hands off of a bottle, somehow. Ol' Mercury, he done dat to me. Ol' debbil planet. Nothin' as it should be. Ol' Man Sun pullin' the innards out of space. Playin' around with things until they ain't the same —"

Craig nodded, almost sympathetically. That *was* the hell of it. Nothing ever was the same on Mercury. Because of the Sun's tremendous mass, light was bent, space was warped and eternally threatening to shift, basic laws required modification. The power of two magnets would not always be the same, the attraction between two electrical charges would be changed. And the worst of it was that a modification which stood one minute would not stand the next.

"Where are we goin' now, boss?"

"We're going out to the space warp that Knut found," said

Craig. "And don't think for a minute I'll turn around and take you back. You got yourself into this, remember."

Rastus's eyes batted rapidly and his tongue ran around his lips. "You said the warp, boss? Did I hear you right? The warp?"

Craig didn't answer. He swung back to his seat, started the jumper once again.

Rastus was staring out of one of the side ports. "There's a Candle followin' us," he announced. "Big blue feller. Skippin' along right with us all the time."

"Nothing funny in that," said Craig. "They often follow us. Whole herds of them."

"Only one this time," said Rastus. "Big blue feller."

Craig glanced at the notation of the space warp's location. Only a few miles distant. He was almost there.

There was nothing to indicate what the warp might be, although the instruments picked it up and charted it as he drew near. Perhaps if a man stood at just the right angle he might detect a certain shimmer, a certain strangeness, as if he were looking into a wavy mirror. But otherwise there probably would be nothing pointing to its presence. Hard to know just where one stopped or started. Hard to keep from walking into one, even with instruments.

Curt shivered as he thought of the spacemen who had walked into just such warps in the early days. Daring mariners of space who had ventured to land their ships on the Sunward side, had dared to take short excursions in their old-type spacesuit. Most of them had died, blasted by the radiations spewed out by the Sun, literally cooked to death. Others had walked across the plain and disappeared. They had walked into the warps and disappeared as if they had melted into thin air. Although, of course, there wasn't any air to melt into – hadn't been for many million years.

On this world, all free elements long ago had disappeared. Those elements that remained, except possibly far underground, were locked so stubbornly in combination that it was impossible to blast them free in any appreciable quantity. That was why liquid air was carted clear from Venus.

96

The tracks in the dust and rubble made by Knut's machine were plainly visible, and Craig followed them. The jumper topped a slight rise and dipped into a slight depression. And in the centre of the depression was a queer shifting of light and dark, as if one were looking into a tricky mirror.

That was the space warp!

Craig glanced at the instruments and caught his breath. Here was a space warp that was really big. Still following the tracks of Knut's machine, he crept down into the hollow, swinging closer and closer to that shifting, almost invisible blotch that marked the warp.

"Golly!" gasped Rastus, and Craig knew the Negro was beside him, for he felt his breath upon his neck.

Here Knut's machine had stopped, and here Knut had gotten out to carry the instruments nearer, the blotchy tracks of his spacesuit like furrows through the powdered soil. And there he had come back. And stopped and gone forward again. And there . . .

Craig jerked the jumper to a halt, stared in amazement and horror through the filter shield. Then, the breath sobbing in his throat, he leaped from the seat, scrambled frantically for a spacesuit.

Outside the car, he approached the dark shape huddled on the ground. Slowly he moved nearer, the hands of fear clutching at his heart. Beside the shape he stopped and looked down. Heat and radiation had gotten in their work, shrivelling, blasting, desiccating – but there could be no doubt.

Staring up at him from where it lay was the dead face of Knut Anderson!

Craig straightened up and looked around. Candles danced upon the ridges, swirling and jostling, silent watchers of his grim discovery. The one lone blue Candle, bigger than the rest, had followed the machine into the hollow, was only a few rods away, rolling restlessly to and fro.

Knut had said something was funny – had shouted it, his voice raspy and battered by the screaming of powerful radiations. Or had that been Knut? Had Knut already died when that message came through?

Craig glanced back at the sand, the blood pounding in his temples. Had the Candles been responsible for this? And if they were, why was he unmolested, with hundreds dancing on the ridge?

And if this was Knut, with dead eyes staring at the black of space, who was the other one – the one who came back?

Candles masquerading as human beings? Was that possible? Mimics the Candles were – but hardly as good as that. There was always something wrong with their mimicry – something ludicrously wrong.

He remembered now the look in the eyes of the returned Knut – that chilly, deadly look – the kind of look one sometimes sees in the eyes of ruthless men. A look that had sent cold chills chasing up his spine.

And Knut, who was no match for Creepy at checkers, but who thought he was because Creepy let him win at regular intervals, had taken six games straight.

Craig looked back at the jumper again, saw the frightened face of Rastus pressed against the filter shield. The Candles still danced upon the hills, but the big blue one was gone.

Some subtle warning, a nasty little feeling between his shoulder blades, made Craig spin around to face the warp. Just in front of the warp stood a man, and for a moment Craig stared at him, frozen, speechless, unable to move.

For the man who stood in front of him, not more than 40ft away, was Curt Craig!

Feature for feature, line for line, that man was himself. A second Curt Craig. As if he had rounded a corner and met himself coming back.

Bewilderment roared through Craig's brain, a baffling bewilderment. He took a quick step forward, then stopped. For the bewilderment suddenly was edged with fear, a knifelike sense of danger.

The man raised a hand and beckoned, but Craig stayed rooted where he stood, tried to reason with his muddled brain. It wasn't a reflection, for if it had been a reflection it would have shown him in a spacesuit, and this man stood without a spacesuit. And if it were a real man, it wouldn't be standing there exposed to the madness of the Sun. Such a thing would have spelled sure and sudden death.

Forty feet away – and yet within that 40ft, perhaps very close, the power of the warp might reach out, might entangle any man who crossed that unseen deadline. The warp was moving, at a few feet an hour, and this spot where he now stood, with Knut's dead body at his feet, had a few short hours ago been within the limit of the warp's influence.

The man stepped forward, and as he did, Craig stepped back, his hands dropping to the gun butts. But with the guns half out he stopped, for the man had disappeared. Had simply vanished. There had been no puff of smoke, no preliminary shimmering as of matter breaking down. The man just simply wasn't there. But in his place was the big blue Candle, rocking to and fro.

Cold sweat broke out upon Craig's forehead and trickled down his face. For he knew he had trodden very close to death – perhaps to something even worse than death. Wildly he swung about, raced for the puddle jumper, wrenched the door open, hurled himself at the controls.

Rastus wailed at him. "What's the matter, boss?"

"We have to get back to the centre," yelled Craig. "Old Creepy is back there all alone! Lord knows what has happened to him – what will happen to him."

"But, boss," yipped Rastus, "what's the matter. Who was back there on the ground?"

"That was Knut," said Craig.

"But Mr Knut is back there at the centre, boss. I know. I seen him with my own eyes."

"Knut isn't at the centre," Craig snapped. "Knut is dead out there by the warp. The thing that's at the centre is a Candle, masquerading as Knut!"

Craig drove like a madman, the cold claws of fear hovering over him. Twice he almost met disaster, once when the jumper bucked through a deep drift of dust, again when it rocketed through a pool of molten tin.

"But them Candles can't do that nohow," argued Rastus. "They can't get nothing right. Every time they try to be a thing they always get it wrong."

"How do you know that?" snapped Craig. "How do you know they couldn't if they tried? And if they could and wanted to use it against us, do you think they would let us see them do it? Through all these years they have done their best to make us lower our guard. They have tried to make us believe they were nothing but a gang of good-natured clowns. That, my boy, is super-plus psychology."

"But why?" demanded Rastus. "Why would they want to do it? We ain't never hurt them."

"Ask me another one," said Craig grimly. "The best answer is that we don't know them. They might have a dozen reasons – reasons we couldn't understand. Reasons no human being could understand because they wouldn't tally with the things we know."

Craig gripped the wheel hard and slammed the jumper up an incline slippery with dust.

Damn it, the thing that had come back as Knut *was* Knut. It knew the things Knut knew, it acted like Knut. It had his mannerisms, it talked in his voice, it actually seemed to think the way Knut would think.

What could a man – what could mankind do against a thing like that? How could it separate the original from the duplicate? How would it know its own?

The thing that had come back to the Centre had beaten Creepy at checkers. Creepy had led Knut to believe he was the old man's equal at the game, although Creepy knew he could beat Knut at any time he chose. But Knut didn't know that – and the thing masquerading as Knut didn't know it. So it had sat down and beaten Creepy six games hand-running, to the old man's horror and dismay.

Did that mean anything or not?

Craig groaned and tried to get another ounce of speed out of the jumper.

"It was that old blue jigger," said Rastus. "He was sashaying all around, and then he disappeared."

Craig nodded. "He was in the warp. Apparently the Candles are able to alter their electronic structures so they may exist within the warp. They lured Knut into the warp by posing as human beings, arousing his curiosity, and when he stepped into its influence it opened the way for their attack. They can't get at us inside a suit, you see, because a suit is a photocell, and they are energy, and in a game of that sort, the cell wins every time.

"That's what they tried to do with me. Lord knows what the warp would have done if I'd stepped into it, but undoubtedly it would have made me vulnerable in the fourth dimension or in some other way. That would have been all they needed."

Rastus's eyes strayed to the litter of glass on the floor by the bunk. "Sho' wish I had me a snort of red-eye," he mourned. "Sho' could do with a little stimulus."

"It was clever of them," Craig said. "A Trojan horse method of attack. First they got Knut, and next they tried to get me, and with two of them in the Centre it would not have been so hard to have gotten you and Creepy."

He slapped the wheel a vicious stroke, venting his anger.

"And the beauty of it was that no one would have known. The oxygen ship could have come from Venus and the men on board would never have been the wiser, for they would have met things that seemed like all four of us. No one would have guessed. They would have had time – plenty of time – to do anything they planned."

"What you figure they was aimin' to do, boss?" queried Rastus. "Figure maybe they meant to blow up that ol' plant?"

"I don't know, Rastus. How could I know? If they were human beings, I could make a guess, because I could put myself in their shoes and try to think the way they did. But with the Candles you can't do that. You can't do anything with the Candles, because you don't know what they are."

"You aimin' to raise hell with dem Candles, boss?"

"With what?" snapped Craig.

"Just give me a razor," exulted Rastus. "Maybe two razors, one for each han'. I'se a powerful dangerous man with a razor blade."

"It'll take more than razors," said Craig. "More than our energy guns, for those things are energy. We could blast them with everything we had, and they'd just soak it up and laugh at us and ask for more."

He skidded the jumper around a ravine head, slashed across the desert. "First thing," he declared, "is to find the one that's masquerading as Knut. Find him and then figure out what to do with him."

But finding the Knut Candle was easier said than done. Craig, Creepy and Rastus, clad in spacesuits, stood in the kitchen at the Centre.

"By cracky," said Creepy, "he must be here somewhere. He must have found him an extra-special hideout that we have overlooked."

Craig shook his head. "We haven't overlooked him, Creepy. We've searched this place from stem to stern. There isn't a crack where he could hide."

"Maybe," suggested Creepy, "he figured the jig was up and took it on the lam. Maybe he scrammed out the lock when I was up there guarding that control room."

"Maybe," agreed Craig. "I had been thinking of that. He smashed the radio – that much we know. He was afraid that we might call for help, and that means he may have had a plan. Even now he may be carrying out that plan."

The Centre was silent, filled with those tiny sounds that only serve to emphasise and deepen a silence. The faint *cluck-cluck* of the machines on the floor below, the hissing and distant chortling of the atmosphere mixer, the chuckling of the water synthesizer.

"Dang him," snorted Creepy, "I knew he couldn't do it. I knew Knut couldn't beat me at checkers honest —"

From the refrigerator came a frantic sound. "Me-ow – me-ow-ow-ow," it wailed.

Rastus leaped for the refrigerator door, grabbing a broom as he went. "It's that Mathilde cat again," he yelled. "She's always sneakin' in on me. Every time my back is turned."

He brandished the broom and addressed the door. "You jus' wait. I'll sure work you over with this here broom. I'll plaster you —"

But Craig had leaped forward, snatched the Negro's hand away from the door. "Wait!" he shouted.

Mathilde yodelled pitifully.

"But, boss, that Mathilde cat —"

"Maybe it isn't Mathilde," Craig rasped grimly.

From the doorway leading out into the corridor came a low purring rumble. The three men whirled about. Mathilde was standing across the threshold, rubbing with arched back against the jamb, plumed tail waving. From inside the refrigerator came a scream of savage feline fury.

Rastus's eyes were popping and the broom clattered to the floor. "But, boss," he shrieked, "there's only one Mathilde!"

"Of course, there's only one Mathilde," snapped Craig. "One of these is her. The other is Knut, or the thing that was Knut."

The lock signal rang shrilly, and Craig stepped swiftly to a port, flipped the shutter up.

"It's Page," he shouted. "Page is back again!"

He turned from the port, face twisted in disbelief. Page had gone out five hours before – without oxygen. Yet here he was, back again. No man could live for over four hours without oxygen.

Craig's eyes hardened, and furrows came between his brows.

"Creepy," he said suddenly. "You open the inner lock. You, Rastus, pick up that cat. Don't let her get away."

Rastus backed off, eyes wide in terror.

"Pick her up," commanded Craig sharply. "Hang onto her."

"But, boss, she —"

"Pick her up, I say!"

Creepy was shuffling down the ramp to the lock. Slowly Rastus moved forward, clumsily reached down and scooped up Mathilde. Mathilde purred loudly, dabbing at his suit-clad fingers with dainty paws.

Page stepped out of the jumper and strode across the garage toward Craig, his boot heels ringing on the floor.

From behind the spacesuit visor, Craig regarded him angrily. "You disobeyed my orders," he snapped. "You went out and caught some Candles."

"Nothing to it, Captain Craig," said Page. "Docile as so many kittens. Make splendid pets."

He whistled sharply, and from the open door of the jumper rolled three Candles, a red one, a green one, a yellow one. Ranged in a row, they lay just outside the jumper, rolling back and forth.

Craig regarded them appraisingly.

"Cute little devils," said Page good-naturedly.

"And just the right number," said Craig.

Page started, but quickly regained his composure. "Yes, I think so, too. I'll teach them a routine, of course, but I suppose the audience reactions will bust that all to hell once they get on the stage."

Craig moved to the rack of oxygen tanks and snapped up the lid.

"There's just one thing I can't understand," he said. "I warned you you couldn't get into this rack. And I warned you that without oxygen you'd die. And yet here you are."

Page laughed. "I had some oxygen hid out, Captain. I anticipated something just like that."

Craig lifted one of the tanks from the rack, held it in his arms. "You're a liar, Page," he said calmly. "You didn't have any other oxygen. You didn't need any. A man would die if he went out there without oxygen – die horribly. But you wouldn't – *because you aren't a man!*"

Page stepped swiftly back, but Craig cried out warningly. Page stopped, as if frozen to the floor, his eyes on the oxygen tank. Craig's finger grasped the valve control.

"One move out of you," he warned grimly, "and I'll let you have it. You know what it is, of course. Liquid oxygen, pressure of two hundred atmospheres. Colder than the hinges of space."

Craig grinned ferociously. "A dose of that would play hell with your metabolism, wouldn't it? Tough enough to keep going here in the dome. You Candles have lived out there on the surface too long. You need a lot of energy, and there isn't much energy here. We have to screen it out or we would die ourselves. And there's a damn sight less energy in liquid oxygen. You met your own environment, all right; you even spread that environment pretty wide, but there's a limit to it."

"You'd be talking a different tune," Page declared bitterly, "if it weren't for those spacesuits."

"Sort of crossed you up, didn't they," said Craig. "We're wearing them because we were tracking down a pal of yours. I think he's in the refrigerator."

"A pal of mine – in a refrigerator?"

"He's the one that came back as Knut," said Craig, "and he turned into Mathilde when he knew we were hunting for him. But he did the job too well. He was almost more Mathilde than he was Candle. So he sneaked into the refrigerator. And he doesn't like it."

Page's shoulders sagged. For a moment his features seemed to blur, then snapped back into rigid lines again.

"The answer is that you do the job too well," said Craig. "Right now you yourself are more Page than Candle, more man than thing of energy."

"We shouldn't have tried it," said Page. "We should have waited until there was someone in your place. You were too frank in your opinion of us. You held none of the amused contempt so many of the others held. I told them they should wait, but a man named Page got caught in a space warp —"

Craig nodded. "I understand. An opportunity you simply couldn't miss. Ordinarily we're pretty hard to get at. You can't fight photocells. But you should strive for more convincing stories. That yarn of yours about capturing Candles —"

"But Page came out for that purpose," insisted the pseudo-Page. "Of course, he would have failed. But, after all, it was poetic justice."

"It was clever of you," Craig said softly. "More clever than you thought. Bringing your sidekicks in here, pretending you had captured them, waiting until we were off our guard."

"Look," said Page, "we know when we are licked. What are you going to do?"

"We'll turn loose the one in the refrigerator," Craig told him. "Then we'll open up the locks and you can go."

"And if we don't want to go?"

"We'd turn loose the liquid oxygen," said Craig. "We have vats of the stuff upstairs. We can close off this room, you know, turn it into a howling hell. You couldn't live through it. You'd starve for energy."

From the kitchen came a hideous uproar, a sound that suggested a roll of barbed wire galloping around a tin roof. The bedlam was punctuated by yelps and howls from Rastus.

Creepy, who had been standing by the lock, started forward, but Craig, never lifting an eye from Page, waved him back.

Down the ramp from the kitchen came a swirling ball of fur, and after it came Rastus, whaling lustily with his broom. the ball of fur separated, became two identical cats, tails five times normal size, backs bristling, eyes glowing with green fury.

"Boss, I jus' got tired of holding Mathilde —" Rastus panted.

"I know," said Craig. "So you chucked her into the refrigerator with the other cat."

"I sho' did," confessed Rastus, "and hell busted loose right underneath my nose."

"All right," snapped Craig. "Now, Page, if you'll tell us which one of those is yours —"

Page spoke sharply and one of the cats melted and flowed. Its outlines blurred and it became a Candle, a tiny, pale-pink Candle.

Mathilde let out one soul-wrenching shriek and fled.

106

"Page," said Craig, "we've never wanted trouble. If you are willing we'd like to be your friends. Isn't there some way?"

Page shook his head. "No, Captain. We're poles apart. I and you have talked here, but we've talked as man to man rather than as a man and a person of my race. Our differences are too great, our minds too far apart."

He hesitated, almost stammering. "You're a good egg, Craig. You should have been a Candle."

"Creepy," said Craig, "open up the lock."

Page turned to go, but Craig called him back. "Just one thing more. A personal favour. Could you tell me what's at the bottom of this?"

"It's hard to explain," said Page. "You see, my friend, it's a matter of culture. That isn't exactly the word, but it's the nearest I can express it in your language.

"Before you came we had a culture, a way of life, a way of thought, that was distinctly our own. We didn't develop the way you developed, we missed this crude, preliminary civilisation you are passing through. We started at a point you won't reach for another million years.

"We had a goal, an ideal, a place we were heading for. And we were making progress. I can't explain it, for – well, there just are no words for it. And then you came along —"

"I think I know," said Craig. "We are a disturbing influence. We have upset your culture, your way of thought. Our thoughts intrude upon you and you see your civilisation turning into a troupe of mimics, absorbing alien ideas, alien ways."

He stared at Page. "But isn't there a way? Damn it, do we have to fight about this?"

But even as he spoke, he knew there was no way. The long role of terrestrial history recorded hundreds of such wars as this – wars fought over forms of faith, over terminology of religion, over ideologies, over cultures. And the ones who fought those wars were members of the same race – not members of two races separated by different origins, by different metabolisms, by different minds.

"No," he said, "there is no way. Some day, perhaps, we will

be gone. Some day we will find another and a cheaper source of power and you will be left in peace. Until that day —" he left the words unspoken.

Page turned away, headed for the lock, followed by the three big Candles and the little pink one.

Ranged together at the port, the three Terrestrials watched the Candles come out of the lock. Page was still in the form of a man, but as he walked away the form ran together and puddled down until he was a sphere.

Creepy cackled at Craig's elbow. "By cracky," he yelped, "he was a purple one!"

Craig sat at his desk, writing his report to the Solar power board, his pen travelling rapidly over the paper:

– they waited for 500 years before they acted. Perhaps this was merely caution or in the hope they might find a better way. Or it may be that time has a different value for them than it has for us. In an existence which stretches into eternity, time would have but little value.

For all those 500 years they have watched and studied us. They have read our minds, absorbed our thoughts, dug out our knowledge, soaked up our personalities. Perhaps they know us better than we know ourselves. Whether their crude mimicry of our thoughts is merely a clever ruse to make us think they are harmless or whether it reflects differing degrees of the art of mimicry – the difference between a cartoon and a masterpiece of painting – I cannot say. I cannot even guess.

Heretofore we have never given thought to protect ourselves against them, for we have considered them, in general, as amusing entities and little else. Whether or not the cat in the refrigerator was the Candle or Mathilde I do not know, but it was the cat in the refrigerator that gave me the idea of using liquid oxygen. Undoubtedly there are better ways. Anything that would swiftly deprive them of energy would serve. Convinced they will try again,

*even if they have to wait another 500 years, I urgently
suggest—*

He stopped and laid down the pen.

From the kitchen below came the faint clatter of pots and pans
as Rastus engineered a dinner. Bellowed snatches of unmusical
song, sandwiched between the clatter of utensils, floated up
the ramp:

> "Chicken in de bread pan,
> Kickin' up de dough —"

The wastebasket in the corner moved slightly and Mathilde
slunk out, tail at half mast. With a look of contempt at Craig,
she stalked to the door and down the ramp.

Creepy was tuning up his fiddle, but only half-heartedly.
Creepy felt badly about Knut. Despite their checker arguments,
the two had been good friends.

Craig considered the things he'd have to do. He'd have to go
out and bring in Knut's body, ship it back to Earth for burial.
But first he was going to sleep. Lord, how he needed sleep!

He picked up the pen and proceeded with his writing:

*— that every effort be bent to the development of some
convenient weapon to be used against them. But to be used
only in defence. A program of extermination, such as has
been carried out on other planets, is unthinkable.*

*To do this it will be necessary that we study them even as
they have studied us. Before we can fight them we must know
them. For the next time their method of attack undoubtedly
will be different.*

*Likewise we must develop a test, to be applied to every
person before entering the Centre, that will reveal whether
he is a Candle or a man.*

*And, lastly, every effort should be made to develop some
other source of universal power against the day when Mercury
may become inaccessible to us.*

109

He reread the report and put it down.

"They won't like that," he told himself. "Especially that last paragraph. But we have to face the truth."

Rastus's voice rose shrilly. "You, Mathilde! You get out of there! Can't turn my back but you're in that icebox —"

A broom thudded with a whack.

There was no sound from the control room. Creepy apparently had put away his fiddle. Probably didn't have the heart to play it.

For a long time Craig sat at his desk, thinking. Then he arose and went to the port.

Outside, on the bitter plains of Mercury, the Candles had paired off, two and two, were monstrous dice, rolling in the dust. As far as the eye could see, the plains were filled with galloping dominoes.

And every pair, at every toss, were rolling sevens!

Buckets of Diamonds

The police picked up Uncle George walking west on Elm Street at 3 o'clock in the morning. He was shuffling along, muttering to himself, and his clothes were soaked, as if he'd been out in the rain – and Cottonwood County for the past three months had been suffering a drought, with the corn withering in the field and day after day not a cloud in sight. He was carrying a good-sized painting underneath one arm and in the other hand he carried a pail filled to the brim with diamonds. He was in his stockinged feet; he'd lost his shoes somewhere. When officer Alvin Saunders picked him up, he asked Uncle George what was going on, and George mumbled something that Alvin couldn't quite make out. He seemed to be befuddled.

So Alvin took him to the station, and it wasn't until then they saw that his pockets bulged. So they emptied his pockets and laid all the stuff out on a table, and when they'd had a good look at it, Sergeant Steve O'Donnell phoned Chief Chet Burnside to ask him what to do. The chief, sore at being hauled out of bed, said to throw George into pokey. So that is what they did. You couldn't really blame the chief, of course. Off and on, for years, Uncle George had given the police force of Willow Grove a fair amount of trouble.

But as soon as Uncle George had a chance to look around and realise where he was, he grabbed up a stool and beat upon the bars, yelling that the dirty fuzz had framed him once again and declaring very loudly that his constitutional rights as a free and upright citizen were being trampled on. "I know my rights," he yelled. "You owe me at least one phone call and when I get out of here I'm going to sue all of you on the grounds of false arrest."

111

So they unlocked the cell and let him make his call. As usual he made the call to me.

"Who is it?" Elsie asked, sitting up in bed.

"It's your Uncle George," I said.

"I knew it!" I said.

"I knew it!" she exclaimed. "Aunt Myrt is off to California to visit relatives. And he's running loose again."

"All right," I said to George, "what could it be this time?"

"You needn't take that tone of voice, John," he said. "It's only once or twice a year I call you. And what's the use of having a lawyer in the family . . ."

"You can skip that part of it," I told him, "and get down to what is going on."

"This time," he said, triumphantly, "I got them dead to rights. This time you get paid off. I'll split the judgment with you. I wasn't doing nothing. I was walking down the street when the fuzz pulled up and hauled me in. I wasn't staggering and I wasn't singing. I was creating no disturbance. I tell you, John, a man has the right to walk the streets, no matter at what hour . . ."

"I'll be right down," I said.

"Don't be too long," said Elsie, "You have a hard day coming up in the court."

"Are you kidding?" I asked. "With Uncle George, the day's already lost."

When I got down to the station, they all were waiting for me. George was sitting beside a table, and on the table stood the pail of diamonds with the junk they'd taken from his pockets and the painting was leaning up against it. The police chief had got there, just a few minutes ahead of me.

"Okay," I said, "let's get down to business. What's the charge?"

The chief still was pretty sore. "We don't need no charge right yet."

"I'll tell you, Chet," I said, "you'll need one badly before the day is over, so you better start to thinking."

112

"I'm going to wait," said Chet, "to see what Charley says."

He meant Charley Nevins, the county attorney.

"All right, then," I said, "if there is no charge as yet, what are the circumstances?"

"Well," said the chief, "George here was carrying a pail of diamonds. And you tell me just how he came by a pail of diamonds."

"Maybe they aren't diamonds," I suggested. "How come you're so sure that they are diamonds?"

"Soon as he opens up, we'll get Harry in to have a look at them."

Harry was the jeweller, who had a shop across the square.

I went over to the table and picked up some of the diamonds. They surely looked like diamonds, but I am no jeweller. They were cut and faceted and shot fire in the light. Some of them were bigger than my fist.

"Even if they should be diamonds," I demanded, "what has that to do with it? There's no law I know of says a man can't carry diamonds."

"That's telling them!" cheered George.

"You shut up," I told him, "and keep out of this. Let me handle it."

"But George here hasn't got no diamonds," said the chief. "These must be stolen diamonds."

"Are you charging him with theft?" I asked.

"Well, not right now," said the chief. "I ain't got no evidence as yet."

"And there's that painting, too," said Alvin Saunders. "It looks to me just like one of them old masters."

"There's one thing," I told them, "that puzzles me exceedingly. Would you tell me where, in Willow Grove, anyone bent on thievery could find an old master or a pail of diamonds?"

That stopped them, of course. There isn't anyone in Willow Grove who has an honest-to-God painting except Banker Amos Stevens, who brought one back from a visit to Chicago; and knowing as little as he does about the world of art he was probably taken.

113

"You'll have to admit, though," said the chief, "there's something funny going on."

"Maybe so," I said, "but I doubt that that alone is sufficient ground to hold a man in jail."

"It ain't the diamonds or the painting so much as this other stuff," declared the chief, "that makes me think there are shenanigans afoot. Look at this will you!"

He picked up a gadget from the table and held it out to me. "Watch out," he warned. "One end of it's hot, and the other end is cold."

It was about a foot in length and shaped something like an hourglass. The hourglass part of it was some sort of transparent plastic, pinched in at the middle and flaring at both ends, and the ends were open. Through the centre of it ran a rod that looked like metal. One end of the metal glowed redly, and when I held my hand down opposite the open end a blast of heat came out. The other end was white, covered by crystals. I turned it around to look.

"Keep away from it," warned the chief. "That end of it is colder than a witch's spit. Them's big ice crystals hanging onto it."

I laid it back upon the table, carefully.

"Well," the chief demanded, "what do you make of it?"

"I don't know," I said.

I never took any more physics in school than had been necessary and I'd long since forgotten all I'd ever known about it. But I knew damn well that the gadget on the table was impossible. But impossible or not, there it was, one end of the rod glowing with its heat, the other frosted by its cold.

"And this," said the chief, picking up a little triangle formed by a thin rod of metal or of plastic. "What do you think of this?"

"What should I think of it?" I asked. "It's just . . ."

"Stick your finger through it," said the police chief triumphantly.

I tried to stick my finger through it and I couldn't. There was nothing there to stop me. My finger didn't hit anything, there was no pressure on it and I couldn't feel a thing, but I couldn't put my finger through the centre of that

114

triangle. It was as if I'd hit a solid wall that I couldn't see or feel.

"Let me see that thing," I said.

The chief handed it to me, and I held it up to the ceiling light and I twisted it and turned it, and so help me, there wasn't anything there. I could see right through it and I could see there was nothing there, but when I tried to put my finger through the centre there was something there to stop it.

I laid it back on the table beside the hourglass thing.

"You want to see more?" asked the chief.

I shook my head. "I'll grant you, Chet, that I don't know what this is all about, but I don't see a thing here that justifies you in holding George."

"I'm holding him," said the chief, "until I can talk to Charley."

"You know, of course, that as soon as court opens, I'll be back here with an order for his release."

"I know that, John," said the chief. "You're a real good lawyer. But I can't let him go."

"If that's the case," I said, "I want a signed inventory of all this stuff you took off of him, and then I want you to lock it up."

"But . . ."

"Theoretically," I said, "it's George's property . . ."

"It couldn't be. You know it couldn't, John. Where would he have gotten . . ."

"Until you can prove that he has stolen it from some specific person, I imagine the law would say that it was his. A man doesn't have to prove where he obtained such property."

"Oh, all right," said the chief. "I'll make out the inventory, but I don't know just what we'll call some of this stuff."

"And now," I said, "I'd like to have a moment to confer with my client."

After balking and stalling around a bit, the chief opened up the city council chamber for us.

"Now, George," I said, "I want you to tell me exactly how

115

it was. Tell me everything that happened and tell it from the start."

George knew I wasn't fooling, and he knew better than to lie to me. I always caught him in his lies.

"You know, of course," said George, "that Myrt is gone . . ."

"I know that," I said.

"And you know that every time she's gone, I go out and get drunk and get into some sort of trouble. But this time I promised myself I wouldn't do any drinking and wouldn't get into any kind of trouble. Myrt's put up with a lot from me, and this time I was set to show her I could behave myself. So last night I was sitting in the living room, with my shoes off, in my stocking feet, with the TV turned on, watching a ball game. You know, John, if them Twins could get a shortstop they might stand a chance next year. A shortstop and a little better pitching and some left-handed batters and . . ."

"Get on with it," I said.

"I was just sitting there," said George, "watching this here ball game and drinking beer. I had got a six-pack and I guess I was on the last bottle of it . . ."

"I thought you said you had promised yourself you would do no drinking."

"Ah, John, this was only beer. I can drink beer all day and never . . ."

"All right, go on," I said.

"Well, I was just sitting there, drinking that last bottle of beer and the game was in the seventh inning and the Yanks had two men on and Mantle coming up . . ."

"Damn it, not the game!" I yelled at him. "Tell me what happened to you. You're the one in trouble."

"That's about all there was to it," said George. "It was the seventh inning and Mantle coming up, and the next thing I knew I was walking on the street and a police car pulling up?"

"You mean you don't know what happened in between? You don't know where you got the pail of diamonds or the painting or all the other junk?"

George shook his head, "I'm telling you just the way it was. I don't remember anything. I wouldn't lie to you. It doesn't pay to lie to you. You always trip me up."

I sat there for a while, looking at him, and I knew it was no use to ask him any more. He probably had told me the truth, but perhaps not all of it, and it would take more time than I had right then to sweat it out of him.

"OK," I said, "we'll let it go at that. You go back and get into that cell and don't let out a whimper. Just behave yourself. I'll be down by nine o'clock or so and get you out. Don't talk to anyone. Don't answer any questions. Volunteer no information. If anyone asks you anything, tell them I've told you not to talk."

"Do I get to keep the diamonds?"

"I don't know," I said. "They may not be diamonds."

"But you asked for an inventory."

"Sure I did," I said, "but I don't know if I can make it stick."

"One thing, John. I got an awful thirst . . ."

"No," I said.

"Three or four bottles of beer. That couldn't hurt much. A man can't get drunk on only three or four. I wasn't drunk last night. I swear to you I wasn't."

"Where would I get beer at this time in the morning?"

"You always have a few tucked away in your refrigerator. And that's only six blocks or so away."

"Oh, all right," I said. "I'll ask the chief about it."

The chief said yes, he guessed it would be all right, so I left to get the beer.

The moon was setting behind the courthouse cupola, and in the courthouse square the Soldier's Monument was alternately lighted and darkened by a street lamp swaying in a little breeze. I had a look at the sky, and it seemed entirely clear. There were no clouds in sight and no chance of rain. The sun, in a few hours more, would blaze down again and the corn would dry a little more and the farmers would watch their wells anxiously

117

as the pumps brought up lessening streams of water for their bawling cattle.

A pack of five or six dogs came running across the courthouse lawn. There was a dog-leashing ordinance, but everyone turned their dogs loose at night and hoped they would come home for breakfast before Virgil Thompson, the city dog catcher, could get wind of them.

I got into the car and drove home and found four bottles of beer in the refrigerator. I took it back to the station, then drove home again.

By this time it was 4.30, and I decided it wasn't worth my while to go back to bed, so I made some coffee and started to fry some eggs. Elsie heard me and came down, and I fried some eggs for her and we sat and talked.

Her Uncle George had been in a lot of scrapes, none of them serious, and I had always managed to get him out of them one way or another. He wasn't a vicious character and he was an honest man, liked by most everyone in town. He ran a junkyard out at the edge of town, charging people for dumping trash, most of which he used to fill in a swampy stretch of ground, salvaging some of the more usable junk and selling it cheap to people who might need it. It wasn't a very elevating kind of business, but he made an honest living at it and in a little town like ours if you made an honest living it counts for quite a lot.

But this scrape was just a little different, and it bothered me. It wasn't exactly the kind of situation that was covered in a law book. The thing that bothered me the most was where George could have gotten the stuff they found on him.

"Do you think we should phone Aunt Myrt?" asked Elsie.

"Not right now," I told her. "Having her here wouldn't help at all. All she'd do would be to scream and wring her hands."

"What are you going to do first of all?" she asked.

"First of all," I said, "I'm going to find Judge Benson and get a writ to spring him out of jail. Unless Charley Nivens can find some grounds for holding him and I don't think he can. Not right away, at least."

But I never got the writ. I was about to leave my office to go over to the courthouse to hunt up the judge when Dorothy Ingles, my old-maid secretary, told me I had a call from Charley.

I picked up the phone, and he didn't even wait for me to say hello. He just started shouting.

"All right," he yelled, "you can start explaining. Tell me how you did it."

"How I did what?" I asked.

"How George broke out of jail."

"But he isn't out of jail. When I left he was locked up and I was just now going over to the courthouse . . ."

"He's not locked up now," yelled Charley. "The cell door still is locked, but he isn't there. All that's left is four empty beer bottles, standing in a row."

"Look, Charley," I said, "I don't know a thing about this. You know me well enough . . ."

"Yeah," yelled Charley, "I know you well enough. There isn't any dirty trick . . ."

He strangled on his words, and it was only justice. Of all the tricky lawyers in the state, Charley is the trickiest.

"If you are thinking," I said, "of swearing out a fugitive warrant for him, you might give a thought to the lack of grounds for his incarceration."

"Grounds!" yelled Charley. "There is that pail of dia-monds."

"If they are really diamonds."

"They are diamonds, that's for sure. Harry Johnson had a look at them this morning and he says that they are diamonds. There is just one thing wrong. Harry says there are no diamonds in the world as big as those. And very few as perfect."

He paused for a moment and then he whispered, hoarsely, "Tell me John, what is going on? Let me in on it."

"I don't know," I said.

"But you talked with him and he told the chief you had told him not to answer any questions."

"That's good legal procedure," I told him. "You can have no quarrel with that. And another thing, I'll hold you responsible for seeing that those diamonds don't disappear somehow. I

have an inventory signed by Chet and there is no charge
. . ."

"What about busting jail?"

"Not unless you can show cause for his being arrested in the first place."

He slammed down the receiver, and I hung up the phone and sat there trying to get the facts straight inside my mind. But they were too fantastic for me to make them spell out any sense.

"Dorothy," I yelled.

She poked her head around the door, her face prissy with her disapproval. Somehow, apparently, she had heard about what had been going on – as, no doubt, had everyone in town – and she was one of the few who held George in very ill-repute. She thought he was a slob. She resented my relationship to him and she often pointed out that he cost me over the years a lot of time and cash, with no money ever coming back. Which was true, of course, but you can't expect a junkyard operator to afford fancy legal fees and, in my case, he was Elsie's uncle.

"Put in a call to Calvin Ross," I told her, "at the Institute of Arts in Minneapolis. He is an old friend of mine and . . ."

Banker Amos Stevens came bursting through the door. He crossed the outer office and brushed past Dorothy as if she weren't there.

"John, do you know what you have got – what you've got down there?"

"No," I said. "Please tell me."

"You have got a Rembrandt."

"Oh, you mean the painting."

"Where do you think George found a Rembrandt? There aren't any Rembrandts except in museums and such."

"We'll soon find out more about it," I told Banker Stevens, Willow Grove's one and only expert in the arts. "I've got a call in now and . . ."

Dorothy stuck her head around the door. "Mr Ross is on the phone," she said.

I picked up the phone and I felt a little funny about it, because Cal Ross and I hadn't seen each other for a good 15 years or more, and I wasn't even sure he would remember me. But I told him who I was and acted as if we'd had lunch together just the day before, and he did the same to me.

Then I got down to business. "Cal, we have a painting out here that maybe you should have a look at. Some people think it might be old and perhaps by one of the old masters. I know that it sounds crazy . . ."

"Where did you say this painting is?" he asked.

"Here in Willow Grove."

"Have you had a look at it?"

"Well, yes," I said, "a glance, but I wouldn't know . . ."

"Tell him," Stevens whispered, fiercely, "that it is a Rembrandt."

"Who owns it?"

"Not really anyone," I said. "It's down at the city jail."

"John, are you trying to suck me into something? As an expert witness, maybe."

"Nothing like that," I said, "but it does have a bearing on a case of mine and I suppose I could dig up a fee . . ."

"Tell him," Stevens insisted, "that it is a Rembrandt."

"Did I hear someone talking about a Rembrandt?" Cal asked.

"No," I said. "No one knows what it is."

"Maybe I could get away," he said.

He was getting interested – well, maybe interested isn't the word; intrigued might be more like it.

"I could arrange a charter to fly you out," I said.

"It's that important, is it?"

"To tell you the truth, Cal, I don't know if it is or not. I'd just like your opinion."

"Fix up the charter, then," he said, "and call me back. I can be at the airport to be picked up within an hour."

"Thanks, Cal," I said. "I'll be seeing you."

Elsie would be sore at me, I knew, and Dorothy would be

furious. Chartering a plane for a small-town lawyer in a place like Willow Grove is downright extravagance. But if we could hang onto those diamonds, or even a part of them, the bill for the charter would be peanuts. If they were diamonds. I wasn't absolutely sure Harry Johnson would know a diamond if he saw one. He sold them in his store, of course, but I suspected that he just took some wholesaler's word that what he had were diamonds.

"Who was that you were talking to?" demanded Banker Stevens.

I told him who it was.

"Then why didn't you tell him it was a Rembrandt?" Stevens raged at me. "Don't you think that I would know a Rembrandt?"

I almost told him no, that I didn't think he would, and then thought better of it. Some day I might have to ask him for a loan.

"Look, Amos," I said, "I didn't want to do anything that would prejudice his judgment. Nothing that would sway him one way or the other. Once he gets here he will no doubt see right away that it is a Rembrandt."

That mollified him a bit, and then I called in Dorothy and asked her to fix up arrangements for Cal to be flown out, and her mouth got grimmer and her face more prissy at every word I said. If Amos hadn't been there, she'd have had something to say about throwing away my money.

Looking at her, I could understand the vast enjoyment she got out of the revival meetings that blossomed out in Willow Grove and other nearby towns each summer. She went to all of them, no matter what the sect, and sat on the hard benches in the summer heat and dropped in her quarter when the collection plate was passed and sucked out of the fire-and-brimstone preaching a vast amount of comfort. She was always urging me to go to them, but I never went. I always had the feeling she thought they might do me a world of good.

"You're going to be late in court," she told me curtly, "and the case this morning is one you've spent a lot of time on."

Which was her way of telling me I shouldn't be wasting any of my time on George.

So I went off to court.

At noon recess, I phoned the jail, and there'd been no sign of George. At three o'clock Dorothy came across the square to tell me Calvin Ross would be coming in at five. I asked her to phone Elsie to be expecting a guest for dinner and maybe one for overnight; and she didn't say anything, but from her face I knew she thought I was a brute and she'd not blame Elsie any if she up and left me. Such inconsideration!

At five o'clock I picked Cal up at our little airport and a fair crowd was on hand. Somehow the word had got around that an art expert was flying out to have a look at the painting George Wetmore had picked up somewhere.

Cal was somewhat older than I had remembered him and age had served to emphasise and sharpen up the dignity that he'd had even in his youth. But he was kind and affable and as enthusiastic about his art as he had ever been. And I realised, with a start, that he was excited. The possibility of finding a long-lost painting of some significance must be, I realised, a dream that is dear to everyone in the field.

I drove him down to the square and we went into the station and I introduced him round. Chet told me there was no sign of George. After a little argument he got out the painting and laid it on the table underneath the ceiling light.

Cal walked over to look down at it and suddenly he froze, like a bird dog on the point. For a long time he stood there, not moving, looking down at it, while the rest of us stood around and tried not to breathe too hard.

Then he took a folding magnifier out of his pocket and unfolded it. He bent above the painting and moved the glass from spot to spot, staring at each spot over which he held the glass for long seconds.

Finally he straightened up.

"John," he said, "would you please tilt it up for me."

I tilted it up on the table and he walked back a ways and had

123

a long look at it from several angles and then came back and examined it with the glass again.

Finally he straightened up again and nodded to Chet.

"Thanks very much," he said. "If I were you, I'd guard that canvas very carefully."

Chet was dying to know what Cal might think, but I didn't give him a chance to ask. I doubt Cal would have told him anything even if he'd asked.

I hustled Cal out of there and got him in the car and we sat there for a moment without either of them saying anything at all.

Then Cal said, "Unless my critical faculties and my knowledge of art have deserted me entirely, that canvas in there is Toulouse-Lautrec's *Quadrille at the Moulin Rouge.*"

So it wasn't Rembrandt! I'd known damn well it wasn't. So much for Amos Stevens!

"I'd stake my life on it," said Cal. "I can't be mistaken. No one could copy the canvas as faithfully as that. There is only one thing wrong."

"What is that?" I asked.

"*Quadrille at the Moulin Rouge* is in Washington at the National Gallery of Art."

I experienced a sinking feeling in my gizzard. If George somehow had managed to rifle the National Gallery both of us were sunk.

"It's possible the painting is missing," said Cal, "and the National Gallery people are keeping quiet about it for a day or two. Allthough ordinarily, they'd notify other large museums and some of the dealers."

He shook his head, perplexed. "But why anyone should steal it is more than I would know. There's always the possibility that it could be sold to some collector who would keep it hidden. But that would require prior negotiations, and few collectors would be so insane as to buy a painting as famous as the *Moulin Rouge.*"

I took some hope from that. "Then there isn't any possibility George could have stolen it."

He looked at me, funny. "From what you tell me," he said, "this George of yours wouldn't know one painting from another."

"I don't think he would."

"Well, that lets him out. He must have just picked it up somewhere. But where – that's the question."

I couldn't help him there.

"I think," said Cal, "I had better make a phone call."

We drove down to the office and climbed the stairs.

Dorothy was waiting for me to come back, and she still was sore at me. "There is a Colonel Sheldon Reynolds in your office," she told me. "He is from the Air Force."

"I can phone out here," said Cal.

"Colonel Reynolds has been waiting for some time," said Dorothy, "and he strikes me as a most patient man."

I could see she didn't approve of me associating with people from the world of art and that she highly disapproved of me meeting with the Air Force and she still was sore at me for giving Elsie such short notice we were to have a dinner guest. She was very properly outraged, although she was too much of a lady and too loyal an employee to bawl me out in front of Cal.

I went into my office, and sure enough, Colonel Reynolds was there, acting most impatient, sitting on the edge of a chair and drumming his fingers on its arms.

He quit his drumming and stood up as soon as I came in.

"Mr Page," he said.

"I'm sorry you had to wait," I said. "What can I do for you?"

We shook hands, and he sat down in the chair and I perched uneasily on the edge of the desk, waiting.

"It has come to my attention," he told me, "that there have been some extraordinary occurrences in town and that there are certain artifacts involved. I've spoken with the county attorney, and he says you are the man I have to talk with. It appears there is some question about the ownership of the artifacts."

"If you're talking about what I think you are," I told him, "there is no question whatsoever. All the articles in question are the property of my client."

125

"I understand your client has escaped from jail."

"Disappeared," I said. "And he was placed in custody originally in an illegal manner. The man was doing nothing except walking on the street."

"Mr Page," said the colonel, "you do not have to convince me I have no interest in the merits of the case. All the Air Force is concerned about are certain gadgets found in the possession of your client."

"You have seen these gadgets?"

He shook his head. "No. The county attorney told me you'd probably crucify him in court if he let me see them. But he said you were a reasonable man and if properly appealed to . . ."

"Colonel," I said, "I'm never a reasonable man where the welfare of my client could be jeopardised."

"You don't know where your client is?"

"I have no idea."

"He must have told you where he found the stuff."

"I don't think he knows himself," I said.

The colonel, I could see, didn't believe a word I told him, for which I couldn't very well blame him.

"Didn't your client tell you he'd contacted a UFO?"

I shook my head, bewildered. That was a new one on me. I'd never thought of it.

"Mr Page," the colonel said, "I don't mind telling you that these gadgets might mean a lot to us. Not to the Air Force alone, but to the entire nation. If the other side should get hold of some of them before we did and . . ."

"Now wait a minute," I interrupted. "Are you trying to tell me there are such things as UFOs?"

He stiffened. "I'm not trying to tell you anything at all," he said. "I an simply asking . . ."

The door opened, and Cal stuck in his head. "Sorry for breaking in like this," he said, "but I have to leave."

"You can't do that," I protested. "Elsie is expecting you for dinner."

"I have to go to Washington," he said. "Your secretary says she will run me to the airport. If the pilot can get me home within an hour or so, I can catch a plane."

"You talked with the National Gallery?"

"The painting is still there," he said. "There is a remote possibility there may have been a substitution, but with the tight security that seems impossible. I don't suppose there would be any chance . . ."

"Not a ghost," I said. "The painting stays right here."

"But it belongs in Washington!"

"Not if there are two of them," I shouted.

"But there can't be."

"There appears to be," I told him. "I'd feel a whole lot better, John, if it were in a safer place."

"The police are guarding it."

"A bank vault would be a whole lot better."

"I'll look into it," I promised. "What did the National Gallery say about it?"

"Not much of anything," said Cal. "They are flabbergasted. You may have them out here."

"I might as well," I said. "I have the Pentagon."

We shook hands, and he left; I went back and perched upon the desk.

"You're a hard man to deal with," said the colonel. "How do I reach you? Patriotism, perhaps?"

"I'm not a patriotic man," I told him, "and I'll instruct my client not to be."

"Money?"

"If there were a lot of it."

"The public interest?"

"You've got to show me it's in the public interest."

We glared at one another. I didn't like this Colonel Sheldon Reynolds, and he reciprocated.

The phone banged at me.

It was Chet down at the police station. His words started tumbling over one another as soon as I picked up the phone.

"George is back!" he shouted. "This time he has got someone

with him and he's driving something that looks like a car, but it hasn't got no wheels . . . !"

I slammed down the phone and ran for the door. Out of the tail of my eye I saw that Reynolds had jumped up and was running after me.

Chet had been right. It looked like a car, but it had no wheels. It was standing in front of the police station, hanging there about two feet off the ground and a gentle thrumming indicated there was some mechanism somewhere inside of it that was running smoothly.

Quite a crowd had gathered and I forced my way through it and got up beside the car.

George was sitting in what appeared to be the driver's seat and sitting beside him was a scarecrow of a fellow with the sourest face I've ever seen on any man.

He wore a black robe that buttoned up the front and up close around his throat and a black skullcap that came down hard against his ears and across his forehead; his hands and face, all of him that showed, were fishbelly white.

"What happened to you?" I demanded of George. "What are you sitting here for?"

"I tell you, John," he said, "I am somewhat apprehensive that Chet will try to throw me into the pokey once again. If he makes a move I'm all ready to go shooting out of here. This here vehicle is the slickest thing there is.

"It'll go along the ground or it will shoot up in the air and make just like a plane. I ain't rightly got the hang of it yet, having hardly driven it, but it handles smooth and easy and it ain't no trick at all to drive it."

"You can tell him," said Charley Nevins, "that he need not fear arrest. There is something most peculiar going on here, but I'm not sure at all there is violation of the law involved."

I looked around in some surprise. I hadn't noticed Charley standing there when I'd pushed through the crowd.

Reynolds shoved in ahead of me and reached up to grab George by the arm.

"I am Colonel Reynolds," he said, "and I am from the Air

128

Force and it's terribly important that I know what this is all about. Where did you get this car?"

"Why," George said, "it was standing there with a pile of other junk, so I took it. Someone threw it away and didn't seem to want it. There were a lot of people there throwing things away that they didn't want."

"And I suppose," yelled Chet, "that someone threw away the painting and the pail of diamonds."

"I wouldn't know about that," George told him. "I don't seem to remember much about that other trip. Except there was this big pile of stuff and that it was raining . . ."

"Shut up, George," I said. He hadn't told me anything about a pile of stuff. Either his memory was improving or he had lied to me.

"I think," said Charley, getting edgy, "that we all better sit down together and see if we can make some sense out of these proceedings."

"That's all right with me," I said, "always remembering that this machine remains technically the property of my client."

"It seems to me," Charley said to me, "that you're being somewhat unreasonable and high-handed in this whole affair."

"Charley," I said, "you know I have to be. If I let down my guard a minute, you and Chet and the Pentagon will tramp all over me."

"Let's get on with it," said Charley. "George, you put that machine down on the ground and come along with us. Chet will stand guard over it and see no one touches it."

"And while you're doing that," I said, "don't take your eyes off the painting and the diamonds. The painting just might be worth an awful lot of money."

"Right now," said Chet, disgusted, "would be a swell time for someone to rob the bank. I'd have the entire force tied up watching all this junk of George's."

"I think, too," said Charley, "we better include this passenger of George's in our little talk. He might be able to add some enlightenment."

*　　*　　*

129

George's passenger didn't pay any attention. He'd been paying no attention all along. He had just been sitting there, bolt upright in his seat, with his face pointing straight ahead.

Chet walked officiously around the car. The passenger said something, at some length, in a high chittering voice. I didn't recognise a word of it but crazy as it sounds, I knew exactly what he said.

"Don't touch me!" he said. "Get away from me. Don't interfere with me."

And, having said this, he opened the door and let himself to the ground. Chet stepped back from him and so did all the others. Silence fell upon the gathering which had been buzzing up until this moment. As he advanced down the street, the crowd parted and pressed back to make way for him. Charley and the colonel stepped backward, bumping into me, pinning me against the car, to get out of his way. He passed not more than 10ft from me and I got a good look at his face. There was no expression on it and it was set in a natural grimness – the way, I imagined, that a judge of the Inquisition might have looked. And there was something else that is very hard to say, an impression that translated itself into a sense of smell, although I was sure there was no actual odour. The odour of sanctity is as close as I can come to it, I guess. Some sort of vibration radiating from the man that impinged upon the senses in the same manner, perhaps, as ultrasonics will impinge without actual hearing upon the senses of a dog.

And then he was past me and gone, walking down the street through the lane of human bodies that stepped aside for him, walking slowly, unconcernedly, almost strolling – walking as if he might have been all alone, apparently unaware of a single one of us.

All of us watched him until he was free of the crowd and had turned a corner into another street. And even for a moment after that we stood uncertain and unmoving until finally someone spoke a whisper and someone answered him and the buzz of the crowd took up again, although now a quieter buzz.

Someone's fingers were digging hard into the muscles of my

upper arm and when I looked around, I saw that it was Charley who had fastened onto me.

Ahead of me, the colonel turned his head to look at me. His face was white and tight and little drops of perspiration stood out along his hairline.

"John," said Charley, quietly, "I think it is important that we all sit down together."

I turned around toward the car and saw that it was now resting on the ground and that George was getting out of it.

"Come along," I said to George.

Charley led, pushing his way through the crowd, with the colonel following and George and me bringing up the rear. We went down the street, without a word among us, to the square and walked across the lawn to the courthouse steps.

When we got in Charley's office, Charley shut the door and dug down into a desk drawer and come up with a jug. He got out four paper cups and poured them almost full.

"No ice," he said, "but what the hell, it's the liquor that we need."

Each of us took a cup and found a place to sit and worked on the booze a while without saying anything.

"Colonel," Charley finally asked, "what do you make of it?"

"It might be a help," the colonel said, "if we could talk with the passenger. I assume some attempt will be made to apprehend the man."

"I suppose we should," said Charley. "Although how one apprehends a bird like that, I don't really know."

"He caught us by surprise," the colonel pointed out. "Next time we'll be ready for him. Plug your ears with cotton, so you cannot hear him . . ."

"It may take more than that," said Charley. "Did anyone actually hear him speak?"

"He spoke, all right," I said. "He uttered words, but there was none I recognised. Just a sort of chirping gibberish."

"But we knew what he meant," said Charley. "Every single one of us knew that. Telepathy, perhaps?"

"I doubt it," the colonel said. "Telepathy is not the simple thing so many people think."

"A new language," I suggested. "A language scientifically constructed. Sounds that are designed to trigger certain understandings. If one dug deep enough into semantics . . ."

Charley interrupted me; apparently he took no stock in my semantics talk.

"George," he asked, "what do you know of him?"

George was sunk back deep into a chair, with his shoeless feet stuck out in front of him. He had his big mitt wrapped around the paper cup and was wriggling his toes and he was content. It did not take an awful lot to make George content.

"I don't know a thing," said George.

"But he was riding with you. He must have told you something."

"He never told me a thing," said George. "He never said a word. I was just driving off and he came running up and jumped into the seat and then . . ."

"You were driving off from where?"

"Well," said George, "there was this big pile of stuff. It must have covered several acres and it was piled up high. It seemed to be in a sort of square, like the courthouse and no lawn, but just a sort of paving that might have been concrete and all around it, everywhere you looked, but quite a distance off, there were big high buildings."

Charley asked, exasperated, "Did you recognise the place?"

"I never saw the place before," said George, "nor no pictures of it, even."

"Perhaps it would be best," suggested Charley, "if you told it from the start."

So George told it the way he had told it to me.

"That first time it was raining pretty hard," he said, "and it was sort of dark, as if evening might be coming on, and all I saw was this pile of junk. I didn't see no buildings."

He hadn't told me he'd seen anything at all. He had claimed

132

he hadn't known a thing until he was back in Willow Grove, walking on the street, with the police car pulling up. But I let it go and kept on listening.

"Then," said George, "after Chet threw me into pokey . . ."

"Now, wait a minute there," said Charley. "I think you skipped a bit. Where did you get the diamonds and the painting and all the other stuff?"

"Why, off the pile of junk," said George. "There was a lot of other stuff and if I'd had the time I might have done some better. But something seemed to warn me that I didn't have much time and it was raining and the rain was cold and the place was sort of spooky. So I grabbed what I could and put it in my pockets and I took the pail of diamonds, although I wasn't sure they were really diamonds, and then I took the painting because Myrt has been yelling that she wants a high-class picture to hang in the dining room . . ."

"And then you were back home again?"

"That is it," said George, "and I am walking down the street, minding my own business and not doing anything illegal . . ."

"And how about the second time?"

"You mean going back again?"

"That's what I mean," said Charley.

"That first time," said George, "it was unintentional. I was just sitting in the living room with my shoes off and a can of beer, watching television and in the seventh inning the Yankees had two on and Mantle coming up to bat – say, I never did find out what Mantle did. Did he hit a homer?"

"He struck out," said Charley.

George nodded sadly; Mickey is his hero.

"The second time," said George, "I sort of worked at it. I don't mind a cell so much, you understand, as the injustice of being there when you ain't done nothing wrong. So I talked John into bringing me some beer and I sat down and started drinking it. There wasn't any television, but I imagined television. I imagined it real hard and I put two men on bases and had Mantle coming up – all in my mind, of course – and I guess it must have worked. I was back again, in the place where there was this pile of junk.

Only you must understand it wasn't really junk. It was all good stuff. Some of it didn't make any sense at all, but a good part of it did; and it was just setting there and no one touching it and every now and then someone would come walking out from some of those tall buildings – and it was quite a walk, I tell you, for those buildings were a long ways off – and they'd be carrying something and they'd throw it on the pile of junk and go walking back."

"I take it," said the colonel, "that you spent more time there on your second trip."

"It was daytime," George explained, "and it wasn't raining and it didn't seem so spooky, although it did seem lonesome. There weren't any people – just the few who came walking to throw something on the pile, and they didn't pay much attention to me; they acted almost as if they didn't see me. You understand, I didn't know if I'd ever get back there again and there was a limit to how much I could carry, so this time I figured I'd do a job of it. I'd look over the pile and figure exactly what I wanted. Maybe I should say that a little differently. There was a lot of it I wanted, but I had to decide what I wanted most. So I started walking around the pile, picking up stuff I thought I wanted until I saw something I took a special liking to then I'd decide between it and something else I had picked up. Sometimes I'd discard the new thing I had picked up and sometimes I'd keep it and drop something else. Because, you see, I could carry just so much, and by this time I was loaded with about all that I could carry. There was a lot of nice items up on the sides of the pile, and once I tried climbing the pile to get a funny-looking sort of gadget, but that stuff was piled loose, just tossed up there, you know; and when I started to climb, the stuff started to shift and I was afraid it might all come down on top of me. So I climbed down again, real careful. After that I had to satisfy myself with whatever I could pick up at the bottom of the pile."

The colonel had become greatly interested, leaning forward in his chair so he wouldn't miss a word. "Some of this junk," he asked. "Could you tell what it was?"

"There was a pair of spectacles," said George, "with some

134

sort of gadget on them and I tried them on and I got so happy that it scared me, so I took them off and I quit being happy; then I put them on again and I was happy right away . . ."

"Happy?" asked Charley. "Do you mean they made you drunk?"

"Not drunk, happy," said George. "Just plain happy, that is all. No troubles and no worries and the world looked good and a man enjoyed living. Then there was another thing, a big square piece of glass. I suppose you'd call it a cube of glass. Like these fortune tellers have, but it was square instead of round. It was a pretty thing, all by itself, but when you looked into it – well, it didn't reflect your face, like a mirror does, but there seemed to be some sort of picture in it, deep inside of it. It looked to me, that first time, like maybe it was a tree and when I looked closer I could see it was a tree. A big, high elm tree like the one that used to stand in my grandfather's yard, the one that had the bobolink's nest way up at the top, and this one, too, I saw, had a bobolink's nest and there was the bobolink, himself, sitting on a limb beside the nest. And then I saw it was the very tree that I remembered, for there was my grandfather's house and the picket fence and the old man sitting in the battered lawn swing, smoking his corncob pipe. You see, that piece of glass showed you anything that you wanted to see. First there was just the tree, then I thought about the nest and the nest was there and then the house showed up and the picket fence and I was all right until I saw the old man himself – and him dead for twenty years or more. I looked at him for a while and then I made myself look away, because I had thought a lot of the old man and seeing him there made me remember too much, so I looked away. By then I thought I knew what this glass was all about so I thought of a pumpkin and the pie was there, with gobs of whipped cream piled on it and then I thought of a stein of beer and the beer was there . . ."

"I don't believe," said Charley, "a single word of this."

"Go on," urged the colonel. "Tell us the rest of it."

"Well," said George, "I guess I must have walked almost all the way around that pile, picking one thing up and throwing

135

another away and I was loaded, I can tell you. I had my arms full and my pockets full and stuff hung around my neck. And suddenly, driving out from those tall buildings came this car, floating about three feet off the ground . . ."

"You mean the vehicle that you have out there?"

"The very one," said George. "There was a sad-looking old geezer driving it, and he ran it up alongside the pile and set it down, then got out of it and started walking back, sort of hobbling. So I went up to it and I dumped all the stuff I had been carrying into the back seat and it occurred to me that with it I could carry away more than I could in my arms. But I thought that first, perhaps, I had ought to see if I could operate it, so I climbed in the driver's seat and there was no trick to it at all. I started it up and began to drive it, slow, around the pile, trying to remember where I had discarded some of the stuff I had picked up earlier – intending to go back and get it and put it in the back seat. I heard the sound of running feet behind me and when I looked around there was this gent all dressed in black. He reached the car and put one hand upon it and vaulted into the seat beside me. The next instant we were in Willow Grove."

"You mean to tell us," cried the colonel, leaping to his feet, "that you have the back seat of that car loaded with some of these things you have been telling us about?"

"Colonel, please sit down," said Charley. "You can't possibly believe any of the things he has been telling us. On the face of them, they are all impossible and . . ."

"Charley," I said, "let me cite a few more impossibilities, like a painting being in the National Gallery of Art and also in Willow Grove, like that car out there without any wheels, like a gadget that is hot at one end and cold at the other."

"God, I don't know," said Charley, desperately. "And I am the guy that has it in his lap."

"Charley," I said, "I don't believe you have anything in your lap at all. I don't think there is a single legal question involved in this whole mess. Taking a car you might say, being of the particular turn of legal mind you are,

136

without the permission of the owner, only it is not a car . . ."

"It's a vehicle!" Charley yelled.

"But the owner had junked it. He'd junked it and walked away and . . ."

"What I want to know," the colonel said, "is where this place is and why the people were discarding their possessions."

"And you'd also," I said, "love to get your hands on some of those possessions."

"You're damned right I would" said the colonel, grimly. "And I'm going to. Do you realise what some of them might mean to this nation of ours? Why, they might spell the margin of difference between us and the other side and I don't intend . . ."

"Colonel," I said, "haul down the flag. There is no use of screaming. I am sure that George would be willing to discuss terms with you."

Feet came pounding up the stairs and down the hall. The door flew open and a deputy sheriff came skidding to a halt.

"Charley," he panted, "I don't know what to do. There's been a crazy-looking coot preaching to a crowd out by the Soldier's Monument. The sheriff, I am told, went out to stop it, him not having any licence to be preaching anywhere, let alone the courthouse square, and then came charging back. I came in the back way, without knowing anything about what was going on, and I found the sheriff collecting up the guns and ammunition and when I asked him what was going on, he wouldn't talk to me, but went walking out the front door and he threw all of them guns and all that ammunition down at the base of the monument. And there are a lot of other people bringing other things and throwing them there, too . . ."

I didn't wait to hear the rest of it. I dodged past the deputy and through the door and down the stairs, heading for the building's front.

The pile had grown to a size that was big enough to cover the base of the monument; and there were, I saw, such things as bicycles, radios, typewriters and 5 sewing machines, electric razors and lawn mowers; and there was a car or two, jammed up against the monument. Dusk had fallen and the farmers were coming into town to trade and people were coming across the square, dark, muffled figures, lugging stuff to throw upon the pile.

There was no sign of the passenger. He had done his dirty work and gone. Standing there in the courthouse square, with the street lamps swinging in the tiny breeze and all those dark-enshrouded figures toiling up the lawn toward the monument, I had the vision of many other towns throughout the country with growing piles of discarded objects bearing testimony to the gullibility of the human race.

My God, I thought, they never understood a word of what he said, not a single syllable of that clacking tongue of his. But the message, as had been the case which we'd pushed back to clear the path for him, had been plain and clear. Thinking about it, I knew I'd been right up there in Charley's office when I'd said it was a matter of semantics.

We had words, of course, lots of words, perhaps more than an ordinary man would ever need, but intellectual words, tailored for their precise statement of one peculiar piece of understanding; and we'd become so accustomed to them, to their endless ebb and flow, that many of them – perhaps most of them – had lost the depth and the precision of their meaning. There had been a time when great orators could catch and hold the public ear with the pure poetry of their speech and men such as these had at times turned the tide of national opinion. Now, however, in large part, spoken words had lost their power to move. But the laugh, I thought, would never lose its meaning. The merry laugh that, even if one were not included in it, could lift the human spirits; the belly laugh that spelled out unthinking fellowship; the quiet laugh of superior, supercilious intellect that could cut the ground beneath one.

Sounds, I thought – sounds, not words – sounds that could trigger basic human reaction. Was it something such as this that the passenger had used? Sounds so laboriously put together, probing so deeply into the human psyche, that they said almost as much as the most carefully constructed sentence of intellectual speech, but with the one advantage that they were convincing as words could never be. Far back in man's prehistory there had been the grunt of warning, the cry of rage, the food-call, the little clucking recognition signals.

Was this strange language of the passenger's no more than a sophisticated extension of these primal sounds?

Old Con Weatherby came tramping stolidly across the lawn to fling his portable television set upon the pile, and behind him came a young housewife I didn't recognise who threw a toaster and a blender and a vacuum cleaner beside Con's television set.

My heart cried out to them in my pity of what was happening and I suppose I should have hurried forth and spoken to them – Old Con at least – trying to stop them, to show them this was all damn foolishness. I knew Old Con had saved dollars here and there, going without the drinks he wanted, smoking only three cigars a day instead of his usual five, so that he and his old lady could have that television set. But, somehow, I knew how useless it would be to stop them, to do anything about it.

I went down across the lawn feeling beat and all played out. Coming up the lawn toward me, staggering under a heavy load, came a familiar figure.

"Dorothy!" I yelled.

Dorothy stopped and some of the books that she was carrying up toward the monument came unstuck from the load and went thumping to the ground. In a flash I knew exactly what they were – my law books.

"Hey!" I yelled. "Take those back. Hey, what is going on!"

I didn't need to ask, of course. Of all the people in Willow Grove, she would have been the one most certain to be on hand to listen to the passenger and the most avid to believe. She could smell out an evangelist 20 miles away and the high moments of her life were those spent with her scrawny little bottom planted on the hardness of a bench in the suffocating air of a tent meeting and listening to some jackleg preacher spout about his hellfire and brimstone. She'd believe anything at all and subscribe to it whole-heartedly so long as it was evangelistic.

I started down the lawn toward her but was distracted.

From the other side of the square came a snarling, yipping sound; out of the dusk came a running figure, with a pack of dogs snapping at his heels. The man had shucked up his robe to give him extra leg room, and he was making exceptionally good time. Every once in a while one of the dogs would get a mouthful of the robe that flowed out behind him, snapping in the wind of his rapid movement, but it didn't slow him down.

It was the passenger, of course, and while he'd done right well with humans, it was quite evident he was doing not so well with dogs. They had just been let loose with the dusk, after being tied up for the day, and they were spoiling for a bit of fun. They didn't understand the talk of the passenger perhaps, or there was something so different about him that they immediately had pegged him as some sort of outlander to be hunted down.

He went across the lawn below me in a rush with the dogs very close behind, and out into the street, and it wasn't until then that I realised where he would be heading.

I let out a whoop and set out after him. He was heading for that car to make his getaway and I couldn't let him do it. That car belonged to George.

I knew I could never catch him, but I pinned my hopes on Chet. Chet would have a man or two guarding the car; and while the passenger would probably talk them out of it, they might slow him a bit, enough for me to catch up with him before he had taken off. He might try, of course, to talk me out of it as well with his chittering gibberish, but I told myself I'd have to do my best to resist whatever he might tell me.

We went whipping down the street, the passenger with the dogs close to his heels, and me close to the dogs; and there, up ahead, stood the car out in front of the station. There still

140

was a fair-sized crowd around it, but the passenger yelled some outlandish sounds at them and they began to scatter.

He didn't even break his stride, and I'll say this much for him – he was quite an athlete. Ten feet or so from the car, he jumped and sailed up through the air and landed in the driver's seat. He was plenty scared of those mutts, of course, and that may have helped him some; under certain crisis circumstances a man can accomplish feats that ordinarily would be impossible. But even so, he had to be fairly athletic to manage what he did.

As he landed in the driver's seat the car immediately took off upward at a slant, and in a couple of seconds had soared above the buildings and was out of sight. The two cops that Chet had detailed to guard the car just stood there with their jaws hanging down, looking up to where the car had gone. The crowd that had been there and scattered when the passenger yelled his gibberish at them now turned about and stared as vacantly, while the dogs circled around, puzzled, sniffing at the ground and every now and then pointing up a nose to bay.

I was standing there like the rest of them when someone came running up behind me and grabbed my arm. It was Colonel Sheldon Reynolds.

"What happened?"

I told him, somewhat bitterly and profanely, exactly what had happened.

"He's gone futureward," the colonel said. "We'll never see him or the car again."

"Futureward?" I asked stupidly.

"That must be it," the colonel said. "There's no other was to explain it. George wasn't in contact with any UFO, as I had thought to be the case. He must have travelled futureward. You probably were right about the way the passenger talked. That was a new semantics. A sort of speech shorthand, made up of basic sounds. I suppose it would be possible, but it would take a long time to develop. Maybe it developed, or was borrowed, when the race went to the stars – a sort of universal language, a vocal version of the sign language used by the Great Plains Indians . . ."

"But that would be time travel," I protested. "Hell, George doesn't know enough . . ."

"Look," said the colonel, "you maybe don't need to know anything to travel in time. You maybe have to feel something; you may have to be in tune. There might be only one man in the entire world today who can feel that way . . ."

"But, colonel," I said, "it makes no sense at all. Let's say George did go into the future – just for the sake of argument, let us say he did. Why should people up in the future be throwing away their things, why should there be the big pile of junk?"

"I don't know," the colonel said. "That is, I couldn't say for sure, but I have a theory."

He waited for me to ask about his theory, but when I didn't ask, he went ahead and told me.

"We've talked a lot," he said, "about contact with other intelligences that live on other stars and we've done some listening in the hope of picking up some signals sent out by peoples many light years distant. We haven't heard any signals yet and we may never hear any because the time span during which any race is technologically oriented may be very short."

I shook my head. "I don't see what you're driving at," I told him. "What has all that had happened here got to do with signals from the stars?"

"Perhaps not very much," he admitted, "except that if contact is ever made it must be made with a technological race very much like ours. And there are sociologists who tell us that the technological phase of any society finds ways and means of destroying itself or it creates stresses and pressures against which the people rebel or it becomes interested in something other than technology and . . ."

"Now hold up a minute," I said. "You are trying to tell me that this junk heap of George's is the result of the human race, in some future day, rejecting a technological society – throwing away technological items? It wouldn't work that way. It would be a gradual rejection, a gradual dying out of technology. People wouldn't just decide they wanted no more of it and go out and throw all their beautiful, comfortable gadgets . . ."

142

"That could happen," the colonel argued. "It could happen if the rejection was the result of a religious or evangelistic movement. The passenger may have been one of their evangelists. Look at what he did right here in a few minutes' time. Typewriters, radios, television sets, vacuum cleaners in that pile on the courthouse lawn – all technological items."

"But a painting isn't technological," I protested. "A pail of diamonds isn't."

Both of us stopped talking and looked at one another in the deepening dusk. Both of us realised, I guess, that there wasn't too much sense of us standing there and arguing over a speculation.

The colonel shrugged. "I don't know," he said. "It was only an idea. The car is lost for good, of course, and all the stuff George had thrown into the back seat. But we have the other stuff . . ."

One of the cops who had been set to guard the car had been standing close and listening to us and now he broke in on us.

"I am sorry sir," he said gulping a little, "but we ain't got none of it. All of it is gone."

"All of it!" I yelled. "The painting and the diamonds. I told Chet . . ."

"Chet, he couldn't do nothing else," said the man. "He had two of us here and he had two inside guarding that other stuff and when the ruckus started up at the courthouse, he needed men and he didn't have them . . ."

"And so he brought the painting and the diamonds and the other stuff out here and put them in the car," I yelled. I knew Chet, I knew how he would think.

"That way he figured we could guard them all," said the man. "And we could have, but . . ."

I turned and started to walk away. I didn't want to hear another word. If Chet had been there, I would have strangled him.

I was walking down the sidewalk, clear of the crowd, and there was someone walking close beside me, just a little way behind. I looked around; it was the colonel.

His mouth shaped a single word as I looked around at him, "George," he said.

We both of us must have had the same idea.

"Are the Yankees and Twins on TV tonight?" I asked.

He nodded.

"For the love of God," I said, "let us get some beer."

We made it in record time, each of us lugging a couple of six-packs.

George had beaten us to it.

He was sitting in front of the TV set, in his stockinged feet, watching the ball game with a can of beer in hand.

We didn't say a word. We just put the beer down beside him so there'd be no danger of his running out of it and went into the dining room and waited in the dark, keeping very quiet.

In the sixth, the Yanks had two men on and Mantle up to bat and Mantle hit a double. But nothing happened. George just went on drinking beer, wriggling his toes and watching television.

"Maybe," said the colonel, "it has to be the seventh."

"And maybe," I said, "a double doesn't count. It may take a strike-out."

We keep on trying, of course, but our hopes are fading. There are only four more Twin and Yankee games on television before the season ends. And someone wrote the other day that next year, for sure, Mantle will retire.

Hunch

Hannibal was daydreaming again and Spencer Chambers wished he'd stop. Chambers, as chairman of the Solar Control Board, had plenty of things to worry about without having his mind cluttered up with the mental pictures Hannibal kept running through his brain. But, Chambers knew, there was nothing he could do about it. Daydreaming was one of Hannibal's habits, and since Chambers needed the spidery little entity, he must put up with it as best he could.

If those mental pictures hadn't been so clear, it wouldn't have been so bad, but since Hannibal was the kind of thing he was they couldn't be anything but clear.

Chambers recognised the place Hannibal was remembering. It wasn't the first time Hannibal had remembered it and this time, as always, it held a haunting tinge of nostalgia. A vast green valley, dotted with red boulders splotched with gray lichens, and on either side of the valley towering mountain peaks that reached spear-point fingers toward a bright-blue sky.

Chambers, seeing the valley exactly as Hannibal saw it, had the uncomfortable feeling that he knew it, too – that in the next instant he could say its name, could give its exact location. He had felt that way before, when the identification of the place, just as now, seemed at his fingertips. Perhaps it was just an emotional hallucination brought about by Hannibal's frequent thinking of the place, by the roseate longing with which he invested it. Of that, however, Chambers could not be sure. At times he would have sworn the feeling was from his own brain, a feeling of his own, set apart and distinct from Hannibal's daydreams.

At one time that green valley might have been Hannibal's

home, although it seemed unlikely. Hannibal had been found in the Asteroid Belt, to this day remained the only one of his species to be discovered. And that valley never could have been in the Asteroids, for the Belt had no green valleys, no blue skies.

Chambers would have liked to question Hannibal, but there was no way to question him – no way to put abstract thoughts into words or into symbols Hannibal might understand. Visual communication, the picturing of actualities, yes – but not an abstract thought. Probably the very idea of direct communication of ideas, in the human sense, was foreign to Hannibal. After months of association with the outlandish little fellow, Chambers was beginning to believe so.

The room was dark except for the pool of light cast upon the desk top by the single lamp. Through the tall windows shone the stars and a silvery sheen that was the rising moon gilding the tops of the pines of the nearby ridge.

But darkness and night meant nothing to either Chambers or Hannibal. For Hannibal could see in the dark, Chambers could not see at all. Spencer Chambers was blind.

And yet, he saw, through the eyes – or, rather, the senses of Hannibal. Saw far plainer and more clearly than if he had seen with his own eyes. For Hannibal saw differently than a man sees – much differently, and better.

That is except when he was daydreaming.

The daydream faded suddenly and Chambers, brain attuned to Hannibal's sensory vibrations, looked through and beyond the walls of his office into the reception room. A man had entered, was hanging up his coat, chatting with Chambers's secretary.

Chambers's lips compressed into straight, tight lines as he watched. Wrinkles creased his forehead and his analytical brain coldly classified and indexed once again the situation which he faced.

Moses Allen, he knew, was a good man, but in this particular problem he had made little progress – perhaps would make little

146

progress, for it was something to which there seemed, at the moment, no answer.

As Chambers watched Allen stride across the reception room his lips relaxed a bit and he grinned to himself, wondering what Allen would think if he knew he was being spied upon. Moses Allen, head of the Solar Secret Services, being spied upon!

No one, not even Allen, knew the full extent of Hannibal's powers of sight. There was no reason, Chambers realised, to have kept it secret. It was just one of his eccentricities, he admitted. A little thing from which he gained a small, smug satisfaction – a bit of knowledge that he, a blind man, hugged close to himself.

Inside the office, Allen sat down in a chair in front of Chambers's desk, lit a cigarette.

"What is it this time, chief?" he asked.

Chambers seemed to stare at Allen, his dark glasses like bowls of blackness against his thin, pale face. His voice was crisp, his words clipped short.

"The situation is getting worse, Moses. I'm discontinuing the station on Jupiter."

Allen whistled. "You'd counted a lot on that station."

"I had," Chambers acknowledged. "Under the alien conditions such as exist on that planet I had hoped we might develop a new chemistry, discover a new pharmacopoeia. A drug, perhaps, that would turn the trick. Some new chemical fact or combination. It was just a shot in the dark."

"We've taken a lot of them," said Allen. "We're just about down to a point where we have to play our hunches. We haven't much else left to play."

Chambers went on, almost as if Allen hadn't spoken. "The relief ship to Jupiter came back today. Brought back one man, mind entirely gone. The rest were dead. One of them had cut his throat. The relief men came back too. Refused to stay after what they saw."

Allen grimaced. "Can't say I blame them."

"Those men were perfectly sane when they went out," declared Chambers. "Psychologists gave every one of them high ratings for

147

mental stability. They were selected on that very point, because we realised Jupiter is bad – probably the most alien place in the entire Solar System. But not so bad every one of them would go mad in three short months."

Chambers matched his fingers. "The psychologists agree with me on that point."

Hannibal stirred a little, sharp claws scratching the desk top. Allen reached out a hand and chucked the little creature under the chin. Hannibal swiped angrily at the hand with an armoured claw.

"I'm getting desperate, Moses," Chambers said.

"I know," said Allen. "Things getting worse all the time. Bad news from every corner of the Solar System. Communications breaking down. Machines standing idle. Vital installations no good because the men crack up when they try to run them."

They sat in silence. Allen scowling at his cigarette, Chambers stiff and straight behind his desk, almost as if he were sitting on the edge of his chair, waiting for something to happen.

"Situational psychoneurosis." said Allen. "That's what the experts call it. Another sixty-four dollar word for plain insanity. Men walking out on their jobs. Men going berserk. The whole Solar System crumbling because they can't do the jobs they're meant to do."

Chambers spoke sharply. "We can't get anywhere by ranting at it, Moses. We have to find the answer or give up. Give up the dream men held before us. The dream of an integrated Solar System, integrated by men and for men, working smoothly, making the life of the human race a better life."

"You mean," said Allen slowly, "what have I done about it?"

Chambers nodded. "I had that in mind, yes."

"I have been working on a lot of angles," Allen declared. "Cancelling out most of them. Really just one big one left. But you won't find the answer in sabotage. Not that I won't work to find it there. Because, you see, that's my business. But I feel in my bones that this really is on the up and up – would know it was, except for one thing. To solve this problem, we have to

148

find a new factor in the human mind, in human psychology – a new approach to the whole problem itself.

"Geniuses are our trouble. It takes geniuses to run a Solar System. Just ordinary intelligence isn't enough to do the job. And geniuses are screwy. You can't depend on them."

"And yet," said Spencer Chambers, almost angrily, "we must depend on them."

And that, Allen knew, was the truth – the bitter truth.

For years now there had been a breakdown of human efficiency. It had started gradually, a few incidents here, a few there. But it had spread, had progressed almost geometrically; had reached a point now where, unless something could be done about it, the Solar System's economic and industrial fabric would go to pot for lack of men to run it and the power plants and laboratories, the mills, the domed cities, the communication system men had built on all the planets encircling the Sun would crumble into dust.

Men were better trained, better equipped mentally, more brilliant than ever before. Of that there was no question. They had to be. Hundreds of jobs demanded geniuses. And there were geniuses, thousands of them, more than ever before. Trouble was they didn't stay geniuses. They went insane.

There had been evidence of a mass insanity trend as far back as the twentieth century, stemming even then from the greater demands which an increasingly complex, rapidly changing, vastly speeded-up civilisation placed upon the human brain, upon human capabilities and skills. With the development of a scientific age, man suddenly had been called upon to become a mental giant. Man had tried, had in part succeeded. But the pace had been too fast – the work of man had outstripped his brain. Now man was losing out.

Today the world was a world of specialisation. To be of economic value, men had to specialise. They had to study harder than ever to fit themselves into their world. College courses were tougher and longer. The very task of educating themselves for a place in their civilisation placed upon them a nervous tension that was only intensified when they took over

149

the strenuous, brain-wearing workaday tasks to which they were assigned.

No wonder, Allen told himself, that there came a time when they threw up their hands, walked out, didn't give a damn.

"You've got to find out what's wrong with the bright boys," he said. "You have to find what's in their make-up that makes them unstable. Maybe there's something wrong with their education, with the way it's dished out to them. Maybe —"

"The educators and psychologists are conducting research along those lines," Chambers reminded him, shortly.

"I get it," said Allen. "I'm to stick to my own field. All right then. I'm going to tell you something that will make you madder than hell."

Chambers sat silent, waiting. Hannibal shifted himself along the desk, edging closer to Allen, almost as if he were listening and didn't want to miss a word.

"It's this Sanctuary business," Allen said. "You've seen the ads —"

He stopped in flustered embarrassment, but Chambers nodded.

"I see them, yes. I read the papers, Moses. I spread them out and Hannibal looks at them and I read them, just as well as you do. You needn't be so sensitive about my blindness."

"Sanctuary has those ads plastered all over the place," said Allen. "In papers, on signboards, everywhere. Sometimes they call themselves a rest home, sometimes a sanatorium. Sometimes they don't even bother to call themselves anything. Just use a lot of white space, with the name 'Sanctuary' in big type. Refined, all of it. Nothing crude. Nothing quackish about it. They've run about all the other mental sanatoriums out of business. Nobody thinks of going anywhere but Sanctuary when they go batty now."

"What are you getting at?" snapped Chambers.

"I told you it would make you sore," Allen reminded him. "They've fooled you, just like they've fooled all the rest of us. Let me tell you what I know about them."

Chambers's lips were thin and straight. "Whatever made you

150

investigate them, Moses? Sanctuary is —" He faltered. "Why, Sanctuary is —"

Allen laughed. "Yes, I know what you mean. Sanctuary is lily-white. Sanctuary is noble. It's a shining haven in a world that's going haywire. Yeah, that's what you think and everyone thinks. I thought so myself. I started looking them up on a hunch. I hated myself. I felt like I ought to go and hide. But I had a hunch, see, and I never pass one up. So I gritted my teeth and went ahead. And I'm convinced that Sanctuary is either the greatest racket the Solar System has ever known or it's tied up with this insanity some way. My best guess is that it's a racket. I can't figure any angles the other way except that maybe they're doing something to drive people nuts just to boost their business and that doesn't add up for a lot of reasons. If it's a racket, I'm wasting my time. There's bigger game to hunt than rackets these days."

He took a deep breath. "First I checked up on Dr Jan Nichols, he's the fellow that runs it. And he's a nobody, far as I can find out. Certainly not a psychiatrist. Was in the Solar Service at one time. Headed a party making a survey of mineral resources out in the Belt. Had a minor degree in mineralogy. Just that, nothing more, no specialisation. An opportunist, I would deduce. Took just enough education to get a job.

"Our records show the whole party dropped out of sight. Listed as lost. All the rest of them still are lost so far as anybody knows.

"I tried to get in touch with Nichols and couldn't do it. There's no way to reach him. No mail service. No radio service. Nothing. Sanctuary is isolated. If you want anything there, you go there personally, yourself."

"I hadn't realised that," said Chambers.

"Neither does anyone else," declared Allen. "No one tries to get in touch with Sanctuary unless they need their services and if they need their services they go there. But you haven't heard the half of it."

Allen lit a cigarette. A clock chimed softly in the room, and

Hannibal, leaning out from the desk, took a swipe at Allen, missed him by bare inches.

The Secret Service man leaned back in his chair. "So, since I couldn't get in touch with Nichols, I sent some of my men out to Sanctuary. Six of them, in fact, at different times —"

He looked at Chambers, face grim.

"They didn't come back."

Chambers started slightly. "They didn't come back. You mean —"

"I mean just that. They didn't come back. I sent them out. Then nothing happened. No word from them. No word of them. They simply disappeared. That was three months ago."

"It seems incredible," declared Chambers. "Never for a moment have we worried about curing or caring for the men who went insane. Sanctuary did that, we thought. Better than anyone else could."

He shot a sudden question. "They do cure them, don't they?"

"Certainly," said Allen. "Certainly, they cure them. I've talked with many they have cured. But those they cure never go back into Solar Service. They are —"

He wrinkled his brow. "It's hard to put into words, chief. They seem to be different people. Their behaviour patterns don't check against their former records. They have forgotten most of their former skills and knowledge. They aren't interested in things they were interested in before. They have a funny look in their eyes. They —"

Chambers waved a hand. "You have to realise they would be changed. The treatment might —"

"Yes, I know," interrupted Allen. "Your reaction is just the same as mine was – as everyone else's would be. It's instinctive to protect Sanctuary, to offer apology for it. Because, you see, every last one of us, some day may need to go there. And knowing that it's there, we feel reassured. Maybe we go batty. So what? Sanctuary will fix us up OK. Won't cost us a cent if we haven't got the money. Even free transportation if we haven't got the fare. It's something to anchor to in this mad world. A sort of faith, even. It's tough to have it knocked from under you."

Chambers shook his head. "I'm almost sorry you started this business, Moses."

Allen rose, smashed out his cigarette in a tray.

"I was afraid you'd be. I hate to drop it now I've gone this far. It may fizzle out, but —"

"No," said Chambers, "don't drop it. We can't afford to drop anything these days. You, yourself, feel almost instinctively, that it will come to nothing, but on the outside chance it may not, you must go ahead."

"There's just one thing more, chief," said Allen. "I've mentioned it before. The people —"

Chambers flipped impatient hands. "I know what you're going to say, Moses. They resent me. They think I've drawn away from them. There have been too many rumours."

"They don't know you're blind," said Allen. "They'd understand if they did know that. Better for them to know the truth than to think all the things they're thinking. I know what they're thinking. It's my business to know."

"Who would follow a blind man?" asked Chambers bitterly. "I'd gain their pity, lose their respect."

"They're baffled," said Allen. "They talk about your illness, say it has changed you, never realising it left you blind. They even say your brain is going soft. They wonder about Hannibal, ask why you never are without him. Fantastic tales have grown up about him. Even more fantastic than the truth."

"Moses," said Chambers, sharply, "we will talk no more about this."

He sat stiff and straight in his chair, staring straight ahead, as Allen left.

Mrs Templefinger's parties were always dull. That was a special privilege she held as society leader of New York's upper crust.

This party was no exception. The amateurish, three-dimensional movies of her trip to the Jovian moons had been bad enough, but the violinist was worse.

Cabot Bond, publisher of the *Morning Spaceways*, fidgeted in his chair, then suddenly relaxed and tried to look at ease as he caught Mrs Templefinger glaring at him. She might be a snooty old dame, he told himself, and a trial to all her friends with her determined efforts to uphold the dignity of one of the Solar System's greatest families, but it definitely was not policy to vex her. She controlled too many advertising accounts.

Cabot Bond knew about advertising accounts. He lived by them and for them. And he worried about them. He was worrying about one of them now. The violin wailed to a stop and the guests applauded politely. The violinist bowed condescendingly. Mrs Templefinger beamed, fingering her famous rope of Asteroid jewels so the gems caught the light and gleamed with slow ripples of alien fire.

The man next to Bond leaned close.

"Great story that – about discovering the Rosetta stone of Mars," he said. "Liked the way your paper handled it. Lots of background. Interpretative writing. None of the sensationalism some of the other papers used. And you put it on the front page too. The *Rocket* stuck it away on an inside page."

Bond wriggled uncomfortably. That particular story he'd just as soon forget. At least he didn't want to talk about it. But the man apparently expected an answer.

"It wasn't a stone," Bond said icily, almost wishing the violin would start up again. "It was a scroll."

"Greatest story of the century," said the man, entirely unabashed. "Why, it will open up all the ancient knowledge of Mars."

The violin shrieked violently as the musician sawed a vicious bow across the strings.

Bond settled back into his chair, returned to his worry once again.

Funny how Sanctuary Inc. had reacted to that story about the Rosetta scroll of Mars. Almost as if they had been afraid to let it come before the public eye. Almost, although this seemed ridiculous, as if they might have been afraid of something that might be found in some old Martian record.

Perhaps he had been wrong in refusing their request to play the story down. Some of the other papers, like the *Rocket*, apparently had agreed. Others hadn't, of course, but most of those were sheets which never had carried heavy Sanctuary lineage, didn't stand to lose much. *Spaceways* did carry a lot of lineage. And it worried Bond.

The violin was racing now, a flurry of high-pitched notes, weaving a barbaric, outlandish pattern – a song of outer space, of cold winds on strange planets, of alien lands beneath unknown stars.

Mrs Templefinger's sudden scream rang through the room, cutting across the shrilling of the music.

"My jewels!" she screamed. "My jewels!"

She had surged to her feet, one hand clutching the slender chain that encircled her throat. The chain on which the Asteroid jewels had been strung.

But now the famous jewels were gone, as if some hand of magic had stripped them from the chain and whisked them into nowhere.

The violinist stood motionless, bow poised, fingers hovering over the strings. A glass tinkled as it slipped from someone's fingers and struck the floor.

"They're gone!" shrieked Mrs Templefinger. "My jewels are gone!"

The butler padded forward silently.

"Perhaps I should call the police, madam."

A strange light came over Mrs Templefinger's face, a soft and human light that smoothed out the lines around her eyes and suddenly made her soft and gracious instead of a glowering old dowager. For the first time in 20 years, Mrs Templefinger smiled a gracious smile.

"No, Jacques," she whispered. "Not the police."

Still smiling, she sat down again, nodded to the violinist. The chain fell from her fingers, almost as if she had forgotten the jewels, almost as if a cool half million dollars' worth of jewellery didn't matter.

The violinist swept the bow across the strings again.

Cabot Bond rose and tiptoed softly from the room. Suddenly it had occurred to him there was something he must do – phone his editor, tell him to play down any more stories the wires might carry on the Rosetta scroll of Mars.

Harrison Kemp, head of the Solar Research Bureau on Pluto, straightened from the microscope, expelling his breath slowly.

His voice was husky with excitement. "Johnny, I really believe you've got it! After all these years . . . after —"

He stopped and stared a stricken stare.

For Johnny Gardner had not heard him. Was not even looking at him. The man sat hunched on his stool, faint starlight from the laboratory port falling across his face, a face that had suddenly relaxed, hung loose and slack, a tired, wan face with haggard eyes and drooping jowls.

Kemp tried to speak, but his lips were dry and his tongue thick and terror dried up his words before they came. From somewhere behind him came the slow *drip-drip* of precious water. Outside, the black spires of Plutonian granite speared up into the inky, starry sky.

And before the port, the hunched figure of a man whose gaze went out into the alien wilderness, yet did not see the jumbled tangle that was Pluto's surface.

"Johnny!" Kemp whispered, and the whisper frightened him as it seemed to scamper like a frightened rat around the room.

Gardner did not answer, did not move. One hand lay loosely in his lap, the other dangled at his side. One foot slipped off the rung of the stool and, just failing to reach the floor, swung slowly to and fro like a ghastly pendulum.

Kemp took a step forward, reaching out a hand that stopped short of Gardner's shoulder.

There was no use, he knew, of trying to do anything. Johnny Gardner was gone. The hulking body still sat on the stool, but the mind, that keen, clear-cut, knifelike mind, was gone. Gone like a dusty mummy falling in upon itself. One moment a mind that could probe to the very depth of life itself – the next moment a mind that was no more than a darkening cavern filled with the hollow hooting of already half-forgotten knowledge.

Fumbling in the darkness, Kemp found another stool, perched wearily on it. Perched and stared at Gardner, while he felt the nameless horror of an alien planet and an alien happening slowly circle over him, like dark wings beating in the starlight.

A small cone of brilliance hung above the workbench, lighting up the electronic microscope. And under the microscope, Kemp knew, was something that came close to being the raw material, the constituent element of life. Something that he and Johnny Gardner and Victor Findlay had sought – for how many years? To Kemp, sitting there in the darkness, it seemed eternity.

An eternity of research, of compiling notes, of seeming triumph, always followed by the blackest of defeat.

"And," said Harrison Kemp, speaking to himself and the silent room and the madman at the port, "here we are again!"

It would be futile, Kemp knew, to try to pick up where Gardner had left off. For Gardner had worked swiftly, had been forced to work swiftly, in those last few minutes. Since there had been no time to jot it down, he had tucked away that final crucial data in his brain. Even under the near-zero conditions to which the protoplasmic molecules had been subjected, they still would be unstable. They would have changed now, would have been rendered useless for further observation – would either have become more complex life or no life at all, having lost that tiny spark that set them off from other molecules.

Kemp knew he and Findlay would have to start over again. Johnny's notes would help them to a certain point – up to that point where he had ceased to write them down, had stored them in his brain. From that point onward they would have to go alone, have to feel their way along the path Johnny Gardner had taken, try to duplicate what he had done. For whatever was in Johnny's brain was lost now – lost completely, gone like a whiff of rocket gas hurled into the maw of space.

157

A door creaked open and Kemp got to his feet, turning slowly to face the man silhouetted against the light from the room beyond.

"Why so quiet?" asked Findlay. "What are you fellows —"

His voice ran down and stopped. He stood rigidly, staring at the star-lighted face of Johnny Gardner.

"It just happened, Vic," said Kemp. "He called me to show me something in the 'scope and while I looked it happened to him. When I looked up again and spoke to him, he was sitting there, just like he is now. He was all right before, just a few seconds before."

"It hits them like that," said Findlay. He stepped into the room, walked close to Kemp. "We should know," he said. "We've seen it happen to enough of them, you and I. Sometimes I have a dream, with you and me the only sane men left in the entire System. Everybody cracking, leaving just the two of us."

"I should have taken your advice," Kemp declared bitterly. "I should have sent him back on the last ship. But he looked all right. He acted OK. And we needed him. He hung out for a long time. I thought maybe he would last."

"Don't blame yourself, chief," said Findlay. "There was no way for you to know."

"But you knew Vic! You warned me. You said he'd crack. How did you know? Tell me, how did —"

"Take it easy," cautioned Findlay. "I didn't know. Nothing definite, at least. Just a feeling I had. A hunch, I guess you'd call it."

They stood together, shoulder to shoulder, as if by standing thus they might beat back the sense of doom, the air of utter human futility that seemed to well within themselves.

"It won't always be like this," said Kemp. "Some day we'll be able to keep men's minds from going haywire. We'll find a way to help the mind keep pace with man's ambitions, to fall in step with progress."

Findlay nodded toward Gardner. "He was on the right track. He took the first long step. Before we even try to study the mind as it should be studied, scientifically, we must know what life is.

158

Before, we've always started in the middle and stumbled back, trying to find the Lord knows what. We can't afford to do that any longer. We have to have a basis, a basic understanding of life to understand ourselves."

Kemp nodded. "You're right, Vic. He took the first long step. And now . . . now, he goes to Sanctuary."

They helped Johnny Gardner from the stool and across the room. He walked like a blind man, stumblingly, muscles uncertain. His eyes stared straight ahead, as if he were watching something no one else could see.

"Thank heaven," said Findlay, "he went this way. Not like Smith."

Kemp shuddered, remembering. Smith had been violent. He had mouthed obscenities, had screamed and shouted, wrecked the laboratory. They had tried to calm him, to reason with him. When he charged Findlay with a steel bar, Kemp had shot him.

Although even that hadn't been any worse than Lempke. Lempke had committed suicide by walking out of the dome into the almost non-existent atmosphere of frigid Pluto without benefit of space gear.

Dr Daniel Monk laid the pencil aside, read once again the laborious lines of translation:

This is the story of . . . who visited the fifth planet from the central sun; not the first to go there, but the first to discover the life that lived thereon, a curious form of life that because of its . . . had not previously been recognised as life—

Outside the thin night wind of Mars had risen and was sweeping the city of Sandebar, whining and moaning among the cornices and columns of the museum. Drift sand pecked with tiny fingers against the windows and the brilliant Martian starlight painted frosty squares on the floor as it came tumbling through the casement.

This is the story of—

Dr Monk frowned at that. The story of whom? Probably, he told himself, he would never know, for the vocabulary made available by the Rosetta scroll did not extend to personal names.

With a wry smile he picked up his pencil again, wrote 'John Doe' in the blank. That was as good as any name.

This is the story of John Doe—

But that didn't answer another question. It didn't tell why the life of the fifth planet had not been recognised as life.

The fifth planet, without a doubt, was the planet which in another eon had travelled an orbit between Mars and Jupiter – the planet now represented by the Asteroid Belt, a maelstrom of planetary debris. It would have been the planet, it and the Earth, most accessible to Mars. It was natural the Martians should have gone there. And that they had known the planet before its disruption gave a breathtaking clue to the incredible antiquity of the scroll from which the passage had been translated.

Perhaps, Monk told himself, one of the other scrolls might tell of the actual breakup of the fifth planet, might give a clue or state a cause for its destruction. There were thousands of other scrolls, the loot of years from the ruins of Martian cities. But until this moment they had been voiceless, mute testimony the Martians had possessed a written language, but telling nothing of that language, revealing none of the vast store of information they held.

A curious form of life that because of its—

Because of its what? What form could life take, what trick could it devise to hide its being? Invisibility? Some variant of protective coloration? But one couldn't write 'invisible' into the text as one had written 'John Doe'.

Perhaps some day, Monk told himself, he might find the answer, might be able to write in that missing word. But not now. Not yet. The Rosetta scroll, for all its importance, still left much to be desired. It necessarily had to leave much to be desired, for it dealt in a language that sprang from a different source than Terrestrial language, developed along alien lines, represented thought processes that could have been – must have been – poles apart from the thoughts of Earth.

All that the Martian language held in common with Earthian language was that both represented thought symbols. That was all; there was very little similarity in the way they went about doing that same thing.

Monk reached out and lifted the heavy metal cylinder from the desk before him. Carefully, almost reverentially, he flipped open the lock that released one end of the cylinder, drew out the heavy, lengthy scroll that had provided the key to the thoughts, the works, the ways of the ancient race of Mars.

He unrolled it slowly, gently, squinting at the faded characters, faint with a million years or more of being buried in the sands of Mars.

A dictionary once – a dictionary again, but in a different way.

Monk wondered what sort of a long-dead personality had penned that dictionary. Scholar, seeking no more than the ways of truth? Businessman, seeking to facilitate a better lingual understanding, therefore a better commercial understanding, between the race of Mars and the now decadent races of the Jovian moons? Statesmen, trying to bring about a good-neighbour policy?

The Martian, however, whoever he might have been, had not understood that Jovian language too well, for some of the words and idioms didn't check with the Jovian language as Earthmen knew it. Or it might have been that the language itself had changed. Perhaps in that long-gone day when the scroll was written the moon men of Jupiter had not been decadent.

On that point, Monk knew, the Jovians themselves could throw little light. There were ruins, of course, and legends, but the legends were utterly crazy and the ruins held no traditional sentiment for the tribes of Europa or Ganymede. Unlike most peoples, they held no racial memories of a more glorious past, of a forgotten golden age.

It was a roundabout way, a long way, an awkward way to read the language of Mars, Monk reflected. Martian to Jovian to Earthian. But it was better than no way at all.

The clock on the manuscript cabinet chimed briefly, apologetically. Monk glanced at it and started in surprise. Midnight. He had not realised it was that late. Suddenly he knew that he was tired and hungry, needed a drink and a smoke.

He rose and walked to a table, found a bottle and glass, poured himself a drink. From somewhere, far in another part of the vast building, came the ghostly sound of a watchman's tread making his rounds. The sand talked and hissed against the window.

Back at his desk, Monk sipped at his drink, staring at the metallic tube, thinking of the faint scrawling on the scroll inside.

A Rosetta stone – the Rosetta stone of Mars. Brought in off the desert by a man who might just as easily have passed it by. Uncovered by shifting sand that in the next hour might just as well have covered it again for all eternity.

Monk lifted his glass to the weathered cylinder.

"To destiny," he said, and drank before he realised how silly it sounded.

Or was it silly? Might there not really be such a thing as destiny? An actual force moving to offset the haphazard course of a vagrant universe? Sometimes it seemed so. Sometimes—

Monk emptied the glass, set it on the desk, dug into his pocket for cigarettes. His fingers closed on a small package and he drew it out wonderingly, brow wrinkled. Then, quickly, he remembered. It had been in his mail box that morning. He had meant to open it later, had forgotten it until now.

He examined it curiously. It bore no return address and his own was laboriously printed by hand. He ripped the fastening tapes with his fingernails, unwrapped the paper.

A jewel box! Monk snapped up the lid and stiffened in surprise.

In its bed of rich velvet lay the gleaming roundness of an Asteroid jewel. It glowed softly under the desk lamp, colours flowing and changing within its heart, almost as if the jewel itself might be in motion.

There was no card. Nothing to indicate who had sent the jewel or, more important, why it had been sent. Asteroid jewels, Monk knew, weren't something to be just sent around to anyone for no reason at all. The stone before him, he realised, had a value that ran close to five figures.

Almost fearfully, he lifted the gem between thumb and forefinger, held it to the light and caught his breath in wonder as it blazed with soul-stirring beauty.

With a feeling that approached awe, he replaced it, sat quietly in his chair watching it.

Queer things, the Asteroid jewels, queer in more ways than one.

No one knew just what they were. No Asteroid jewel had ever been analysed. Spectrographically, they were like nothing science had ever known. They could be broken down chemically, of course, but even then they were impossible of analysis. Something there to analyse, naturally, but with certain baffling characteristics no chemist had yet been able to tie down and catalogue.

Found nowhere else in the Solar System, they were the magic that drove men to lives of bitter privation in the Belt, searching among the debris of dead planet for that tiny gleam in the jumbled rocks that would spell riches. Most of them, as could be expected, died without ever finding a single jewel; died in one of a vast variety of horrible, lonely ways a man can die among the Asteroids.

Monk found a cigarette and lighted it, listening to the pelting of the sand against the window. But there was a strange sound, too. Something that was not sand tapping on the panes, nor yet the shrill keening of the savage wind that moaned against the building. A faint whining that bore a pattern of melody, the sobbing of music – music that sneaked in and out of the wind blasts until one wondered if it was really there or was just imagination.

Monk sat stiffly, poised, cigarette drooping, ears straining.

It came again, the cry of strings, the breath of lilting cadence, until it was a thing apart from the wind and the patter of the sand.

A violin! Someone playing a violin inside the museum!

Monk leaped to his feet and suddenly the violin screamed in singing agony.

And even as that melodic scream ran full-voiced through the hall outside, a sharp bell of warning clanged inside Monk's brain.

Acting on impulse, his hand shot down and snatched up the Asteroid jewel. Clutching it savagely, he hurled it viciously against the metallic side of the manuscript cabinet.

It flashed for a moment in the light as it exploded into tiny bits of glowing dust. And even as it splashed to shards, it changed – or tried to change. For just a moment it was not a jewel, but something else, a fairylike thing – but a crippled fairy. A fairy with humped back and crooked spine and other curious deformities.

Then there was no twisted fairy, but only jewel dust twinkling on the floor and the sound of running feet far down the corridor.

Monk did not try to give chase to the man outside. Instead, he stood as if frozen, listening to the wind and the sand dance on the window, staring at the sparkle on the floor.

He slowly closed and opened his right hand, trying to remember just how the jewel had felt at the instant he had clutched it. Almost as if it might have been alive, were struggling to get out of his clutches, fighting to attain some end, to carry out some destiny.

His eyes still were upon the floor.

"Now," he said aloud, amazement in his words, "I wonder why I did that?"

Standing in front of Spencer Chambers's desk, Harrison Kemp was assailed by doubt, found that in this moment he could not reconcile himself to the belief he had done the right thing. If he were wrong, he had deserted a post he should have kept. Even if he were right, what good could his action do?

"I remember you very well," he heard Chambers say. "You

164

have been out on Pluto. Life research. Some real achievements in that direction."

"We have failed too often," Kemp told him flatly.

Chambers matched his fingers on the desk in front of him. "We all fail too often," Chambers said. "And yet, some day, some one of us will succeed, and then it will be as if all of us succeeded. We can write off the wasted years."

Kemp stood stiff and straight. "Perhaps you wonder why I'm here."

Chambers smiled a little. "Perhaps I do. And yet, why should I? You have been gone from Earth for a long time. Perhaps you wanted to see the planet once again."

"It wasn't that," Kemp told him. "It's something else. I came because I am about to go insane."

Chambers gasped involuntarily.

"Say that again," he whispered. "Say it slowly. Very slowly."

"You heard me," said Kemp. "I came because I'm going to crack. I came here first. Then I'm going out to Sanctuary. But I thought you'd like to know – well, know that a man can tell it in advance."

"Yes," said Chambers, "I want to know. But even more than that. I want to know how you can tell."

"I couldn't myself," Kempt told him. "It was Findlay who knew."

"Findlay?"

"A man who worked with me on Pluto. And he didn't really know. What I mean is he had no actual evidence. But he had a hunch."

"A hunch?" asked Spencer Chambers. "Just a hunch? That's all?"

"He's had them before," Kemp declared. "And they're usually right. He had one about Johnny Gardner before Johnny cracked up. Told me I should send him back. I didn't. Johnny cracked."

"Only about Johnny Gardner?"

"No, about other things as well. About ways to go about

165

our research, ways that aren't orthodox. But they usually bring results. And about what will happen the next day or the day after that. Just little inconsequential things. Has a feeling, he says – a feeling for the future."

Chambers stirred uneasily. "You've been thinking about this?" he asked. "Trying to puzzle it out. Trying to explain it."

"Perhaps I have," admitted Kemp, "but not in the way you mean. I'm not crazy yet. May not be tomorrow or next week or even next month. But I've watched myself and I'm pretty sure Findlay was right. Small things that point the way. Things most men would just pass by, never give a second thought. Laugh and say they were growing old or getting clumsy."

"Like what?" asked Chambers.

"Like forgetting things I should know. Elemental facts, even. Having to think before I can tell you what seven times eight equals. Facts that should be second nature. Trying to recall certain laws and fumbling around with them. Having to concentrate too hard upon laboratory technique. Getting it all eventually, even quickly, but with a split-second lag."

Chambers nodded. "I see what you mean. Maybe the psychologists could help —"

"It wouldn't work," declared Kemp. "The lag isn't so great but a man could cover up. And if he knew someone was watching he would cover up. That would be instinctive. When it becomes noticeable to someone other than yourself it's gone too far. It's the brain running down, tiring out, beginning to get fuzzy. The first danger signals."

"That's right," said Chambers. "There is another answer, too. The psychologists, themselves, would go insane."

He lifted his head, appeared to stare at Kemp.

"Why don't you sit down?" he asked.

"Thank you," said Kemp. He sank into a chair. On the desk the spidery little statue moved with a scuttling shamble and Kemp jumped in momentary fright.

Chambers laughed quietly. "That's only Hannibal."

Kemp stared at Hannibal and Hannibal stared back, reached out a tentative claw.

166

"He likes you," said Chambers in surprise. "You should consider that a compliment, Kemp. Usually he simply ignores people."

Kemp stared stonily at Hannibal, fascinated by him. "How do you know he likes me?"

"I have ways of knowing," Chambers said.

Kemp extended a cautious finger and for a moment Hannibal's claw closed about it tightly, but gently. Then the grotesque little being drew away, squatted down, became a statue once again.

"What is he?" Kemp asked.

Chambers shook his head. "No one knows. No one can even guess. A strange form of life. You are interested in life, aren't you, Kemp?"

"Naturally," said Kemp. "I've lived with it for years, wondering what it is, trying to find out."

Chambers reached out and picked up Hannibal, put him on his shoulder. Then he lifted a sheaf of papers from his desk, shuffled through them, picked out half a dozen sheets.

"I have something here that should interest you," he said. "You've heard of Dr Monk?"

Kemp nodded. "The man who found the Rosetta scroll of Mars."

"Ever meet him?"

Kemp shook his head.

"Interesting chap," said Chambers. "Buried neck-deep in his beloved Martian manuscripts. Practically slavering in anticipation, but getting just a bit afraid."

He rustled the sheets. "I heard from him last week. Tells me he has found evidence that life, a rather queer form of life, once existed on the fifth planet before it disrupted to form the Asteroids. The Martians wrote that this life was able to encyst itself, live over long periods in suspended animation. Not the mechanically induced suspended animation the human race has tried from time to time, but a natural encystation, a variation of protective coloration."

"Interesting," said Kemp, "but a bit out of my line. It suggests

167

many possibilities. Shows the almost endless flexibility of life as such."

Chambers nodded. "I thought maybe you would have that reaction. It was mine, too, but I'm not an expert on that sort of thing. Monk hints that life form may still exist. Hints at other things, too. He seemed to be upset when he wrote the letter. Almost as if he were on the verge of a discovery he himself couldn't quite believe. A little frightened at it, even. Not wanting to say too much, you see, until he was absolutely sure."

"Why should something like that upset him?" demanded Kemp. "It's information out of the past. Surely something he finds in those old scrolls can't reach out —"

Chambers lifted his hand. "You haven't heard it all. The Martians were afraid of that life on the fifth planet, Kemp. Deathly afraid of it! So afraid of it they blew up the planet, blasted it, destroyed it, thinking that in doing so they would wipe out the life it bore."

Chambers's face did not change. He did not stir.

"Monk believes they failed," he said.

The room swam in almost frightened silence. Hannibal stirred uneasily on his perch on Chambers's shoulder.

"Can you imagine —" Chambers's voice was almost a whisper. "Can you imagine a fear so great that a race would blow up, destroy another planet to rid themselves of it?"

Kemp shook his head. "It seems rather hard, and yet, given a fear great enough —"

He stopped and shot a sudden look at Chambers. "Why have you bothered to tell me this?" he asked.

"Why, don't you see?" said Chambers smoothly. "Here might be a new kind of life – a different kind of life, developed millions of years ago under another environment. It might have followed a divergent quirk of development, just some tiny, subtle difference that would provide a key."

"I see what you're driving at," said Kemp. "But not me. Findlay is your man. I haven't got the time. I'm living on borrowed sanity. And, to start with, you haven't even got that life. You hardly would know what to look for. An encysted form of life. That could be anything. Send a million men out into the Asteroids to hunt for it and it might take a thousand years.

"The idea is sound, of course.We've followed it in other instances, without success. The moon men of Jupiter were no help. Neither were the Venusians. The Martians, of course, were out of the picture to start with. We don't even know what they were like. Not even a skeleton of them has been found. Maybe the race they were afraid of got them after all – did away with them completely."

Chambers smiled bleakly. "I should have known it was no use."

"I'm sorry," said Kemp. "I have to go to Sanctuary. I've seen some others when it happened to them. Johnny Gardner and Smith and Lempke. It's not going to happen to me that way if I can help it."

Chambers matched his fingers carefully. "You've been in the service a long time, Kemp."

"Ten years," said Kemp.

"During those ten years you have worked with scarcely a thought of yourself," said Chambers quietly. "There is no need to be modest. I know your record. You have held a certain ideal. An ideal for a better Solar System, a better human life. You would have given your right arm to have done something that would actually have contributed to the betterment of mankind. Like finding out what life is, for example. You came here now because you thought what you had to tell might help."

Kemp sat without speaking.

"Isn't that it?" insisted Chambers.

"Perhaps it is," admitted Kemp. "I've never thought of it in just those words. To me it was a job."

"Would you do another job?" asked Chambers. "Another job for mankind? Without knowing why you did it? Without asking any questions?"

Kemp leaped to his feet. "I've told you I was going to Sanctuary," he shouted. "I have done what I can, all I can. You can't ask me to wait around for —"

"You will go to Sanctuary," said Chambers sharply.

"But this job —"

"When you go to Santuary I want you to take Hannibal along."

Kemp gasped. "Hannibal?"

"Exactly," said Chambers. "Without asking me why."

Kemp opened his mouth to speak, closed it.

"Now?" he finally asked.

"Now," said Chambers. He rose, lifted Hannibal from his shoulder. Kemp felt the sharp claws digging through his clothing, into his flesh, felt one tiny arm pawing at his neck, seeking a hold.

Chambers patted Hannibal on the head. Tears welled out of his sightless eyes behind the large dark glasses.

Sanctuary was a place of beauty, a beauty that gripped one by the throat and held him, as if against a wall.

Once, a few years ago, Kemp realised, it had been a barren hunk of rock, five miles across at most, tumbling through space on an eccentric orbit. No air, no water – nothing but stark stone that glinted dully when the feeble rays of the distant sun chanced to fall across its surface.

But now it was a garden with lacy waterfalls and singing streams arched by feathery trees in whose branches flitted warbling birds. Cleverly concealed lighting held the black of space at bay and invested the tiny planetoid with a perpetual just-before-dusk, a soft and radiant light that dimmed to purple shadows where the path of flagging ran up the jagged hill crowned by a classic building of shining white plastic.

A garden built by blasting disintegrators that shaped the face of the rock to an architect's blueprint, that gouged deep wells for the gravity apparatus, that chewed the residue of its labour into the basis for the soil in which the trees and other vegetation grew. A garden made livable by machines that manufactured air and water, that screened out the lashing radiations that move through naked space – and yet no less beautiful because it was man and machine-made.

Kemp hesitated beside a deep, still pool just below a stretch of white-sprayed, singing water crossed by a rustic bridge and drank in the scene that ran up the crags before him. A scene that whispered with a silence made up of little sounds. And as he stood there a deep peace fell upon him, a peace he could almost feel, feel it seeping into his brain, wrapping his body – almost as if it were something he could reach and grasp.

It was almost as if he had always lived here, as if he knew and loved this place from long association. The many black years on Pluto were dimmed into a distant memory and it seemed as if weight had fallen from his shoulders, from the shoulders of his soul.

A bird twittered sleepily and the water splashed on stones. A tiny breeze brought the swishing of the waterfall that feathered down the cliff and a breath of fragrance from some blooming thing. Far off, a bell chimed softly, like a liquid note running on the scented air.

Something scurried in the bushes and scuttled up the path and, looking down, Kemp saw Hannibal and at the sight of the grinning face of the little creature his thoughts were jerked back into pattern again.

"Thank goodness you decided to show up." said Kemp. "Where you been? What's the idea of hiding out on me?"

Hannibal grimaced at him.

Well, thought Kemp, that was something less to worry about now. Hannibal was in Sanctuary and technically that carried out the request Chambers had made of him. He remembered the minute of wild panic when, landing at Sanctuary spaceport, he had been unable to find the creature. Search of the tiny one-man ship in which he had come to Sanctuary failed to locate the missing Hannibal, and Kemp had finally given up, convinced that somehow during the past few hours, Chambers's pet had escaped into space, although that had seemed impossible.

"So you hid out somewhere," Kemp said. "Scared they'd find you, maybe, and refuse to let you in. You needn't have worried, though, for they didn't pay any attention to me or to the ship. Just gave me a parking ticket and pointed out the path."

He stooped and reached for Hannibal, but the creature backed away into the bushes.

"What's the matter with you?" snapped Kemp. "You were chummy enough until just —"

His voice fell off, bewildered. He was talking to nothing. Hannibal was gone.

For a moment Kemp stood on the path, then turned slowly and started up the hill. And as he followed the winding trail that skirted the crags, he felt the peace of the place take hold of him again and it was as if he walked an old remembered way, as if he begrudged every footstep for the beauty that he left behind, but moved on to a newer beauty just ahead.

He met the old man halfway up the hill and stood aside because there was not room for both to keep the path. For some reason the man's brown robe reaching to his ankles and his bare feet padding in the little patches of dust that lay among the stones, even his flowing white beard did not seem strange but something that fitted in the picture.

"Peace be on you," the old man said, and then stood before him quietly, looking at him out of calm blue eyes.

"I welcome you to Sanctuary," the old man said. "I have something for you."

He thrust his hand into a pocket of his robe and brought out a gleaming stone, held it toward Kemp.

Kemp stared at it.

"For you, my friend," the old man insisted.

Kemp stammered. "But it's . . . it's an Asteroid jewel."

"It is more than that, Harrison Kemp," declared the oldster. "It is much more than that."

"But even —"

The other spoke smoothly, unhurriedly. "You still react as you did on Earth – out in the old worlds, but here you are in a new world. Here values are different, standards of life are not the same. We do not hate, for one thing. Nor do we question kindness, rather we expect it – and give it. We are not suspicious of motives."

172

"But this is a sanatorium," Kemp blurted out. "I came here to be treated. Treated for insanity."

A smile flicked at the old man's lips. "You are wondering where you'll find the office and make arrangements for treatment."

"Exactly," said Kemp.

"The treatment," declared the oldster, "has already started. Somewhere along this path you found peace – a greater, deeper peace than you've ever known before. Don't fight that peace. Don't tell yourself it's wrong for you to feel it. Accept it and hold it close. The insanity of your worlds is a product of your lives, your way of life. We offer you a new life. That is our treatment."

Hesitantly, Kemp reached out and took the jewel. "And this is a part of that new way of life?"

The old man nodded. "Another part is a little chapel you will find along the way. Stop there for a moment. Step inside and look at the painting you will find there."

"Just look at a painting?"

"That's right. Just look at it."

"And it will help me?"

"It may."

The old man stepped down the path. "Peace go with you," he said and paced slowly down the hill.

Kemp stared at the jewel in his palm, saw the slow wash of colour stir within its heart.

"Stage setting," he told himself, although he didn't say it quite aloud.

A pastoral scene of enchanting beauty, a man who wore a brown robe and a long white beard, the classic white lines of the building on the plateau, the chapel with a painting. Of course a man would find peace here. How could a man help but find peace here? It was designed and built for the purpose – this scene. Just as an architect would design and an engineer would build a spaceship. Only a spaceship was meant to travel across the void, and this place, this garden, was meant to bring peace to troubled men, men with souls so troubled that they were insane.

173

Kemp stared at a flowering crab-apple tree that clung to the rocks above him, and even as he watched a slight breeze shook the tree and a shower of petals cascaded down toward him. Dimly, Kemp wondered if that tree kept on blooming over and over again. Perhaps it did. Perhaps it never bore an apple, perhaps it just kept on flowering. For its function here in Sanctuary was to flower, not to fruit. Blossoms had more psychological value as a stage setting than apples – therefore, perhaps, the tree kept on blossoming and blossoming.

Peace, of course. But how could they make it stick? How could the men who ran Sanctuary make peace stay with a man? Did the painting or the Asteroid jewel have something to do with it? And could peace alone provide the answer to the twisted brains that came here?

Doubt jabbed at him with tiny spears, doubt and skepticism – the old skepticism he had brought with him from the dusty old worlds, the frigid old worlds, the bitter old worlds that lay outside the pale of Sanctuary.

And yet doubt, even skepticism, quailed before the beauty of the place, faltered when he remembered the convincing sincerity of the old man in the brown robe, when he remembered those calm blue eyes and the majesty of the long white beard. It was hard to think, Kemp told himself, that all of this could be no more than mere psychological trappings.

He shook his head, bewildered, brushed clinging apple blossoms from his shoulder and resumed his climb, Asteroid jewel still clutched tightly in his hand. The path narrowed until it was scarcely wide enough to walk upon, with the sheer wall on his right knifing up toward the plateau, the precipice to his left dropping abruptly into a little valley where the brook gurgled and laughed beneath the waterfall that loomed just ahead.

At the second turn he came upon the chapel. A little place, it stood close to the path, recessed a little into the wall of rock. The door stood ajar, as if inviting him.

Hesitating for a moment, Kemp stepped into the recess, pushed gently on the door and stepped inside. Stepped inside and halted, frozen by the painting that confronted him. Set in a rocky alcove in the wall, it was lighted by a beam that speared down from the ceiling just above the door.

As if it were a scene one came upon through an open window rather than one caught upon a canvas, the city stood framed within the flare of light – a weird, fantastic city sprawled on some outer world. Bizarre architecture rearing against an outlandish background; towers leaping upward and fading into nothing, showing no clear-cut line where they left off; spidery sky bridges coiling and looping among the spires and domes that somehow were not the way spires and domes should be – the city looked like the impassioned chisellings of some mad sculptor.

And as Kemp stood transfixed before the city in the wall, a bell clanged far above him, one sharp clear note that lanced into his brain and shook him like an angry fist.

Something stirred within his hand, something that came to life and grew and wanted to be free. With a wild exclamation, Kemp jerked his hand in front of him, shaking it to free it of the thing that moved within it – repugnance choking him, an instinctive gesture born in the human race by spiders in dark caves, by crawling things that dropped off jungle leaves and bit.

But it was no spider, no crawling thing. Instead it was a light, a little point of light that slipped from between his fingers and rose and swiftly faded into nothing. And even as it faded, Kemp felt cool fingers on his jumping nerves, fingers that soothed them and quieted them until he felt peace flow toward him once again, but this time a deeper, calmer, vaster peace that took in all the universe, that left him breathless with the very thought of it.

Claws rustled on the floor behind him and a dark form sailed through the air to land upon his shoulder.

"Hannibal!" yelled the startled Kemp.

But, even as he yelled, Hannibal launched himself into the air again, straight from Kemp's shoulder into empty air, striking viciously at something that was there, something that fought back, but something Kemp could not see at all.

"Hannibal!" Kemp shrieked again, and the shriek was raw

175

and vicious as he realised that his new-found peace had been stripped from him as one might strip a cloak, leaving him naked in the chill of sudden fear.

Hannibal was fighting something, of that there was no doubt. An invisible something that struggled to get free. But Hannibal had a death grip. His savage jaws were closed upon something that had substance, his terrible claws raked at it, tore at it.

Kemp backed away until he felt the stone wall at his back, then stood and stared with unbelieving eyes.

Hannibal was winning out, was dragging the thing in the air down to the ground. As if he were performing slow-motion acrobatics, he twisted and turned in the air, was slowly sinking toward the floor. And never for a moment were those scythe-like claws idle. They raked and slashed and tore and the thing that fought them was weakening, dropped faster and faster.

Just before they reached the floor, Hannibal relaxed his grip for a moment, twisted in mid-air like a cat and pounced again. For a fleeting second Kemp saw the shape of the thing Hannibal held between his jaws, the thing he shook and shook, then cast contemptuously aside – a shimmery, fairy-like thing with dragging wings and a moth-like body. Just a glimpse, that was all.

"Hannibal," gasped Kemp. "Hannibal, what have you done?"

Hannibal stood on bowed legs and stared back at him, with eyes in which Kemp saw the smoky shine of triumph. Like a cat might look when it has caught a bird, like a man might look when he kills a mortal enemy.

"It gave me peace," said Kemp. "Whatever it was, it gave me peace. And now —"

He took a slow step forward and Hannibal backed away.

But Kemp stopped as a swift thought struck him.

The Asteroid jewel!

Slowly he lifted his two hands and looked at them and found them empty. The jewel, he remembered, had been clutched in his right hand and it had been from that hand that the shining thing arose.

He caught his breath, still staring at his hands.

An Asteroid jewel one moment, and the next, when the bell chimed, a spot of glowing light – then nothing. And yet something, for Hannibal had killed something, a thing that had a moth-like body and still could not have been a moth, for a man can see a moth.

Kemp's anger at Hannibal faded and in its place came a subtle fear, a fear that swept his brain and left it chisel-sharp and cold with the almost certain knowledge that here he faced an alien threat, a siren threat, a threat that was a lure.

Chambers had told him about a life that could encyst itself, could live in suspended animation; had voiced a fear that the old Martians, who had tried to sweep that life away, had failed.

Could it be that the Asteroid jewels were the encysted life?

Kemp remembered things about the jewels. They never had been analysed. They were found nowhere else except upon the Asteroids.

The bell might have been the signal for them to awake, a musical note that broke up the encystation, that returned the sleeping entity to its original form.

Entities that could cure the twisted brains of men, probably by some subtle change of outlook, by the introduction of some mental factor that man had never known before.

Kemp remembered, with a sudden surge of longing, a stinging sense of loss, the mental peace that had reached out to him – for a fleeting moment felt a deep and sharp regret that it had been taken from him.

But despite that ability to give peace the Martians had feared them, feared them with a deep and devastating fear – a fear so great they had destroyed a planet to rid the System of them. And the Martians were an old race and a wise race.

If the Martians had feared them, there was at least good grounds to suspect Earthmen should fear them, too.

And as he stood there, the horror of the situation seeped into Kemp's brain. A sanatorium that cured mental cases by the simple process of turning those mental cases over to an

177

alien life which had the power to impose upon the mind its own philosophy, to shape the human mind as it willed it should be shaped. A philosophy that started out with the concept of mental peace and ended – where?

But that was something one couldn't figure out, Kemp knew – something there was no way to figure out. It could lead anywhere. Especially since one had no way of knowing what sort of mental concepts the aliens of the fifth planet might hold. Concepts that might be good or ill for the human race, but concepts that certainly would not be entirely human.

Clever! So clever that Kemp wondered now why he had not suspected sooner, why he had not smelled a certain rottenness. First the garden to lull one into receptiveness – that odd feeling one had always known this place, making him feel that he was at home so he would put his guard down. Then the painting – meant, undoubtedly to establish an almost hypnotic state, designed to hold a man transfixed in rapt attention until it was too late to escape the attention of the reawakened life. If, in fact, anyone would have wanted to escape.

That was the insidious part of it – they gave a man what he wanted, what he longed for, something he missed out in the older worlds of struggle and progress. Like a drug—

Claws rattled on the floor.

"Hannibal!" yelled Kemp. But Hannibal didn't stop.

Kemp plunged toward the door, still calling. "Hannibal! Hannibal, come back here!"

Far up the slope there was a rustle in the bushes. A tiny pebble came tapping down the hill.

"Peace be on you," said a familiar voice, and Kemp spun round. The old man with the brown robe and the long white whiskers stood in the narrow path.

"Is there anything wrong?"asked the oldster.

"No," said Kemp. "Not yet. But there's going to be!"

"I do not —"

"Get out of my way," snapped Kemp. "I'm going back!"

178

The blue eyes were as calm as ever, the words as unhurried. "No one ever goes back, son."

"Gramp," warned Kemp grimly, "if you don't get out of my way so I can go down the path —"

The old man's hands moved quickly, plunging into the pockets of his robe. Even as Kemp started forward they came out again, tossed something upward and for one breathless instant Kemp saw a dozen or more gleaming Asteroid jewels shimmering in the air, a shower of flashing brilliance.

Bells were clamouring, bells all over the Asteroid, chiming out endlessly that one clear note, time after time, stabbing at Kemp's brain with the clarity of their tones – turning those sparkling jewels into things that would grasp his mind and give him peace and make him something that wasn't quite human.

With a bellow of baffled rage, Kemp charged. He saw the old man's face in front of him, mouth open, those calm eyes now deep pools of hatred, tinged with a touch of fear. Kemp's fist smacked out, straight into the face, white whiskers and all. The face disappeared and a scream rang out as the oldster toppled off the ledge and plunged toward the rocks below.

Cool fingers touched Kemp's brain, but he plunged on, almost blindly, down the path. The fingers slipped away and others came and for a moment the peace rolled over him once again. With the last dregs of willpower he fought it off, screaming like a tortured man, keeping his legs working like pistons. The wind brought the scent of apple blossoms to him and he wanted to stop beside the brook and take off his shoes and know the feel of soft green grass beneath his feet.

But that, one cold corner of his brain told him, was the way they wanted him to feel, the very thing Sanctuary wanted him to do. Staggering, he ran, reeling drunkenly.

He staggered, and as he fell his hand struck something hard and he picked it up. It was a branch, a dead branch fallen from some tree. Grimly, he tested it and found it hard and strong, gripped it in one hand and stumbled down the path.

The club gave him something – some strange psychological advantage – a weapon that he whirled around his head

179

when he screamed at the things that would have seized his mind.

Then there was hard ground beneath his feet – the spaceport. Men ran toward him, yelling at him, and he sprinted forward to meet them, a man that might have been jerked from the caves of Europe half a million years before – a maddened, frothing man with a club in hand, with a savage gleam in his eyes, hair tousled, shirt ripped off.

The club swished and a man slumped to the ground. Another man charged in and the club swished and Harrison Kemp screamed in killing triumph.

The men broke and ran, and Kemp, roaring, chased them down the field.

Somehow he found his ship and spun the lock.

Inside, he shoved the throttle up the rack, fogetting about the niceties of take-off, whipping out into the maw of space with a jerk that almost broke his neck, that gouged deep furrows in the port and crumpled one end of the hangar.

Kemp glanced back just once at the glowing spot that was Sanctuary. After that he kept his face straight ahead. The knotted club still lay beside his chair.

Dr Daniel Monk ran his finger around the inside of his collar, seemed about to choke.

"But you told me," he stammered. "You sent for me —"

"Yes," agreed Spencer Chambers, "I did tell you I had a Martian. But I haven't got him now. I sent him away."

Monk stared blankly.

"I had need of him elsewhere," Chambers explained.

"I don't understand," Monk declared weakly. "Perhaps he will be coming back."

Chambers shook his head. "I had hoped so, but now I am afraid . . . afraid —"

"But you don't realise what a Martian would mean to us!" Monk blurted.

"Yes, I do," declared Chambers. "He could read the manu-scripts. Much more easily, much more accurately than they can be translated. That was why I sent for you. That, in fact, was how I knew he was a Martian in the first place. He read some of the photostatic copies of the manuscripts you sent me."

Monk straightened in his chair. "He read them! You mean you could talk with him!"

Chambers grinned. "Not exactly talk with him, Monk. That is, he didn't make sounds like you and I do."

The chairman of the Solar Control Board leaned across the desk.

"Look at me," he commanded. "Look closely. Can you see anything wrong?"

Monk stammered. "Why, no. Nothing wrong. Those glasses, but a lot of people wear them."

"I know," said Chambers. "A lot of people wear them for effect. Because they think it's smart. But I don't. I wear mine to hide my eyes."

"Your eyes!" whispered Monk. "You mean there's some-thing —"

"I'm blind," said Chambers. "Very few people know it. I've kept it a careful secret. I haven't wanted the world's pity. I don't want the knowledge I can't see hampering my work. People wouldn't trust me."

Monk started to speak, but his words dribbled into silence.

"Don't feel sorry for me," snapped Chambers. "That's the very thing I've been afraid of. That's why no one knows. I wouldn't have told you except I had to tell to explain about Hannibal."

"Hannibal?"

"Hannibal," said Chambers, "is the Martian. People thought he was my pet. Something I carried around with me because of vanity. Because I wanted something different. Something to catch the headlines. But he was more than a pet. He was a Seeing-eye dog. He was my eyes. With Hannibal around I could see. Better than I could see with my own eyes. Much better."

Monk started forward, then settled back. "You mean Hannibal was telepathic?"

Chambers nodded. "Naturally telepathic. Perhaps it was the way the Martians talked. The only way they could talk. He telepathed perfect visual images of everything he saw and in my mind I could see as clearly, as perfectly as if I had seen with my own eyes. Better even, for Hannibal had powers of sight a human does not have."

Monk tapped his fingers on the chair arm, staring out of the window at the pines that marched along the hill.

"Hannibal was found out in the Asteroids, wasn't he?" Monk asked suddenly.

"He was," said Chambers. "Until a few days ago I didn't know what he was. No one knew what he was. He was just a thing that saw for me. I tried to talk with him and couldn't. There seemed no way in which to establish a communication of ideas. Almost as if he didn't know there were such things as ideas. He read the newspapers for me. That is, he looked at the page, and in my mind I saw the page and read it. But I was the one that had to do the reading. All Hannibal did was telepath the picture of the paper to me and my mind would do the work. But when I picked up the manuscript photostats it was Hannibal who read. To me they meant nothing – just funny marks. But Hannibal knew. He read them to me. He made me see the things they said. I knew then he was a Martian. No one else but a Martian, or Dr Monk, could read that stuff."

He matched his fingers carefully. "I've wondered how, since he was a Martian, he got into the Belt. How he could have managed to survive. When we first found him there was no reason to suspect he was a Martian. After all, we didn't know what a Martian was. They left no description of themselves. No paintings, no sculptures."

"The Martians," said Monk, "didn't run to art. They were practical, deadly serious, a race without emotion."

He drummed his fingers along the chair arm again. "There's just one thing. Hannibal was your eyes. You needed him. In such a case I can't imagine why you would have parted with him."

"I needed to see," said Chambers, "in a place I couldn't go."

"You . . . you. What was that?"

"Exactly what I said. There was a place I had to see. A place I had to know about. For various reasons it was closed to me. I could not, dare not, go there. So I sent Hannibal. I sent my eyes there for me."

"And you saw?"

"I did."

"You mean you could send him far away —"

"I sent him to the Asteroids," said Chambers. "To be precise, to Sanctuary. Millions of miles. And I saw what he saw. Still see what he sees, in fact. I can't see you because I'm blind. But I see what's happening on Sanctuary this very moment. Distance has no relation to telepathy. Even the first human experiments in it demonstrated that."

The phone on Chambers's desk buzzed softly. He groped for the receiver, finally found it, lifted it. "Hello," he said.

"This is Moses Allen," said the voice on the other end. "Reports are just starting to come in. My men are rounding up the Asteroid jewels. Got bushels of them so far. Putting them under locks you'd have to use atomics to get open."

Worry edged Chambers's voice. "You made sure there was no slip? No way anyone could get wind of what we're doing and hide out some of them."

Allen chuckled. "I got thousands of men on the job. All of them hit at the same minute. First we checked records of all sales. To be sure we knew just who had them and how many. We haven't got a few of them yet, but we know who's got them. Some of the owners are a little stubborn, but we'll sweat it out of them. We know they've got them cached away somewhere."

He laughed. "One funny thing, chief. Old Lady Templefinger – the society dame, you know – had a rope of them, some of the finest in the world. We can't find them. She claims they disappeared. Into thin air, just like that. One night at a concert. But we —"

"Wait a second," snapped Chambers. "A concert, you said?"

"Sure, a concert. Recital, I guess, is a better name for it. Some long-haired violinist."

"Allen," rapped Chambers, "check up on that recital. Find out who was there. Drag them in. Hold them on some technical charge. Anything at all, just so you hold them. Treat them just as if they were people who had been cured by Sanctuary. Grab on to them and don't let them go."

"Cripes, chief," protested the Secret Service man, "we might run into a barrel of trouble. The old lady would've had some big shots —"

"Don't argue," shouted Chambers. "Get going. Pick them up. And anyone else who was around when any other jewels evaporated. Check up on all strange jewel disappearances. No matter how far back. Don't quit until you're sure in every case. And hang onto everybody. Everyone who's ever had anything to do with Sanctuary."

"OK," agreed Allen. "I don't know what you're aiming at, but we'll do —"

"Another thing," said Chambers. "How about the whispering campaign?"

"We've got it started," Allen said. "And it's a lulu, chief. I got busy-bodies tearing around all over the Solar System. Spreading the word. Nothing definite. Just whispers. Something wrong with Sanctuary. Can't trust them. Can't tell what happens to you when you go there. Why, I heard about a guy just the other day —"

"That's the idea," approved Chambers. "We simply can't tell the real story, but we have to do something to stop people from going there. Frighten them a bit, make them wonder."

"Come morning," said Allen, "and the whole System will be full of stories. Some of them probably even better than those we started with. Sanctuary will starve to death waiting for business after we get through with them."

"That," said Chambers, "is just exactly what we want."

He hung up the phone, fumbling awkwardly, then turned his head toward Monk.

"You heard?" he asked.

"Enough," said Monk. "If it's something I should forget —"

"It's nothing you should forget," Chambers told him. "You're in this with me. Clear up to the hilt."

"I've guessed some of it," said Monk. "A lot of it, in fact. Found some of it from hints in the manuscripts. Some from what I've heard you say. I've been sitting here, trying to straighten it out, trying to make all the factors fall together. The Asteroid jewels, of course, are the encysted life form from the fifth planet and someone on Sanctuary is using them to do to us just what they planned to do to the Martian race – may have done to the Martian race."

"The man out on Sanctuary," said Chambers, "is Jan Nichols, but I doubt if he is using the asterites. More probably they are using him. Some years ago he headed an expedition into the Belt and disappeared. When he came to light again he was the head of Sanctuary. Somehow, while he was out there, he must have come under control of the asterites. Maybe someone played a violin, struck just the right note when he had an Asteroid jewel on his person. Or it might have happened some other way. There's no way of knowing. The worst of it is that now he probably is convinced he is engaged in a great crusade. That's the most dangerous thing about the asterites or the fifth-planet people or whatever you want to call them. Their propaganda is effective because once one is exposed to them he becomes one of them, in philosophy if not in fact and, after all, it's the philosophy, the way of thinking that counts."

Chambers shuddered, as if a cold wind might be sweeping through the room. "It's a beautiful philosophy, Monk. At least, on the surface. God knows what it is underneath. I gained a glimpse of it, several times, through Hannibal. It was that strong, strong enough even to force its way through the veil of hatred that he held for them, powerful enough to reach through the vengeance in his mind. The vengeance that's driving him out there now."

"Vengeance?" asked Monk.

"He's killing them," said Chambers. "As you and I might kill vermin. He's berserk, killing mad. I've tried to call him back. Tried to get him to hide so we can rescue him without the certainty of losing every man we sent out. For some reason, perhaps because he knows them better, hates them more, Hannibal can stand against them. But a man couldn't, a man wouldn't have a chance. Sanctuary is stirred up like a nest of maddened bees."

Chambers's faced sagged. "But I can't call him back. I can't even reach him any more. I still see the things he sees. He still keeps contact with me, probably because he wants me to observe, through his mind, as long as possible. Hoping, perhaps, that the human race will take up where he left off – if he leaves off."

"Hannibal is carrying out his destiny," Monk said gravely. "I can patch it together now. Things I didn't understand before. Things I found in the manuscripts. Hannibal slept through time for this very day."

Chambers snapped his head erect, questioningly.

"That's right," said Monk. "The Martians, in their last days, perfected a fairly safe method of suspended animation. Perhaps they used principles they stole from the fifth planet, perhaps not. It doesn't matter. They placed a number of their people in suspended animation. How many, I don't know. The number's there, but I can't read it. It might be a hundred or a thousand. Anyway, it was a lot of them. And they scattered them all over the Solar System. They took some to the Asteroids, some to Earth, some to the Jovian moons, some even out to Pluto. They left them everywhere. They left them in those different places and then the rest of the race went home to die. I wondered why they did it. The symbol was there to tell me, but I couldn't read the symbol."

Chambers nodded. "You have to fill in too many things, the translation leaves too many blanks."

"I had a hunch," Monk said. "It might have been an attempt to preserve the race. A wild throw, you know. A desperate people will try almost anything. Where there's life, there's hope. Hang on long enough and something's bound to happen.

"But I was wrong. I can see that now. They did it for revenge. It ties in with the other things we know about the Martians. Perhaps the asterites had destroyed them. They had tried to destroy the asterites, were sure that they had failed. So they left behind a mop-up squad. The rest of them died, but the mop-up squad slept on against a distant day, playing the million-to-one chance. In Hannibal's case, the long shot paid out. He's doing some mopping-up out in Sanctuary now. It's the last brave gesture of a race that's dead these million years."

"But there are others," said Chambers. "There are —"

"Don't get your hopes up," Monk warned. "Remember the odds. Hannibal carried out his destiny. Even that was more than could have been logically expected. The others —"

"I'm not doing any hoping," Chambers declared. "Not on my own account, anyhow. There's a job to do. We have to do it the best we can. We must guard against the human race going down before the philosophy of these other people. We must keep the human race – human.

"The asterites' creed, on the surface, is beautiful, admittedly. What it is beneath the surface, of course, we cannot know. But admitting that it is all that it appears and nothing more, it is not a human creed. It's not the old hell-for-leather creed that has taken man up the ladder, that will continue to take him up the ladder if he hangs onto it. It would wipe out all the harsher emotions and we need those harsher emotions to keep climbing. We can't lie in the sun, we can't stand still, we can't, not yet, even take the time to stand off and admire the things that we have done.

"Peace, the deeper concept of peace, is not for the human race, never was meant for the human race. Conflict is our meat. The desire to beat the other fellow to it, the hankering for glorification, the tendency to heave out one's chest and say, 'I'm the guy that done it,' the satisfaction of tackling a hard job and doing it, even looking for a hard job just for the hell of doing it."

A springtime breeze blew softly through the window. A bird sang and a hushed clock ticked.

There were faces in the blackness that loomed before the speeding spaceship. Faces that swirled in the blacknesss and shouted. All

sorts of faces. Old men and babies. Well-dressed man-about-town
and tramp in tattered rags. Women, too. Women with flying hair
and tear-streaked cheeks. All shouting, hooked hands raised
in anger.

Faces that protested. Faces that pleaded. Faces that damned
and called down curses.

Harrison Kemp passed a hand slowly across his eyes and
when he took it away the faces were gone. Only space leered
back at him.

But he couldn't shake from his mind the things those mouths
had said, the words the tongues had shaped.

"What have you done? You have taken Sanctuary from us!"

Sanctuary! Something the race had leaned upon, had counted
on, the assurance of a cure, a refuge from the mental mania that
ranged up and down the worlds.

Something that was almost God. Something that was the
people's friend – a steadying hand in the darkness. It was
something that was there, always would be there, a shining
light in a troubled world, a comforter, something that would
never change, something one could tie to.

And now?

Kemp shuddered at the thought.

One word and he could bring all that structure tumbling down
about their ears. With one blow he could take away their faith
and their assurance. With one breath he could blow Sanctuary
into a flimsy house of cards.

For him, he knew, Sanctuary was gone forever. Knowing what
he knew, he never could go back. But what about those others?
What about the ones who still believed? Might it not be better
that he left them their belief? Even if it led down a dangerous
road. Even if it were a trap.

But was it a trap? That was a thing, of course, that he could
not know. Perhaps, rather, it was the way to a better life.

Perhaps he had been wrong. Perhaps he should have stayed
and accepted what Sanctuary offered.

If a human being, as a human being, could not carry out his
own destiny, if the race were doomed to madness, if evolution

had erred in bringing man along the path he followed what then? If the human way of life were basically at fault, would it not be better to accept a change before it was too late? On what basis, after all, could mankind judge?

In years to come, working through several generations, Sanctuary might mould mankind to its pattern, might change the trend of human thought and action, point out a different road to travel.

And if that were so, who could say that it was wrong?

Bells were ringing. Not the bells he had heard back on Sanctuary, nor yet the bells he remembered of a Sunday morning in his own home town, but bells that came hauntingly from space. Bells that tolled and blotted out his thoughts.

Madness. Madness stalking the worlds. And yet, need there be madness? Findlay wasn't mad – probably never would go mad.

Kemp's brain suddenly buzzed with a crazy-quilt of distorted thought:

Sanctuary . . . Pluto . . . Johnny Gardner . . . what is life . . . we'll try again—

Unsteadily he reached out for the instrument board, but his fingers were all thumbs. His mind blurred and for one wild moment of panic he could not recognise the panel before him – for one long instant it was merely a curious object with coloured lights and many unfamiliar mechanisms.

His brain cleared momentarily and a thought coursed through it – an urgent thought. *Man need not go mad!*

Spencer Chambers! Spencer Chambers had to know!

He reached for the radio and his fingers wouldn't work. They wouldn't go where he wanted them to go.

Kemp set his teeth and fought his hand, fought it out to the radio-control knobs, made his fingers do the job his brain wanted them to do, made them work the dials, forced his mouth to say the things that must be said.

"Kemp calling Earth. Kemp calling Earth. Kemp calling —"

A voice said, "Earth. Go ahead, Kemp."

His tongue refused to move. His hand fell from the set, swayed limply at his side.

"Go ahead, Kemp," the voice urged. "Go ahead Kemp. Go ahead, Kemp."

Kemp grappled with the greyness that was dropping over him, fought it back by concentrating on the simple mechanics of making his lips and tongue move as they had to move.

"Spencer Chambers," he croaked.

"You should have stayed in Sanctuary," blared a voice in his head. *"You should have stayed. You should have —"*

"Spencer Chambers speaking," said a voice out of the radio. "What is it, Kemp?"

Kemp tried to answer, couldn't.

"Kemp!" yelled Chambers. "Kemp, where are you? What's the matter? Kemp —"

Words came from Kemp's mouth, distorted words, taking a long time to say, jerky —

"No time . . . one thing. Hunch. That's it. Chambers . . . hunch —"

"What do you mean, lad?" yelled Chambers.

"Hunches. Have to play . . . hunches. Everyone hasn't . . . got . . . them. Find . . . those . . . who . . . have —"

There was silence. Chambers was waiting. A wave of greyness blotted out the ship, blotted out space – then light came again.

Kemp gripped the side of his chair with one hand while the other swayed limply at his side. What had he been saying? Where was he? One word buzzed in his brain. What was that word?

Out of the past came a snatch of memory.

"Findlay," he said.

"Yes, what about Findaly?"

"Hunches like . . . instinct. See . . . into . . . future —"

The radio bleated at him. "Kemp! What's the matter? Go on. Do you mean hunches are a new instinct? Tell me. Kemp!"

Harrison Kemp heard nothing. The greyness had come again, blotting out everything. He sat in his chair and his hands hung dangling. His vacant eyes stared into space.

The ship drove on.

On the floor lay a stick, a club Harrison Kemp had picked up on Sanctuary.

The intercommunications set buzzed. Fumbling, Chambers snapped up the tumbler.

"Mr Allen is here," said the secretary's voice.

"Send him in," said Chambers.

Allen came in, flung his hat on the floor beside a chair, sat down.

"Boys just reported they found Kemp's ship," he said. "Easy to trace it. Radio was wide open."

"Yes?" asked Chambers.

"Loony," said Allen.

Chambers's thin lips pressed together. "I was afraid so. He sounded like it. Like he was fighting it off. And he did fight it off. Long enough, at least, to tell us what he wanted us to know."

"It's queer," Monk said, "that we never thought of it. That someone didn't think of it. It had to wait until a man on the verge of insanity could think of it."

"It may not work," said Chambers, "but it's worth a try. Hunches, he said, are instinct – a new instinct, the kind we need in the sort of world we live in. Once, long ago, we had instinct the same as animals, but we got rid of it, we got civilised and lost it. We didn't need it any longer. We substituted things for it. Like law and order, houses and other safeguards against weather and hunger and fear.

"Now we face new dangers. Dangers that accompany the kind of civilisation we have wrought. We need new instinct to protect us against those dangers. Maybe we have it in hunches or premonition or intuition or whatever name you want to hang on it. Something we've been developing for a long time, for the past ten thousand years, perhaps, never realising that he had it."

"All of us probably haven't got it," Monk reminded him. "It would be more pronounced in some of us than others."

"We'll find the ones who have it," declared Chambers. "We'll place them in key positions. The psychologists will develop tests for it. We'll see if we can't improve it, develop it. Help it along.

"You have it, Monk. It saved you when the asterites tried to get you that night in Sandebar. Something told you to heave that jewel against the manuscript case. You did it, instinctively, wondering why. You said that afterward you even speculated on why you did it, couldn't find an answer. And yet it was the proper thing to do.

"Findlay out on Pluto has it. Calls it a feeling for the future, the ability to look just a little way ahead. That looking just a way ahead will help us keep one jump beyond our problems.

"Allen has it. He investigated Sanctuary on a hunch, even felt ashamed of himself for doing it, but he went ahead and played his hunch."

"Just a second, chief," Allen interrupted. "Before you go any further there's something to be done. We got to go out and bring in Hannibal. Even if it takes the whole fleet —"

"There's no use," said Chambers.

He rose and faced them.

"Hannibal," he said, "died half an hour ago. They killed him."

Slowly he walked around the desk, felt his way across the room toward the window. Once he stumbled on a rug, once he ran into a chair.

The Big Front Yard

Hiram Taine came awake and sat up in his bed.

Towser was barking and scratching at the floor.

"Shut up," Taine told the dog.

Towser cocked quizzical ears at him and then resumed the barking and scratching at the floor.

Taine rubbed his eyes. He ran a hand through his rat's nest head of hair. He considered lying down again and pulling up the covers.

But not with Towser barking.

"What's the matter with you, anyhow?" he asked Towser, with not a little wrath.

"*Whuff*," said Towser, industriously proceeding with his scratching at the floor.

"If you want out," said Taine, "All you got to do is open the screen door. You know how it is done. You do it all the time."

Towser quit his barking and sat down heavily, watching his master getting out of bed.

Taine put on his shirt and pulled on his trousers, but didn't bother with his shoes.

Towser ambled over to a corner, put his nose down to the baseboard and snuffled moistly.

"You got a mouse?" asked Taine.

"*Whuff*," said Towser, most emphatically.

"I can't ever remember you making such a row about a mouse," Taine said, slightly puzzled. "You must be off your rocker."

It was a beautiful summer morning. Sunlight was pouring through the open window.

Good day for fishing, Taine told himself, then remembered

193

that there'd be no fishing, for he had to go out and look up that old four-poster maple bed that he had heard about up Woodman way. More than likely, he thought, they'd want twice as much as it was worth. It was getting so, he told himself, that a man couldn't make an honest dollar. Everyone was getting smart about antiques.

He got up off the bed and headed for the living room.

"Come on," he said to Towser.

Towser came along, pausing now and then to snuffle into corners and to whuffle at the floor.

"You got it bad," said Taine.

Maybe it's a rat, he thought. The house was getting old.

He opened the screen door and Towser went outside.

"Leave the woodchuck be today," Taine advised him. "It's a losing battle. You'll never dig him out."

Towser went around the corner of the house.

Taine noticed that something has happened to the sign that hung on the post beside the driveway. One of the chains had become unhooked and the sign was dangling.

He padded out across the driveway slab and the grass, still wet with dew, to fix the sign. There was nothing wrong with it – just the unhooked chain. Might have been the wind, he thought, or some passing urchin. Although probably not an urchin. He got along with kids. They never bothered him, like they did some others in the village. Banker Stevens, for example. They were always pestering Stevens.

He stood back a way to be sure the sign was straight.

It read, in big letters:

HANDY MAN

And under that, in smaller lettering:

I fix anything

And under that:

194

What have you got to trade?

Maybe, he told himself, he ought to have two signs, one for his fix-it shop and one for antiques and trading. Some day, when he had the time, he thought, he'd paint a couple of new ones. One for each side of the driveway. It would look neat that way.

He turned around and looked across the road at Turner's Woods. It was a pretty sight, he thought. A sizeable piece of woods like that right at the edge of town. It was a place for birds and rabbits and woodchucks and squirrels and it was full of forts built through generations by the boys of Willow Bend.

Some day, of course, some smart operator would buy it up and start a housing development or something equally objectionable and when that happened a big slice of his own boyhood would be cut out of his life.

Towser came around the corner of the house. He was sidling along, sniffing at the lowest row of siding and his ears were cocked with interest.

"That dog is nuts," said Taine and went inside.

He went into the kitchen, his bare feet slapping on the floor.

He filled the teakettle, set it on the stove and turned the burner on underneath the kettle.

He turned on the radio, forgetting that it was out of kilter.

When it didn't make a sound, he remembered and, disgusted, snapped it off. That was the way it went, he thought. He fixed other people's stuff, but never got around to fixing any of his own.

He went into the bedroom and put on his shoes. He threw the bed together.

Back in the kitchen the stove had failed to work again. The burner beneath the kettle still was cold.

Taine hauled off and kicked the stove. He lifted the kettle and held his palm above the burner. In a few seconds he could detect some heat.

"Worked again," he told himself.

Some day, he knew, kicking the stove would fail to work. When that happened, he'd have to get to work on it. Probably wasn't more than a loose connection.

He put the kettle back onto the stove.

There was a clatter out in front and Taine went out to see what was going on.

Beasly, the Horton's yardboy-chauffeur-gardener-et-cetera was backing a rickety old truck up the driveway. Beside him sat Abbie Horton, the wife of H. Henry Horton, the village's most important citizen. In the back of the truck, lashed on with ropes and half-protected by a garish red and purple quilt, stood a mammoth television set. Taine recognised it from of old. It was a good ten years out of date and still, by any standard, it was the most expensive set ever to grace any home in Willow Bend.

Abbie hopped out of the truck. She was an energetic, bustling, bossy woman.

"Good morning, Hiram," she said. "Can you fix this set again?"

"Never saw anything that I couldn't fix," said Taine, but nevertheless he eyed the set with something like dismay. It was not the first time he had tangled with it and he knew what was ahead.

"It might cost you more than it's worth," he warned her. "What you really need is a new one. This set is getting old and —"

"That's just what Henry said," Abbie told him, tartly. "Henry wants to get one of the colour sets. But I won't part with this one. It's not just TV, you know. It's a combination with radio and a record player and the wood and style are just right for the other furniture, and besides —"

"Yes, I know," said Taine, who'd heard it all before.

Poor old Henry, he thought. What a life the man must lead. Up at the computer plant all day long, shooting off his face and bossing everyone, then coming home to a life of petty tyranny.

"Beasly," said Abbie, in her best drill-sergeant voice, "you get right up there and get that thing untied."

196

"Yes'm," Beasly said. He was a gangling, loose-jointed man who didn't look too bright.

"And see you be careful with it. I don't want it all scratched up."

"Yes'm," said Beasly.

"I'll help," Taine offered.

The two climbed into the truck and began unlashing the old monstrosity.

"It's heavy," Abbie warned. "You two be careful of it."

"Yes'm," said Beasly.

It was heavy and it was an awkward thing to boot, but Beasly and Taine horsed it around to the back of the house and up the stoop and through the back door and down the basement stairs, with Abbie following eagle-eyed behind them, alert to the slightest scratch.

The basement was Taine's combination workshop and display room for antiques. One end of it was filled with benches and with tools and machinery and boxes full of odds and ends and piles of just plain junk were scattered everywhere. The other end housed a collection of rickety chairs, sagging bedposts, ancient highboys, equally ancient lowboys, old coal scuttles painted gold, heavy iron fireplace screens and a lot of other stuff that he had collected from far and wide for as little as he could possibly pay for it.

He and Beasly set the TV down carefully on the floor. Abbie watched them narrowly from the stairs.

"Why, Hiram," she said, excited, "you put a ceiling in the basement. It looks a whole lot better.

"Huh?" asked Taine.

"The ceiling. I said you put in a ceiling."

Taine jerked his head up and what she said was true. There was a ceiling there, but he'd never put it in.

He gulped a little and lowered his head, then jerked it quickly up and had another look. The ceiling was still there.

"It's not that block stuff," said Abbie with open admiration.

"You can't see any joints at all. How did you manage it?"

Taine gulped again and got back his voice. "Something I thought up," he told her weakly.

"You'll have to come over and do it to our basement. Our basement is a sight. Beasly put the ceiling in the amusement room, but Beasly is all thumbs."

"Yes'm," Beasly said contritely.

"When I get the time," Taine promised, ready to promise anything to get them out of there.

"You'd have a lot more time," Abbie told him acidly, "if you weren't gadding around all over the country buying up that broken-down old furniture that you call antiques. Maybe you can fool the city folks when they come driving out here, but you can't fool me."

"I make a lot of money out of some of it," Taine told her calmly.

"And lose your shirt on the rest of it," she said.

"I got some old china that is just the kind of stuff you are looking for," said Taine. "Picked it up just a day or two ago. Made a good buy on it. I can let you have it cheap."

"I'm not interested," she said and clamped her mouth tight shut.

She turned around and went back up the stairs.

"She's on the prod today," Beasly said to Taine. "It will be a bad day. It always is when she starts early in the morning."

"Don't pay attention to her," Taine advised.

"I try not to, but it ain't possible. You sure you don't need a man? I'd work for you cheap."

"Sorry, Beasly. Tell you what – come over some night soon and we'll play checkers."

"I'll do that, Hiram. You're the only one who ever asks me over. All the others ever do is laugh at me or shout."

Abbie's voice came bellowing down the stairs. "Beasly, are you coming? Don't go standing there all day. I have rugs to beat."

"Yes'm," said Beasly, starting up the stairs.

At the truck, Abbie turned on Taine with determination: "'You'll get that set fixed right away? I'm lost without it.'"

"Immediately," said Taine.

He stood and watched them off, then looked around for Towser, but the dog had disappeared. More than likely he was at the woodchuck hole again, in the woods across the road. Gone off, thought Taine, without his breakfast, too.

The teakettle was boiling furiously when Taine got back to the kitchen. He put coffee in the maker and poured in the water. Then he went downstairs.

The ceiling was still there.

He turned on all the lights and walked around the basement, staring up at it.

It was a dazzling white material and it appeared to be translucent – up to a point, that is. One could see into it, but he could not see through it. And there were no signs of seams. It was fitted neatly and tightly around the water pipes and the ceiling lights.

Taine stood on a chair and rapped his knuckles against it sharply. It gave out a bell-like sound, almost exactly as if he'd rapped a fingernail against a thinly-blown goblet.

He got down off the chair and stood there, shaking his head. The whole thing was beyond him. He had spent part of the evening repairing Banker Stevens's lawnmower and there'd been no ceiling then.

He rummaged in a box and found a drill. He dug out one of the smaller bits and fitted it in the drill. He plugged in the cord and climbed on the chair again and tried the bit against the ceiling. The whirling steel slid wildly back and forth. It didn't make a scratch. He switched off the drill and looked closely at the ceiling. There was not a mark upon it. He tried again, pressing against the drill with all his strength. The bit went *ping* and the broken end flew across the basement and hit the wall.

Taine stepped down off the chair. He found another bit and fitted it in the drill and went slowly up the stairs, trying to think. But he was too confused to think. That ceiling should not be up there, but there it was. And unless he was stark, staring crazy and forgetful as well, he had not put it there.

In the living room, he folded back one corner of the worn and faded carpeting and plugged in the drill. He knelt and started drilling in the floor. The bit went smoothly through the old oak flooring, then stopped. He put on more pressure and the drill spun without getting any bite.

And there wasn't supposed to be anything underneath that wood! Nothing to stop a drill. Once through the flooring, it should have dropped into the space between the joists.

Taine disengaged the drill and laid it to one side.

He went into the kitchen and the coffee now was ready. But before he poured it, he pawed through a cabinet drawer and found a pencil flashlight. Back in the living room he shone the light into the hole that the drill had made.

There was something shiny at the bottom of the hole.

He went back to the kitchen and found some day-old doughnuts and poured a cup of coffee. He sat at the kitchen table, eating doughnuts and wondering what to do.

There didn't appear, for the moment at least, much that he could do. He could putter around all day trying to figure out what had happened to his basement and probably not be any wiser than he was right now.

His money-making Yankee soul rebelled against such a horrid waste of time.

There was, he told himself, that maple four-poster that he should be getting to before some unprincipled city antique dealer should run afoul of it. A piece like that, he figured, if a man had any luck at all, should sell at a right good price. He might turn a handsome profit on it if he only worked it right.

Maybe, he thought, he could turn a trade on it. There was the table model TV set that he had traded a pair of ice skates for last winter. Those folks out Woodman way might conceivably be happy to trade the bed for a reconditioned TV set, almost like brand new. After all, they probably weren't using the bed and, he hoped fervently, had no idea of the value of it.

He ate the doughnuts hurriedly and gulped down an extra cup of coffee. He fixed a plate of scraps for Towser and set it outside the door. Then he went down into the basement and got the table TV set and put it in the pickup truck. As an afterthought, he added a reconditioned shotgun which would be perfectly all right if a man were careful not to use these far-reaching, powerful shells, and a few other odds and ends that might come in handy on a trade.

He got back late, for it had been a busy and quite satisfactory day. Not only did he have the four-poster loaded on the truck, but he had as well a rocking chair, a fire screen, a bundle of ancient magazines, an old-fashioned barrel churn, a walnut highboy and a Governor Winthrop on which some half-baked, slaphappy decorator had applied a coat of apple-green paint. The television set, the shotgun and five dollars had gone into the trade. And what was better yet, he'd managed it so well that the Woodman family probably was dying of laughter at this very moment about how they'd taken him.

He felt a little ashamed of it – they'd been such friendly people. They had treated him so kindly and had him stay for dinner and had sat and talked with him and shown him about the farm and even asked him to stop by if he went through that way again.

He's wasted the entire day, he thought, and he rather hated that, but maybe it had been worth it to build up his reputation out that way as the sort of character who had softening of the head and didn't know the value of a dollar. That way, maybe some other day, he could do some more business in the neighbourhood.

He heard the television set as he opened the back door, sounding loud and clear, and he went clattering down the basement stairs in something close to a panic. For now that he'd traded the table model Abbie's set was the only one downstairs and Abbie's set was broken.

It was Abbie's set, all right. It stood just where he and Beasly had put it down that morning and there was nothing wrong with it – nothing wrong at all. It was even televising colour.

Television colour!

He stopped at the bottom of the stairs and leaned against the railing for support.

The set kept on televising colour.

Taine stalked the set and walked around behind it. The back of the cabinet was off, leaning against the bench that stood behind the set, and he could see the innards of it glowing cheerily.

He squatted on the basement floor and squinted at the lighted innards and they seemed a good deal different from the way that they should be. He'd repaired the set many times before and he thought he had a good idea of what the working parts would look like. And now they all seemed different, although just how he couldn't tell.

A heavy step sounded on the stairs and a hearty voice came booming down to him.

"Well, Hiram, I see you got it fixed."

Taine jackknifed upright and stood there slightly frozen and completely speechless.

Henry Horton stood four-squarely and happily on the stairs looking very pleased.

"I told Abbie that you wouldn't have it done, but she said for me to come over anyway. Hey, Hiram, it's in colour. How did you do it, man?"

Taine grinned sickly. "I just got fiddling around," he said.

Henry came down the rest of the stairs with a stately step and stood before the set, with his hands behind his back, staring at it fixedly in his best executive manner.

He slowly shook his head, "I never would have thought," he said, "that it was possible."

"Abbie mentioned that you wanted colour."

"Well, sure. Of course I did. But not on this old set. I never would have expected to get colour on this set. How did you do it, Hiram?"

Taine told the solemn truth. "I can't rightly say," he said.

Henry found a nail keg standing in front of one of the benches and rolled it out in front of the old-fashioned set. He sat down warily and relaxed into solid comfort.

"That's the way it goes," he said. "There are men like you, but not very many of them. Just Yankee tinkerers. You keep messing around with things, trying one thing here and another there and before you know it you come up with something."

He sat on the nail keg, staring at the set.

"It's sure a pretty thing," he said. "It's better than the colour they have in Minneapolis. I dropped in at a couple of the places the last time I was there and looked at the colour sets. And I tell you honest, Hiram, there wasn't one of them that was as good as this."

Taine wiped his brow with his shirt sleeve. Somehow or other, the basement seemed to be getting warm. He was fine sweat all over.

Henry found a big cigar in one of his pockets and held it out to Taine.

"No, thanks. I never smoke."

"Perhaps you're wise," said Henry. "It's a nasty habit."

He stuck the cigar into his mouth and rolled it east to west.

"Each man to his own," he proclaimed expansively. "When it comes to a thing like this, you're the man to do it. You seem to think in mechanical contraptions and electronic circuits. Me, I don't know a thing about it. Even in the computer game, I still don't know a thing about it; I hire men who do. I can't even saw a board or drive a nail. But I can organise. You remember, Hiram, how everybody snickered when I started up the plant?"

"Well, I guess some of them did, at that."

"You're darn tooting they did. They went around for weeks with their hands up to their faces to hide smart aleck grins. They said, what does Henry think he's doing, starting up a computer factory out here in the sticks; he doesn't think he can compete with those big companies in the east, does he? And they didn't stop their grinning until I sold a couple of dozen units and had orders for a year or two ahead."

He fished a lighter from his pocket and lit the cigar carefully, never taking his eyes off the television set.

"You got something there," he said, judiciously, "that may be worth a mint of money. Some simple adaptation that will fit on any set. If you can get colour on this old wreck, you can get colour on any set that's made."

He chuckled moistly around the mouthful of cigar. "If RCA knew what was happening here this minute, they'd go out and cut their throats."

"But I don't know what I did," protested Taine.

"Well, that's all right," said Henry, happily. "I'll take this set up to the plant tomorrow and turn loose some of the boys on it. They'll find out what you have here before they're through with it."

He took the cigar out of his mouth and studied it intently, then popped it back in again.

"As I was saying, Hiram, that's the difference in us. You can do the stuff, but you miss the possibilities. I can't do a thing, but I can organise it once the thing is done. Before we get through with this, you'll be wading in twenty dollar bills clear up to your knees."

"But I don't have —"

"Don't worry. Just leave it all to me. I've got the plant and whatever money we may need. We'll figure out a split."

"That's fine of you," said Taine mechanically.

"Not at all," Henry insisted, grandly. "It's just my aggressive, grasping sense of profit. I should be ashamed of myself, cutting in on this."

He sat on the keg, smoking and watching the TV perform in exquisite colour.

"You know, Hiram," he said, "I've often thought of this, but never got around to doing anything about it. I've got an old computer up at the plant that we will have to junk because it's taking up room that we really need. It's one of our early models, a sort of experimental job that went completely sour. It sure is a screwy thing. No one's ever been able to make much out of it. We tried some approaches that probably were wrong — or maybe they were right, but we didn't know enough to make them quite come off. It's been standing in a corner all these years and I should have junked it long ago. But I sort of hate to do it. I wonder if you might not like it — just to tinker with."

"Well, I don't know," said Taine.

Henry assumed an expansive air. "No obligation, mind you.

You may not be able to do a thing with it – I'd frankly be surprised if you could, but there's no harm in trying. Maybe you'll decide to tear it down for the salvage you can get. There are several thousand dollars worth of equipment in it. Probably you could use most of it one way or another."

"It might be interesting," conceded Taine, but not too enthusiastically.

"Good," said Henry with an enthusiasm that made up for Taine's lack of it. "I'll have the boys cart it over tomorrow. It's a heavy thing. I'll send along plenty of help to get it unloaded and down into the basement and set up."

Henry stood up carefully and brushed cigar ashes off his lap.

"I'll have the boys pick up the TV set at the same time," he said. "I'll have to tell Abbie you haven't got it fixed yet. If I ever let it get into the house, the way it's working now, she'd hold onto it."

Henry climbed the stairs heavily and Taine saw him out of the door into the summer night.

Taine stood in the shadow, watching Henry's shadowed figure go across the Widow Taylor's yard to the next street behind his house. He took a deep breath of the fresh night air and shook his head to try to clear his buzzing brain, but the buzzing went right on.

Too much had happened, he told himself. Too much for any single day – first the ceiling and now the TV set. Once he had a good night's sleep he might be in some sort of shape to try to wrestle with it.

Towser came around the corner of the house and limped slowly up the steps to stand beside his master. He was mud up to his ears.

"You had a day of it, I see," said Taine. "And, just like I told you, you didn't get the woodchuck."

"*Woof*," said Towser, sadly.

"You're just like a lot of the rest us," Taine told him, severely.

205

"Like me and Henry Horton and all the rest of us. You're chasing something and you think you know what you're chasing, but you really don't. And what's even worse, you have no faint idea of why you're chasing it."

Towser thumped a tired tail upon the stoop.

Taine opened the door and stood to one side to let Towser in, then went in himself.

He went through the refrigerator and found part of a roast, a slice or two of luncheon meat, a dried-out slab of cheese and half a bowl of cooked spaghetti. He made a pot of coffee and shared the food with Towser.

Then Taine went back downstairs and shut off the television set. He found a trouble lamp and plugged it in and poked the light into the innards of the set.

He squatted on the floor, holding the lamp, trying to puzzle out what had been done to the set. It was different, of course, but it was a little hard to figure out in just what ways it was different. Someone had tinkered with the tubes and had them twisted out of shape and there were little white cubes of metal tucked here and there in what seemed to be an entirely haphazard and illogical manner – although, Taine admitted to himself, there probably was no haphazardness. And the circuit, he saw, had been rewired and a good deal of wiring had been added.

But the most puzzling thing about it was that the whole thing seemed to be just jury-rigged – as if someone had done no more than a hurried, patch-up job to get the set back in working order on an emergency and temporary basis.

Someone, he thought!

And who had that someone been?

He hunched around and peered into the dark corners of the basement and he felt innumerable and many-legged imaginary insects running on his body.

Someone had taken the back off the cabinet and leaned it against the bench and had left the screws which held the back laid neatly in a row upon the floor. Then they had jury-rigged the set and jury-rigged it far better than it had ever been before.

If this was a jury-job, he wondered, just what kind of job

would it have been if they had had the time to do it up in style?

They hadn't had the time, of course. Maybe they had been scared off when he had come home – scared off even before they could get the back off the set again.

He stood up and moved stiffly away.

First the ceiling in the morning – and now, in the evening, Abbie's television set.

And the ceiling, come to think of it, was not a ceiling only. Another liner, if that was the proper term for it, of the same material as the ceiling, had been laid beneath the floor, forming a sort of boxed-in area between the joists. He had struck that liner when he had tried to drill into the floor.

And what, he asked himself, if all the house were like that, too?

There was just one answer to it all: *There was something in the house with him!*

Towser had heard that *something* or smelled it or in some other manner sensed it and had dug frantically at the floor in an attempt to dig it out, as if it were a woodchuck.

Except that this, whatever it might be, certainly was no woodchuck.

He put away the trouble light and went upstairs.

Towser was curled up on a rug in the living room beside the easy chair and beat his tail in polite decorum in greeting to his master.

Taine stood and stared down at the dog. Towser looked back at him with satisfied and sleepy eyes, then heaved a doggish sigh and settled down to sleep.

Whatever Towser might have heard or smelled or sensed this morning, it was quite evident that as of this moment he was aware of it no longer.

Then Taine remembered something else.

He had filled the kettle to make water for the coffee and had set it on the stove. He had turned on the burner and it had worked the first time.

He hadn't had to kick the stove to get the burner going.

207

He woke in the morning and someone was holding down his feet and he sat up quickly to see what was going on.

But there was nothing to be alarmed about; it was only Towser who had crawled into bed with him and now lay sprawled across his feet.

Towser whined softly and his back legs twitched as he chased dream rabbits.

Taine eased his feet from beneath the dog and sat up, reaching for his clothes. It was early, but he remembered suddenly that he had left all of the furniture he had picked up the day before out there in the truck and should be getting it downstairs where he could start reconditioning it.

Towser went on sleeping.

Taine stumbled to the kitchen and looked out of the window and there, squatted on the back stoop, was Beasly, the Horton man-of-all-work.

Taine went to the back door to see what was going on.

"I quit them, Hiram," Beasly told him. "She kept on pecking at me every minute of the day and I couldn't do a thing to please her, so I up and quit."

"Well, come on in," said Taine. "I suppose you'd like a bite to eat and a cup of coffee."

"I was kind of wondering if I could stay here, Hiram. Just for my keep until I can find something else."

"Let's have breakfast first," said Taine, "then we can talk about it."

He didn't like it, he told himself. He didn't like it at all. In another hour or so Abbie would show up and start stirring up a ruckus about how he'd lured Beasly off. Because, no matter how dumb Beasly might be, he did a lot of work and took a lot of nagging and there wasn't anyone else in town who would work for Abbie Horton.

"Your ma used to give me cookies all the time," said Beasly. "Your ma was a real good woman, Hiram."

"Yes, she was," said Taine.

"My ma used to say that you folks were quality, not like the rest in town, no matter what kind of airs they were always putting on. She said your family was among the first settlers. Is that really true, Hiram?"

"Well, not exactly first settlers, I guess, but this house has stood here for almost a hundred years. My father used to say there never was a night during all those years that there wasn't at least one Taine beneath its roof. Things like that, it seems, meant a lot to father."

"It must be nice," said Beasly, wistfully, "to have a feeling like that. You must be proud of this house, Hiram."

"Not really proud; more like belonging. I can't imagine living in any other house."

Taine turned on the burner and filled the kettle. Carrying the kettle back, he kicked the stove. But there wasn't any need to kick it; the burner was already beginning to take on a rosy glow.

Twice in a row, Taine thought. This thing is getting better!

"Gee, Hiram," said Beasly, "this is a dandy radio."

"It's no good," said Taine. "It's broke. Haven't had the time to fix it."

"I don't think so, Hiram. I just turned it on. It's beginning to warm up."

"It's beginning to – Hey, let me see!" yelled Taine.

Beasly told the truth. A faint hum was coming from the tubes.

A voice came in, gaining in volume as the set warmed up.

It was speaking gibberish.

"What kind of talk is that?" asked Beasly.

"I don't know," said Taine, close to panic now.

First the television set, then the stove and now the radio!

He spun the tuning knob and the pointer crawled slowly across the dial face instead of spinning across as he remembered it, and station after station sputtered and went past.

He tuned in the next station that came up and it was strange lingo, too – and he knew by then exactly what he had.

Instead of $39.50 job, he had here on the kitchen table an all-band receiver like they advertised in the fancy magazines.

209

He straightened up and said to Beasly: "See if you can get someone speaking English. I'll get on with the eggs."

He turned on the second burner and got out the frying pan. He put it on the stove and found eggs and bacon in the refrigerator.

Beasly got a station that had band music playing.

"How's that?" he asked.

"That's fine," said Taine.

Towser came out from the bedroom, stretching and yawning. He went to the door and showed he wanted out.

Taine let him out.

"If I were you," he told the dog, "I'd lay off that woodchuck. You'll have all the woods dug up."

"He ain't digging after any woodchuck, Hiram."

"Well, a rabbit, then."

"Not a rabbit, either. I snuck off yesterday when I was supposed to be beating rugs. That's what Abbie got so sore about."

Taine grunted, breaking eggs into the skillet.

"I snuck away and went over to where Towser was. I talked with him and he told me it wasn't a woodchuck or a rabbit. He said it was something else. I pitched in and helped him dig. Looks to me like he found an old tank of some sort buried out there in the woods."

"Towser wouldn't dig up any tank," protested Taine. "He wouldn't care about anything except a rabbit or a wood-chuck."

"He was working hard," insisted Beasly. "He seemed to be excited."

"Maybe the woodchuck just dug his hole under this old tank or whatever it might be."

"Maybe so," Beasly agreed. He fiddled with the radio some more. He got a disk jockey who was pretty terrible.

Taine shovelled eggs and bacon onto plates and brought them to the table. He poured big cups of coffee and began buttering the toast.

"Dive in," he said to Beasly.

"This is good of you, Hiram, to take me in like this. I won't stay no longer than it takes to find a job."

"Well, I didn't exactly say —"

"There are times," said Beasly, "when I get to thinking I haven't got a friend and then I remember your ma, how nice she was to me and all —"

"Oh, all right," said Taine.

He knew when he was licked.

He brought the toast and a jar of jam to the table and sat down, beginning to eat.

"Maybe you got something I could help you with," suggested Beasly, using the back of his hand to wipe eggs of his chin.

"I have a load of furniture out in the driveway, I could use a man to help me get it down into the basement."

"I'll be glad to do that," said Beasly. "I am good and strong. I don't mind work at all. I just don't like people jawing at me."

They finished breakfast and then carried the furniture down into the basement. They had some trouble with the Governor Winthrop, for it was an unwieldly thing to handle.

When they finally horsed it down, Taine stood off and looked at it. The man, he told himself, who slapped paint onto that beautiful cherrywood had a lot to answer for.

He said to Beasly: "We have to get the paint off that thing there. And we must do it carefully. Use paint remover and a rag wrapped around a spatula and just sort of roll it off. Would you like to try it?"

"Sure, I would. Say, Hiram, what will we have for lunch?"

"I don't know," said Taine. "We'll throw something together. Don't tell me you're hungry."

"Well, it was sort of hard work, getting all that stuff down here."

"There are cookies in the jar on the kitchen shelf," said Taine. "Go and help yourself."

When Beasly went upstairs, Taine walked slowly around the basement. The ceiling, he saw, was still intact. Nothing else seemed to be disturbed.

Maybe that television set and the stove and radio, he thought,

211

was just their way of paying rent to me. And if that were the case, he told himself, whoever they might be, he'd be more than willing to let them stay right on.

He looked around some more and could find nothing wrong.

He went upstairs and called to Beasly in the kitchen.

"Come on out to the garage, where I keep the paint. We'll hunt up some remover and show you how to use it."

Beasly, a supply of cookies clutched in his hand, trotted willingly behind him.

As they rounded the corner of the house they could hear Towser's muffled barking. Listening to him, it seemed to Taine that he was getting hoarse.

Three days, he thought – or was it four?

"If we don't do something about it," he said, "that fool dog is going to get himself wore out."

He went into the garage and came back with two shovels and a pick.

"Come on," he said to Beasly. "We have to put a stop to this before we have any peace."

Towser had done himself a noble job of excavation. He was almost completely out of sight. Only the end of his considerably bedraggled tail showed out of the hole he had clawed in the forest floor.

Beasly had been right about the tank-like thing. One edge of it showed out of one side of the hole.

Towser backed out of the hole and sat down heavily, his whiskers dripping clay, his tongue hanging out of the side of his mouth.

"He says that it's about time that we showed up," said Beasly.

Taine walked around the hole and knelt down. He reached down a hand to brush the dirt off the projecting edge of Beasly's tank. The clay was stubborn and hard to wipe away, but from the feel of it the tank was heavy metal.

212

Taine picked up a shovel and rapped it against the tank. The tank gave out a clang.

They got to work, shovelling away a foot or so of topsoil that lay above the object. It was hard work and the thing was bigger than they had thought and it took some time to get it uncovered, even roughly.

"I'm hungry," Beasly complained.

Taine glanced at his watch. It was almost one o'clock.

"Run on back to the house," he said to Beasly. "You'll find something in the refrigerator and there's milk to drink."

"How about you, Hiram? Ain't you ever hungry?"

"You could bring me back a sandwich and see if you can find a trowel."

"What you want a trowel for?"

"I want to scrape the dirt off this thing and see what it is."

He squatted down beside the thing they had unearthed and watched Beasly disappear into the woods.

"Towser," he said, "this is the strangest animal you ever put to ground."

A man, he told himself, might better joke about it – if to do no more than keep his fear away.

Beasly wasn't scared, of course. Beasly didn't have the sense to be scared of a thing like this.

Twelve feet wide by twenty long and oval shaped. About the size, he thought, of a good-size living room. And there never had been a tank of that shape or size in all of Willow Bend.

He fished his jackknife out of his pocket and started to scratch away the dirt at one point on the surface of the thing. He got a square inch of free dirt and it was no metal such as he had ever seen. It looked for all the world like glass.

He kept on scraping at the dirt until he had a clean place as big as an outstretched hand.

It wasn't any metal. He'd almost swear to that. It looked like cloudy glass – like the milk-glass goblets and bowls he was always on the lookout for. There were a lot of people who were plain nuts about it and they'd pay fancy prices for it.

He closed the knife and put it back into his pocket and

213

squatted, looking at the oval shape that Towser had discovered.

And the conviction grew: Whatever it was that had come to live with him undoubtedly had arrived in this same contraption. From space or time, he thought, and was astonished that he thought it, for he'd never thought such a thing before.

He picked up his shovel and began to dig again, digging down this time, following the curving side of this alien thing that lay within the earth.

And as he dug, he wondered. What should he say about this – or should he say anything? Maybe the smartest course would be to cover it again and never breathe a word about it to a living soul.

Beasly would talk about it, naturally. But no one in the village would pay attention to anything that Beasly said. Everyone in Willow Bend knew Beasly was cracked.

Beasly finally came back. He carried three inexpertly-made sandwiches wrapped in an old newspaper and a quart bottle almost full of milk.

"You certainly took your time," said Taine, slightly irritated.

"I got interested," Beasly explained.

"Interested in what?"

"Well, there were three big trucks and they were lugging a lot of heavy stuff down into the basement. Two or three big cabinets and a lot of other junk. And you know Abbie's television set? Well, they took the set away. I told them that they shouldn't, but they took it anyway."

"I forgot," said Taine. "Henry said he'd send the computer over and I plumb forgot."

Taine ate the sandwiches, sharing them with Towser, who was very grateful in a muddy way.

Finished, Taine rose and picked up his shovel.

"Let's get to work," he said.

"But you got all that stuff down in the basement."

"That can wait," said Taine. "This job we have to finish."

It was getting dusk by the time they finished.

Taine leaned wearily on his shovel.

Twelve feet by twenty across the top and ten feet deep – and all of it, every bit of it, made of the milk-glass stuff that sounded like a bell when you whacked it with a shovel.

They'd have to be small, he thought, if there were many of them, to live in a space that size, especially if they had to stay there very long. And that fitted in, of course, for if they weren't small they couldn't now be living in the space between the basement joists.

If they were really living there, thought Taine. If it wasn't all just a lot of supposition.

Maybe, he thought, even if they had been living in the house, they might be there no longer – for Towser had smelled or heard or somehow sensed them in the morning, but by that very night he'd paid them no attention.

Taine slung his shovel across his shoulder and hoisted the pick.

"Come on," he said, "let's go. We've put in a long, hard day."

They tramped out through the brush and reached the road. Fireflies were flickering off and on in the woody darkness and the street lamps were swaying in the summer breeze. The stars were hard and bright.

Maybe they were still in the house, thought Taine. Maybe when they found out that Towser had objected to them, they had fixed it so he'd be aware of them no longer.

They probably were highly adaptive. It stood to good reason they would have to be. It hadn't taken them too long, he told himself grimly, to adapt to a human house.

He and Beasly went up the gravel driveway in the dark to put the tools away in the garage and there was something funny going on, for there was no garage.

There was no garage and there was no front on the house and the driveway was cut off abruptly and there was nothing but the curving wall of what apparently had been the end of the garage.

They came up to the curving wall and stopped, squinting unbelieving in the summer dark.

215

There was no garage, no porch, no front of the house at all. It was as if someone had taken the opposite corners of the front of the house and bent them together until they touched, folding the entire front of the building inside the curvature of the bent-together corners.

Taine now had a curved-front house. Although it was, actually, not as simple as all that, For the curvature was not in proportion to what actually would have happened in case of such a feat. The curve was long and graceful and somehow not quite apparent. It was as if the front of the house had been eliminated and an illusion of the rest of the house had been summoned to mask the disappearance.

Taine dropped the shovel and the pick and they clattered on the driveway gravel. He put his hand up to his face and wiped it across his eyes, as if to clear his eyes of something that could not possibly be there.

And when he took the hand away it had not changed a bit.

There was no front to the house.

Then he was running around the house, hardly knowing he was running, and there was a fear inside him at what had happened to the house.

But the back of the house was all right. It was exactly as it had always been.

He clattered up the stoop with Beasly and Towser running close behind him. He pushed open the door and burst into the entry and scrambled up the stairs into the kitchen and went across the kitchen in three strides to see what had happened to the front of the house.

At the door between the kitchen and the living room he stopped and his hands went out to grasp the door jamb as he stared in disbelief at the windows of the living room.

It was night outside. There could be no doubt of that. He had seen the fireflies flickering in the brush and weeds and the street lamps had been lit and the stars were out.

But a flood of sunlight was pouring through the windows of the living room and out beyond the windows lay a land that was not Willow Bend.

216

"Beasly," he gasped, "look out there in front!"

Beasly looked.

"What place is that?" he asked.

"That's what I'd like to know."

Towser had found his dish and was pushing it around the kitchen floor with his nose, by way of telling Taine that it was time to eat.

Taine went across the living room and opened the front door. The garage, he saw, was there. The pickup stood with its nose against the open garage door and the car was safe inside.

There was nothing wrong with the front of the house at all.

But if the front of the house was all right, that was all that was.

For the driveway was chopped off just a few feet beyond the tail end of the pickup and there was no yard or woods or road. There was just a desert – a flat, far-reaching desert, level as a floor, with occasional boulder piles and haphazard clumps of vegetation and all of the ground covered with sand and pebbles. A big blinding sun hung just above the horizon that seemed much too far away and a funny thing about it was that the sun was in the north, where no proper sun should be. It had a peculiar whiteness, too.

Beasly stepped out on the porch and Taine saw that he was shivering like a frightened dog.

"Maybe," Taine told him kindly, "you'd better go back in and start making us some supper."

"But, Hiram —"

"It's all right," said Taine. "It's bound to be all right."

"If you say so, Hiram."

He went in and the screen door banged behind him and in a minute Taine heard him in the kitchen.

He didn't blame Beasly for shivering, he admitted to himself. It was a sort of shock to step out of your front door into an unknown land. A man might eventually get used to it, of course, but it would take some doing.

He stepped down off the porch and walked around the truck and around the garage corner and when he rounded the corner

217

he was half prepared to walk back into familiar Willow Bend – for when he had gone in the back door the village had been there.

There was no Willow Bend. There was more of the desert, a great deal more of it.

He walked around the house and there was no back to the house. The back of the house now was just the same as the front had been before – the same smooth curve pulling the sides of the house together.

He walked on around the house to the front again and there was desert all the way. And the front was still all right. It hadn't changed at all. The truck was there on the chopped-off driveway and the garage was open and the car inside.

Taine walked out a way into the desert and hunkered down and scooped up a handful of the pebbles and the pebbles were just pebbles.

He squatted there and let the pebbles trickle through his fingers.

In Willow Bend there was a back door and there wasn't any front. Here, wherever here might be, there was a front door, but there wasn't any back.

He stood up and tossed the rest of the pebbles away and wiped his dusty hands upon his breeches.

Out of the corner of his eye he caught a sense of movement on the porch and there they were.

A line of tiny animals, if animals they were, came marching down the steps, one behind another. They were four inches high or so and they went on all four feet, although it was plain to see that their front feet were really hands, not feet. They had ratlike faces that were vaguely human, with noses long and pointed. They looked as if they might have scales instead of hide, for their bodies glistened with a rippling motion as they walked. And all of them had tails that looked very much like the coiled-wire tail one finds on certain toys and the tails stuck straight up above them, quivering as they walked.

They came down the steps in single file, in perfect military order, with half a foot or so of spacing between each one of them.

They came down the steps and walked out into the desert in a straight, undeviating line as if they knew exactly where they might be bound. There was something deadly purposeful about them and yet they didn't hurry.

Taine counted 16 of them and he watched them go out into the desert until they were almost lost to sight.

There go the ones, he thought, who came to live with me. They are the ones who fixed up the ceiling and who repaired Abbie's television set and jiggered up the stove and radio. And more than likely, too, they were the ones who had come to Earth in the strange milk-glass contraption out there in the woods.

And if they had come to Earth in that deal out in the woods, then what sort of place was this?

He climbed the porch and opened the screen door and saw the neat, 6in circle his departing guests had achieved in the screen to get out of the house. He made a mental note that some day, when he had the time, he would have to fix it.

He went in and slammed the door behind him.

"Beasly," he shouted.

There was no answer.

Towser crawled from beneath the love seat and apologised.

"It's all right, pal," said Taine. "That outfit scared me, too."

He went into the kitchen. The dim ceiling light shone on the overturned coffee pot, the broken cup in the centre of the floor, the upset bowl of eggs. One broken egg was a white and yellow gob on the linoleum.

He stepped down on the landing and saw that the screen door in the back was wrecked beyond repair. Its rusty mesh was broken – exploded might have been a better word – and a part of the frame was smashed.

Taine looked at it in wondering admiration.

"The poor fool," he said. "He went straight through it without opening it at all."

He snapped on the light and went down the basement stairs. Halfway down he stopped in utter wonderment.

To his left was a wall – a wall of the same sort of material as had been used to put in the ceiling.

219

He stooped and saw that the wall ran clear across the basement, floor to ceiling, shutting off the workshop area.

And inside the workshop, what?

For one thing, he remembered, the computer that Henry had sent over just this morning. Three trucks, Beasly had said – three truckloads of equipment delivered straight into their paws!

Taine sat down weakly on the steps.

They must have thought, he told himself, that he was co-operating! Maybe they had figured that he knew what they were about and so went along with them. Or perhaps they thought he was paying them for fixing up the TV set and the stove and radio.

But to tackle first things first, why had they repaired the TV set and the stove and radio? As a sort of rental payment? As a friendly gesture? Or as a sort of practice run to find out what they could about this world's technology? To find, perhaps, how their technology could be adapted to the materials and conditions on this planet they had found?

Taine raised a hand and rapped with his knuckles on the wall beside the stairs and the smooth white surface gave out a pinging sound.

He laid his ear against the wall and listened closely and it seemed to him he could hear a low-key humming, but if so it was so faint he could not be absolutely sure.

Banker Stevens's lawnmower was in there, behind the wall, and a lot of other stuff waiting for repair. They'd take the hide right off him, he thought, especially Banker Stevens. Stevens was a tight man.

Beasly must have been half crazed with fear, he thought. When he had seen those things coming up out of the basement, he'd gone clean off his rocker. He'd gone straight through the door without even bothering to try to open it and now he was down in the village yapping to anyone who'd stop to listen to him.

No one ordinarily would pay Beasly much attention, but if he yapped long enough and wild enough, they'd probably do some checking. They'd come storming up here and they'd give the place a going over and they'd stand goggle-eyed at what they found in front and pretty soon some of them would have worked their way around to sort of running things.

And it was none of their business, Taine stubbornly told himself, his ever-present business sense rising to the fore. There was a lot of real estate lying around out there in his front yard and the only way anyone could get to it was by going through the house. That being the case, it stood to reason that all that land out there was his. Maybe it wasn't any good at all. There might be nothing there. But before he had other people overrunning it, he'd better check and see.

He went up the stairs and out into the garage.

The sun was still just above the northern horizon and there was nothing moving.

He found a hammer and some nails and a few short lengths of plank in the garage and took them in the house.

Towser, he saw, had taken advantage of the situation and was sleeping in the gold-upholstered chair. Taine didn't bother him.

Taine locked the back door and nailed some planks across it. He locked the kitchen and the bedroom windows and nailed planks across them too.

That would hold the villagers for a while, he told himself, when they came tearing up there to see what was going on.

He got his deer rifle, a box of cartridges, a pair of binoculars and an old canteen out of a closet. He filled the canteen at the kitchen tap and stuffed a sack with food for him and Towser to eat along the way, for there was no time to wait and eat.

Then he went into the living room and dumped Towser out of the gold-upholstered chair.

"Come on Tows," he said. "We'll go and look things over."

He checked the gasoline in the pick-up and the tank was almost full.

He and the dog got in and he put the rifle within easy reach. Then he backed the truck and swung it around and headed out, north, across the desert.

It was easy travelling. The desert was as level as a floor. At times it got a little rough, but no worse than a lot of the back roads he travelled hunting down antiques.

The scenery didn't change. Here and there were low hills, but the desert itself kept on mostly level, unravelling itself into that far-off horizon. Taine kept on driving north, straight into the sun. He hit some sandy stretches, but the sand was firm and hard and he had no trouble.

Half an hour out he caught up with the band of things – all 16 of them – that had left the house. They were still travelling in line at their steady pace.

Slowing down the truck, Taine travelled parallel with them for a time, but there was no profit in it; they kept on travelling their course, looking neither right nor left.

Speeding up, Taine left them behind.

The sun stayed in the north, unmoving, and that certainly was queer. Perhaps, Taine told himself, this world spun on its axis far more slowly than the Earth and the day was longer. From the way the sun appeared to be standing still, perhaps a good deal longer.

Hunched above the wheel, staring out into the endless stretch of desert, the strangeness of it struck him for the first time with its full impact.

There was another world – there could be no doubt of that – another planet circling another star, and where it was in actual space no one on Earth could have the least idea. And yet, through some machination of those 16 things walking straight in line, it also was lying just outside the front door of his house.

Ahead of him a somewhat larger hill loomed out of the flatness of the desert. As he drew nearer to it, he made out a row of shining objects lined upon its crest. After a time he stopped the truck and got out with the binoculars.

Through the glasses, he saw that the shining things were the same sort of milk-glass contraptions as had been in the woods. He counted eight of them, shining in the sun, perched upon some sort of rock-grey cradles. And there were other cradles empty.

He took the binoculars from his eyes and stood there for a moment, considering the advisability of climbing the hill and investigating closely. But he shook his head. There'd be time for that later on. He'd better keep on moving. This was not a real exploring foray, but a quick reconnaissance.

He climbed into the truck and drove on, keeping watch upon the gas gauge. When it came close to half full he'd have to turn around and go back home again.

Ahead of him he saw a faint whiteness above the dim horizon line and he watched it narrowly. At times it faded away and then came in again, but whatever it might be was so far off he could make nothing of it.

He glanced down at the gas gauge and it was close to the halfway mark. He stopped the pick-up and got out with the binoculars.

As he moved around to the front of the machine he was puzzled at how slow and tired his legs were and then remembered – he should have been in bed many hours ago. He looked at his watch and it was two o'clock and that meant, back on Earth, two o'clock in the morning. He had been awake for more than 20 hours and much of that time he had been engaged in the back-breaking work of digging out the strange thing in the woods.

He put up the binoculars and the elusive white line that he had been seeing turned out to be a range of mountains. The great, blue, craggy mass towered up above the desert with the gleam of snow on its peaks and ridges. They were a long way off, for even the powerful glasses brought them in as little more than a misty blueness.

He swept the glasses slowly back and forth and the mountains extended for a long distance above the horizon line. He brought the glasses down off the mountains and examined the desert that stretched ahead of him. There was more of the same that he had been seeing – the same floor-like levelness, the same occasional mounds, the self-same scraggy vegetation.

And a house!

His hands trembled and he lowered the glasses, then put them up to his face again and had another look. It was a house, all right. A funny-looking house standing at the foot of one of the hillocks, still shadowed by the hillock so that one could not pick it out with the naked eye.

It seemed to be a small house. Its roof was like a blunted cone and it lay tight against the ground, as if it hugged or crouched against the ground. There was an oval opening that probably was a door, but there was no sign of windows.

He took the binoculars down again and stared at the hillock. Four or five miles away, he thought. The gas would stretch that far and even if it didn't he could walk the last few miles into Willow Bend.

It was queer, he thought, that a house should be all alone out here. In all the miles he'd travelled in the desert he'd seen no sign of life beyond the sixteen little rat-like things that marched in single file, no sign of artificial structure other than the eight milk-glass contraptions resting in their cradles.

He climbed into the pick-up and put it into gear. Ten minutes later he drew up in front of the house, which still lay within the shadow of the hillock.

He got out of the pick-up and hauled his rifle after him. Towser leaped to the ground and stood with his hackles up, a deep growl in his throat.

"What's the matter, boy?" asked Taine.

Towser growled again.

The house stood silent. It semed to be deserted.

The walls were built, Taine saw, of rude, rough masonry crudely set together, with a crumbling, mud-like substance used in lieu of mortar. The roof originally had been of sod and that was queer, indeed, for there was nothing that came close to sod upon this expanse of desert. But now, although one could see the lines where the sod strips had been fitted together, it was nothing more than earth baked hard by the desert sun.

The house itself was featureless, entirely devoid of any ornament, with no attempt at all to soften the harsh utility of it as a simple shelter. It was the sort of thing that a shepherd people might have put together. It had the look of age about it; the stone had flaked and crumbled in the weather.

Rifle slung beneath his arm, Taine paced toward it. He

reached the door and glanced inside and there was darkness and no movement.

He glanced back for Towser and saw that the dog had crawled beneath the truck and was peering out and growling.

"You stick around," said Taine. "Don't go running off."

With the rifle thrust before him, Taine stepped through the door into the darkness. He stood for a long moment to allow his eyes to become accustomed to the gloom.

Finally he could make out the room in which he stood. It was plain and rough, with a rude stone bench along one wall and queer unfunctional niches hollowed in another. One rickety piece of wooden furniture stood in a corner, but Taine could not make out what its use might be.

An old and deserted place, he thought, abandoned long ago. Perhaps a shepherd people might have lived here in some long-gone age, when the desert had been a rich and grassy plain.

There was a door into another room and as he stepped through it he heard the faint, far-off booming sound and something else as well – the sound of pouring rain! From the open door that led out through the back he caught a whiff of salty breeze and he stood there frozen in the centre of that second room.

Another one!

Another house that led to another world!

He walked slowly forward, drawn toward the outer door, and he stepped out into a cloudy, darkling day with the rain streaming down from wildly racing clouds. Half a mile away, across a field of jumbled broken, iron-grey boulders, lay a pounding sea that raged upon the coast, throwing great spumes of angry spray high into the air.

He walked out from the door and looked up at the sky, and the rain drops pounded at his face with a stinging fury. There was a chill and a dampness in the air and the place was eldritch, uncanny – a world jerked straight from some ancient Gothic tale of goblin and of sprite.

He glanced around and there was nothing he could see, for the rain blotted out the world beyond this stretch of coast, but behind

225

the rain he could sense or seemed to sense a presence that sent shivers down his spine. Gulping in fright, Taine turned around and stumbled back again through the door into the house.

One world away, he thought, was far enough; two worlds away was more than one could take. He trembled at the sense of utter loneliness that tumbled in his skull and suddenly this long-forsaken house became unbearable and he dashed out of it.

Outside the sun was bright and there was welcome warmth. His clothes were damp from rain and little beads of moisture lay on the rifle barrel.

He looked around for Towser and there was no sign of the dog. He was not underneath the pick-up; he was nowhere in sight.

He walked around the house, looking for the dog, and there was no back door to the house. The rough rock walls of the sides of the house pulled in with that funny curvature and there was no back to the house at all.

But Taine was not interested; he had known how it would be. Right now he was looking for his dog and he felt the panic rising in him. Somehow it felt a long way from home.

He spent three hours at it. He went back into the house and Towser was not there. He went into the other world again and searched among the tumbled rocks and Towser was not there. He went back to the desert and walked around the hillock and then he climbed to the crest of it and used the binoculars and saw nothing but the lifeless desert, stretching far in all directions.

Dead-beat with weariness, stumbling, half asleep even as he walked, he went back to the pick-up.

He leaned against it and tried to pull his wits together.

Continuing as he was would be a useless effort. He had to get some sleep. He had to go back to Willow Bend and fill the tank and get some extra fuel so that he could range further afield in his search for Towser.

He couldn't leave the dog out here – that was unthinkable. But he had to plan, he had to act intelligently. He would be doing Towser no good by stumbling around in his present shape.

He pulled himself into the truck and headed back for Willow

Bend, following the occasional faint impression that his tires had made in the sandy places, fighting a half-dead drowsiness that tried to seal his eyes shut.

Passing the higher hill on which the milk-glass things had stood, he stopped to walk around a bit so he wouldn't fall asleep behind the wheel. And now, he saw, there were only seven of the things resting in their cradles.

But that meant nothing to him now. All that meant anything was to hold off the fatigue that was closing down upon him, to cling to the wheel and wear and wear off the miles, to get back to Willow Bend and get some sleep and then come back again to look for Towser.

Slightly more than halfway home he saw the other car and watched in numb befuddlement, for this truck that he was driving and the car at home in his garage were the only two vehicles this side of his house.

He pulled the pick-up to a halt and tumbled out of it.

The car drew up and Henry Horton and Beasly and a man who wore a star leaped quickly out of it.

"Thank God we found you, man!" cried Henry, striding over to him.

"I wasn't lost," protested Taine. "I was coming back."

"He's all beat out," said the man who wore the star.

"This is Sheriff Hanson," Henry said. "We were following your tracks."

"I lost Towser," Taine mumbled. "I had to go and leave him. Just leave me be and go and hunt for Towser. I can make it home."

He reached out and grabbed the edge of the pick-up's door to hold himself erect.

"You broke down the door," he said to Henry. "You broke into my house and you took my car —"

"We had to do it, Hiram. We were afraid that something might have happened to you. The way that Beasly told it, it stood your hair on end."

"You better get him in the car," the sheriff said. "I'll drive the pick-up back."

"But I have to hunt for Towser!"

"You can't do anything until you've had some rest."

Henry grabbed him by the arm and led him to the car and Beasly held the rear door open.

"You got any idea what this place is?" Henry whispered conspiratorially.

"I don't positively know," Taine mumbled. "Might be some other —"

Henry chuckled. "Well, I guess it doesn't really matter. Whatever it may be, it's put us on the map. We're in all the newscasts and the papers are plastering us in headlines and the town is swarming with reporters and cameramen and there are big officials coming. Yes, sir, I tell you, Hiram, this will be the making of us —"

Taine heard no more. He was fast asleep before he hit the seat.

He came awake and lay quietly in the bed and he saw the shades were drawn and the room was cool and peaceful.

It was good, he thought, to wake in a room one knew – in a room that one had known for one's entire life, in a house that had been the Taine house for almost a hundred years.

Then memory clouted him and he sat bolt upright.

And now he heard it – the insistent murmur from outside the window.

He vaulted from the bed and pulled one shade aside. Peering out, he saw the cordon of troops that held back the crowd that overflowed his back yard and the back yards back of that.

He let the shade drop back and started hunting for his shoes, for he was fully dressed. Probably Henry and Beasly, he told himself, had dumped him into bed and pulled off his shoes and let it go at that. But he couldn't remember a single thing of it. He must have gone dead to the world the minute Henry had bundled him into the back seat of the car.

He found the shoes on the floor at the end of the bed and sat down upon the bed to pull them on.

And his mind was racing on what he had to do.

He'd have to get some petrol somehow and fill up the truck and stash an extra can or two into the back and he'd have to take some food and water and perhaps his sleeping bag. For he wasn't coming back until he found his dog.

He got on his shoes and tied them, then went out into the living room. There was no one there, but there were voices in the kitchen.

He looked out of the window and the desert lay outside, unchanged. The sun, he noticed, had climbed higher in the sky, but out in his front yard it was still forenoon.

He looked at his watch and it was six o'clock and from the way the shadows had been falling when he'd peered out of the bedroom window, he knew that it was 6.00 p.m. He realised with a guilty start that he must have slept almost around the clock. He had not meant to sleep that long. He hadn't meant to leave Towser out there that long.

He headed for the kitchen and there were three persons there – Abbie and Henry Horton and a man in military garb.

"There you are," cried Abbie merrily. "We were wondering when you would wake up."

"You have some coffee cooking, Abbie?"

"Yes, a whole pot full of it. And I'll cook up something else for you."

"Just some toast," said Taine. "I haven't got much time. I have to hunt for Towser."

"Hiram," said Henry, "this is Colonel Ryan, National Guard. He has his boys outside."

"Yes, I saw them through the window."

"Necessary," said Henry. "Absolutely necessary. The sheriff couldn't handle it. The people came rushing in and they'd have torn the place apart. So I called the governor."

"Taine," the colonel said, "sit down. I want to talk with you."

"Certainly," said Taine, taking a chair. "Sorry to be in such a rush, but I lost my dog out there."

"This business," said the colonel, smugly, "is vastly more important than any dog could be."

229

"Well, colonel, that just goes to show that you don't know Towser. He's the best dog I ever had and I've had a lot of them. Raised him from a pup and he's been a good friend all these years —"

"All right," the colonel said, "so he is a friend. But still I have to talk with you."

"You just sit and talk," Abbie said to Taine. "I'll fix up some cakes and Henry brought over some of that sausage that we get out on the farm."

The back door opened and Beasly staggered in to the accompaniment of a terrific metallic banging. He was carrying three empty five-gallon gas cans in one hand and two in the other hand and they were bumping and banging together as he moved.

"Say," yelled Taine, "what's going on here?"

"Now, just take it easy," Henry said. "You have no idea the problems that we have. We wanted to get a big gas tank moved through here, but we couldn't do it. We tried to rip out the back of the kitchen to get it through, but we couldn't."

"You did what?"

"We tried to rip out the back of the kitchen," Henry told him calmly. "You can't get one of those big storage tanks through an ordinary door. But when we tried, we found that the entire house is boarded up inside with the same kind of material that you used down in the basement. You hit it with an axe and it blunts the steel —"

"But, Henry, this is my house and there isn't anyone who has the right to start tearing it apart."

"Fat chance," the colonel said. "What I would like to know, Taine, what is that stuff that we couldn't break through?"

"Now you take it easy, Hiram," cautioned Henry. "We have a big new world waiting for us out there —"

"It isn't waiting for you or anyone," yelled Taine.

"And we have to explore it and to explore it we need a stockpile of gasoline. So since we can't have a storage tank, we're getting together as many gas cans as possible and then we'll run a hose through here —"

"But, Henry —"

"I wish," said Henry sternly, "that you'd quit interrupting me and let me have my say. You can't even imagine the logistics that we face. We're bottlenecked by the size of a regulation door. We have to get supplies out there and we have to get transport. Cars and trucks won't be so bad. We can disassemble them and lug them through piecemeal, but a plane will be a problem."

"You listen to me, Henry. There isn't anyone going to haul a plane through here. This house has been in my family for almost a hundred years and I own it and I have a right to it and you can't come in high-handed and start hauling stuff through it."

"But," said Henry plaintively, "we need a plane real bad. You can cover so much more ground when you have a plane."

Beasly went banging through the kitchen with his cans and out into the living room.

The colonel sighed. "I had hoped, Mr Taine, that you would understand how the matter stood. To me it seems very plain that it's your patriotic duty to co-operate with us in this. The government, of course, could exercise the right of eminent domain and start condemnation action, but it would rather not do that. I'm speaking unofficially, of course, but I think it's safe to say the government would much prefer to arrive at an amicable agreement."

"I doubt," Taine said, bluffing, not knowing anything about it, "that the right to eminent domain would be applicable. As I understand it, it applies to buildings and to road —"

"This is a road," the colonel told him flatly. "A road right through your house to another world."

"First," Taine declared, "the government would have to show it was in the public interest and that refusal of the owner to relinquish title amounted to an interference in government procedure and —"

"I think," the colonel said, "that the government can prove it is in the public interest."

"I think," Taine said angrily, "I better get a lawyer."

"If you really mean that," Henry offered, ever helpful, "and you want to get a good one – and I presume you do – I would be

231

pleased to recommend a firm that I am sure would represent your interests most ably and be, at the same time, fairly reasonable in cost."

The colonel stood up, seething. "You'll have a lot to answer, Taine. There'll be a lot of things the government will want to know. First of all, they'll want to know just how you engineered this. Are you ready to tell that?"

"No," said Taine, "I don't believe I am."

And he thought with some alarm: They think that I'm the one who did it and they'll be down on me like a pack of wolves to find out just how I did it. He had visions of the FBI and the State Department and the Pentagon and, even sitting down, he felt shaky in the knees.

The colonel turned around and marched stiffly from the kitchen. He went out the back and slammed the door behind him.

Henry looked at Taine speculatively.

"Do you really mean it?" he demanded. "Do you intend to stand up to them?"

"I'm getting sore," said Taine. "They can't come in here and take over without even asking me. I don't care what anyone may think, this is my house. I was born here and I've lived here all my life and I like the place and —"

"Sure," said Henry. "I know just how you feel."

"I suppose it's childish of me, but I wouldn't mind so much if they showed a willingness to sit down and talk about what they meant to do once they'd taken over. But there seems no disposition to even ask me what I think about it. And I tell you, Henry, this is different than it seems. This isn't a place where we can walk in and take over, no matter what Washington may think. There's something out there and we better watch our step —"

"I was thinking," Henry interrupted, "as I was sitting here, that your attitude is most commendable and deserving of support. It has occurred to me that it would be most unneighbourly of me to go on sitting here and leave you in the fight alone. We could hire ourselves a fine array of legal talent and we could fight the case and in the meantime we could form a land and development

232

company and that way we could make sure that this new world of yours is used the way it should be used.

"It stands to reason, Hiram, that I am the one to stand beside you, shoulder to shoulder in this business since we're already partners in this TV deal."

"What's this about TV?" shrilled Abbie, slapping a plate of cakes down in front of Taine.

"Now, Abbie," Henry said patiently, "I have explained to you already that your TV set was down in the basement and they took it out."

"Yes, I know," said Abbie, bringing a platter of sausages and pouring a cup of coffee.

Beasly came in from the living room and went bumbling out the back.

"After all," said Henry, pressing his advantage, "I would suppose I had some hand in it. I doubt you could have done much without the computer I sent over."

And there it was again, thought Taine. Even Henry thought he'd been the one who did it.

"But didn't Beasly tell you?"

"Beasly said a lot, but you know how Beasly is."

And that was it, of course. To the villagers it would be no more than another Beasly story – another whopper that Beasly had dreamed up. There was no one who believed a word that Beasly said.

Taine picked up the cup and drank his coffee, gaining time to shape an answer and there wasn't any answer. If he told the truth, it would sound far less believable than any lie he'd tell.

"You can tell me, Hiram. After all, we're partners."

He's playing me for a fool, thought Taine. Henry thinks he can play anyone he wants for a fool and sucker.

"You wouldn't believe me if I told you, Henry."

"Well," Henry said, resignedly, getting to his feet, "I guess that part of it can wait."

Beasly came tramping and banging through the kitchen with another load of cans.

233

"I'll have to have some gasoline," said Taine, "if I'm going out for Towser."

"I'll take care of that right away," Henry promised smoothly. "I'll send Ernie over with his tank wagon and we can run a hose through here and fill up those cans. And I'll see if I can find someone who'll go along with you."

"That's not necessary. I can go alone."

"If we had a radio transmitter. Then you could keep in touch."

"But we haven't any. And, Henry, I can't wait. Towser's out there somewhere —"

"Sure, I know how much you thought of him. You go out and look for him if you think you have to and I'll get started on this other business. I'll get some lawyers lined up and we'll draw up some sort of corporate papers for our land development —"

"And, Hiram," Abbie said, "will you do something for me, please?"

"Why, certainly," said Taine.

"Would you speak to Beasly. It's senseless the way he's acting. There wasn't any call for him to up and leave us. I might have been a little sharp with him, but he's so simple-minded he's infuriating. He ran off and spent half a day helping Towser at digging out that woodchuck and —"

"I'll speak to him," said Taine.

"Thanks, Hiram. He'll listen to you. You're the only one he'll listen to. And I wish you could have fixed my TV set before all this came about. I'm just lost without it. It leaves a hole in the living room. It matched my furniture, you know."

"Yes I know," said Taine.

"Coming, Abbie?" Henry asked, standing at the door.

He lifted a hand in a confidential farewell to Taine. "I'll see you later, Hiram. I'll get it all fixed up."

I just bet you will, thought Taine.

He went back to the table, after they were gone, and sat down heavily in a chair.

The front door slammed and Beasly came panting in, excited.

234

"Towser's back," he yelled. "He's coming back and he's driving in the biggest woodchuck you ever clapped your eyes on."

Taine leaped to his feet.

"Woodchuck! That's an alien planet. It hasn't any woodchucks."

"You come and see," yelled Beasly.

He turned and raced back out again, with Taine following close behind.

It certainly looked considerably like a woodchuck – a sort of man-size woodchuck. More like a woodchuck out of a children's book, perhaps, for it was walking on its hind legs and trying to look dignified even while it kept a weather eye on Towser.

Towser was back a hundred feet or so, keeping a wary distance from the massive chuck. He had the pose of a good shepherding dog, walking in a crouch, alert to head off any break that the chuck might make.

The chuck came up close to the house and stopped. Then it did an about-face so that it looked back across the desert and it hunkered down.

It swung its massive head to gaze at Beasly and Taine and in the limpid brown eyes Taine saw more than the eyes of an animal.

Taine walked swiftly out and picked up the dog in his arms and hugged him tight against him. Towser twisted his head around and slapped a sloppy tongue across his master's face.

Taine stood with the dog in his arms and looked at the man-size chuck and felt great relief and an utter thankfulnesss.

Everything was all right now, he thought. Towser had come back.

He headed for the house and out into the kitchen.

He put Towser down and got a dish and filled it at the tap. He placed it on the floor and Towser lapped at it thirstily, slopping water all over the linoleum.

"Take it easy, there," warned Taine. "You don't want to overdo it."

He hunted in the refrigerator and found some scraps and put them in Towser's dish.

Towser wagged his tail with doggish happiness.

"By rights," said Taine, "I ought to take a rope to you, running off like that."

Beasly came ambling in.

"That chuck is a friendly cuss," he announced. "He's waiting for someone."

"That's nice," said Taine, paying no attention.

He glanced at the clock.

"It's seven-thirty," he said. "We can catch the news. You want to get it, Beasly?"

"Sure. I know right where to get it. That fellow from New York."

"That's the one," said Taine.

He walked into the living room and looked out of the window. The man-size chuck had not moved. He was sitting with his back to the house, looking back the way he'd come.

Waiting for someone, Beasly had said, and it looked as if he might be, but probably it was all just in Beasly's head.

And if he were waiting for someone, Taine wondered, who might that someone be? *What* might that someone be? Certainly by now the word had spread out that there was a door into another world. And how many doors, he wondered, had been opened through the ages?

Henry had said that there was a big new world out there waiting for Earthmen to move in. And that wasn't it at all. It was the other way around.

The voice of the news commentator came blasting from the radio in the middle of a sentence:

". . . finally got into the act. Radio Moscow said this evening that the Soviet delegate will make representations in the UN tomorrow for the internationalisation of this other world and the gateway to it.

"From that gateway itself, the home of a man named Hiram Taine, there is no news. Complete security had been clamped down and a cordon of troops form a solid wall around the house, holding back the crowds. Attempts to telephone the residence are blocked by a curt voice which says that no calls

236

are being accepted for that number. And Taine himself has not stepped from the house."

Taine walked back into the kitchen and sat down.

"He's talking about you," Beasly said importantly.

"Rumour circulated this morning that Taine, a quiet village repair man and dealer in antiques, and until yesterday a relative unknown, had finally returned from a trip which he made out into this new unknown land. But what he found, if anything, no one yet can say. Nor is there any further information about this other place beyond the fact that it is a desert and, at the moment, lifeless.

"A small flurry of excitement was occasioned late yesterday by the finding of some strange object in the woods across the road from the residence, but this area likewise was swiftly cordoned off and at the moment Colonel Ryan, who commands the troops, will say nothing of what actually was found.

"Mystery man of the entire situation is one Henry Horton, who seems to be the only unofficial person to have entry to the Taine house. Horton, questioned earlier today, had little to say, but managed to suggest an air of great conspiracy. He hinted he and Taine were partners in some mysterious venture and left hanging in mid-air the half impression that he and Taine had collaborated in opening the new world.

"Horton, it is interesting to note, operates a small computer plant and it is understood on good authority that only recently he delivered a computer to Taine, or at least some sort of machine to which considerable mystery is attached. One story is that this particular machine had been in the process of development for six or seven years.

"Some of the answers to the matter of how all this did happen must wait upon the findings of a team of scientists who left Washington this evening after an all-day conference at the White House, which was attended by representatives from the military, the State Department, the security division and the special weapons section.

"Throughout the world the impact of what happened yesterday at Willow Bend can only be compared with the sensation of the news of the dropping of the first atomic bomb. There is some tendency among many observers to believe that the implications of Willow Bend, in fact, may be even more earth-shaking than were those at Hiroshima.

"Washington insists, as is only natural, that this matter is of internal concern only and that it intends to handle the situation as it best affects the national welfare.

"But abroad there is a rising storm of insistence that this is not a matter of national policy concerning one nation, but that it necessarily must be a matter of worldwide concern.

"There is an unconfirmed report that a UN observer will arrive in Willow Bend almost momentarily. France, Britain, Bolivia, Mexico and India have already requested permission of Washington to send observers to the scene and other nations undoubtedly plan to file similar requests.

"The world sits on edge tonight, waiting for the word from Willow Bend and —"

Taine reached out and clicked the radio to silence.

"From the sound of it," said Beasly, "we're going to be overrun by a batch of foreigners."

Yes, thought Taine, there might be a batch of foreigners, but not exactly in the sense that Beasly meant. The use of the word, he told himself, so far as any human was concerned, must be outdated now. No man of Earth ever again could be called a foreigner with alien life next door – literally next door. What were the people of the stone house?

And perhaps not the alien life of one planet only, but the alien life of many. For he himself had found another door into yet another planet and there might be many more such doors and what would these other worlds be like, and what was the purpose of the doors?

Someone, *something*, had found a way of going to another planet short of spanning light years of lonely space – a simpler and a shorter way than flying through the gulfs of space. And once the way was open, then the way stayed open and it was as easy as walking from one room to another.

But one thing – one ridiculous thing – kept puzzling him

238

and that was the spinning and the movement of the connected planets, of all the planets that must be linked together. You could not, he argued, establish solid, factual links between two objects that move independently of one another.

And yet, a couple of days ago, he would have contended just as stolidly that the whole idea on the face of it was fantastic and impossible. Still it had been done. And once one impossibility was accomplished, what logical man could say with sincerity that the second could not be?

The doorbell rang and he got up to answer it. It was Ernie, the oil man.

"Henry said you wanted some gas and I came to tell you I can't get it until morning."

"That's all right," said Taine. "I don't need it now."

And swiftly slammed the door.

He leaned against it, thinking: I'll have to face them sometime. I can't keep the door locked against the world. Sometime, sooner or later, the Earth and I will have to have this out.

And it was foolish, he thought, for him to think like this, but that was the way it was.

He had something here that the Earth demanded; something that Earth wanted or thought it wanted. And yet, in the last analysis, it was his responsibility. It had happened on his land, it had happened in his house; unwittingly, perhaps, he'd even aided and abetted it.

And the land and house are mine, he fiercely told himself, and that world out there was an extension of his yard. No matter how far or where it went, an extension of his yard.

Beasly had left the kitchen and Taine walked into the living room. Towser was curled up and snoring gently in the gold-upholstered chair.

Taine decided he would let him stay there. After all, he thought, Towser had won the right to sleep anywhere he wished.

He walked past the chair to the window and the desert stretched to its far horizon and there before the window sat the man-size woodchuck and Beasly side by side, with their backs turned to the window and staring out across the desert.

Somehow it seemed natural that the chuck and Beasly should be sitting there together – the two of them, it appeared to Taine, might have a lot in common.

And it was a good beginning – that a man and an alien creature from this other world should sit down companionably together.

He tried to envision the set-up of these linked worlds, of which Earth was now a part, and the possibilities that lay inherent in the fact of linkage rolled thunder through his brain.

There would be contact between the Earth and these other worlds and what would come of it?

And come to think of it, the contact had been made already, but so naturally, so undramatically, that it failed to register as a great, important meeting. For Beasly and the chuck out there were contact and if it all should go like that, there was absolutely nothing for one to worry over.

This was no haphazard business, he reminded himself. It had been planned and executed with the smoothness of long practice. This was not the first world to be opened and it would not be the last.

The little rat-like things had spanned space – how many light years of space one could not even guess – in the vehicle which he had unearthed out in the woods. They then had buried it, perhaps as a child might hide a dish by shoving it into a pile of sand. Then they had come to this very house and had set up the apparatus that had made this house a tunnel between one world and another. And once that had been done, the need of crossing space had been cancelled out forever. There need be but one crossing and that one crossing would serve to link the planets.

And once the job was done the little rat-like things had left, but not before they had made certain that this gateway to their planet would stand against no matter what assault. They had sheathed the house inside the studdings with a wonder material that would resist an axe and that, undoubtedly, would resist much more than a simple axe.

And they had marched in drill order, single file out to the

hill where eight more of the space machines had rested in their cradles. And now there were only seven there, in their cradles on the hill, and the rat-like things were gone and, perhaps, in time to come, they'd land on another planet and another doorway would be opened, a link to yet another world.

But more, Taine thought, than the linking of mere worlds. It would be, as well, the linking of the peoples of those worlds.

The little rat-like creatures were the explorers and the pioneers who sought out other Earth-like planets and the creature waiting with Beasly just outside the window must also serve its purpose and perhaps in time to come there would be a purpose which man would also serve.

He turned away from the window and looked around the room and the room was exactly as it had been ever since he could remember it. With all the change outside, with all that was happening outside, the room remained unchanged.

This is the reality, thought Taine, this is all the reality there is. Whatever else may happen, this is where I stand – this room with its fireplace blackened by many winter fires, the bookshelves with the old thumbed volumes, the easy chair, the ancient worn carpet – worn by beloved and unforgotten feet through the many years.

And this also, he knew, was the lull before the storm.

In just a little while the brass would start arriving – the team of scientists, the governmental functionaries, the military, the observers from the other countries, the officials from the UN.

And against all these, he realised, he stood weaponless and shorn of his strength. No matter what a man might say or think, he could not stand off the world.

This was the last day that this would be the Taine house. After almost a hundred years, it would have another destiny.

And for the first time in all those years there'd be no Taine asleep beneath its roof.

He stood looking at the fireplace and the shelves of books and he sensed the old, pale ghosts walking in the room and he lifted a hesitant hand as if to wave farewell, not only to

241

the ghosts but to the room as well. But before he got it up, he dropped it to his side.

What was the use, he thought.

He went out to the porch and sat down on the steps.

Beasly heard him and turned around.

"He's nice," he said to Taine, patting the chuck upon the back. "He's exactly like a great big teddy bear."

"Yes, I see," said Taine.

"And best of all, I can talk with him."

"Yes, I know," said Taine, remembering that Beasly could talk with Towser, too.

He wondered what it would be like to live in the simple world of Beasly. At times, he decided, it would be comfortable.

The rat-like things had come in the spaceship, but why had they come to Willow Bend, why had they picked this house, the only house in all the village where they would have found the equipment that they needed to built their apparatus so easily and so quickly? For there was no doubt that they had cannibalised the computer to get the equipment they needed. In that, at least, Henry had been right. Thinking back on it, Henry, after all, had played quite a part in it.

Could they have foreseen that on this particular week in this particular house the probability of quickly and easily doing what they had come to do had stood very high?

Did they, with all their other talents and technology, have clairvoyance as well?

"There's someone coming," Beasly said.

"I don't see a thing."

"Neither do I," said Beasly, "but Chuck told me that he saw them."

"Told you!"

"I told you we been talking. There, I can see them too."

They were far off, but they were coming fast – three dots rode rapidly out of the desert.

He sat and watched them come and he thought of going in to get the rifle, but he didn't stir from his seat upon the steps. The rifle would do no good, he told himself. It would be a senseless thing to get it; more than that, a senseless attitude. The least that man could do, he thought, was to meet these creatures of another world with clean and empty hands.

They were closer now and it seemed to him that they were sitting in invisible chairs that travelled very fast.

He saw that they were humanoid, to a degree at least, and there were only three of them.

They came in with a rush and stopped very suddenly a hundred feet or so from where he sat upon the steps.

He didn't move or say a word – there was nothing he could say. It was too ridiculous.

They were, perhaps, a little smaller than himself, and black as the ace of spades, and they wore skin-tight shorts and vests that were somewhat oversize and both the shorts and vests were the blue of April skies.

But that was not the worst of it.

They sat on saddles, with horns in front and stirrups and a sort of bedroll tied on the back, but they had no horses.

The saddles floated in the air, with the stirrups about 3ft above the ground and the aliens sat easily in the saddles and stared at him and he stared back at them.

Finally he got up and moved forward a step or two and when he did that the three swung from the saddles and moved forward, too, while the saddles hung there in the air, exactly as they'd left them.

Taine walked forward and the three walked forward until they were no more than 6ft apart.

"They say hello to you," said Beasly. "They say welcome to you."

"Well, all right, then, tell them – Say, how do you know all this?"

"Chuck tells me what they say and I tell you. You tell me and I tell him and he tells them. That's the way it works. That is what he's here for."

"Well, I'll be —" said Taine. "So you can really talk to him."

"I told you that I could," stormed Beasly. "I told you that

I could talk to Towser, too, but you thought that I was crazy."

"Telepathy," said Taine. And it was worse than ever now. Not only had the rat-like things known all the rest of it, but they'd known of Beasly, too.

"What was that you said, Hiram?"

"Never mind," said Taine. "Tell that friend of yours to tell them I'm glad to meet them and what can I do for them?"

He stood uncomfortably and stared at the three and he saw that their vests had many pockets and that the pockets were crammed, probably with their equivalent of tobacco and handkerchiefs and pocket knives and such.

"They say," said Beasly, "that they want to dicker."

"Dicker?"

"Sure, Hiram. You know, trade."

Beasly chuckled thinly. "Imagine them laying themselves open to a Yankee trader. That's what Henry says you are. He says you can skin a man on the slickest –"

"Leave Henry out of this," snapped Taine. "Let's leave Henry out of something."

He sat down on the ground and the three sat down to face him.

"Ask them what they have in mind to trade."

"Ideas," Beasly said.

"Ideas! That's a crazy thing —"

And then he saw it wasn't.

Of all the commodities that might be exchanged by an alien people, ideas would be the most valuable and the easiest to handle. They'd take no cargo room and they'd upset no economies – not immediately, that is – and they'd make a bigger contribution to the welfare of the cultures than trade in actual goods.

"Ask them," said Taine, "what they'll take for the idea back of those saddles they are riding."

"They say, what have you to offer?"

And that was the stumper. That was the one that would be hard to answer.

244

Automobiles and trucks, the internal gas engine – well, probably not. Because they already had the saddles. Earth was out of date in transportation from the viewpoint of these people.

Housing architecture – no, that was hardly an idea and, anyhow, there was that other house, so they knew of houses.

Cloth? No, they had cloth.

Paint, he thought. Maybe paint was it.

"See if they are interested in paint," Taine told Beasly.

"They say, what is it? Please explain yourself."

"OK, then. Let's see. It's a protective device to be spread over almost any surface. Easily packaged and easily applied. Protects against weather and corrosion. It's decorative, too. Comes in all sorts of colours. And it's cheap to make."

"They shrug in their mind," said Beasly. "They're just slightly interested. But they'll listen more. Go ahead and tell them."

And that was more like it, thought Taine.

That was the kind of language that he could understand.

He settled himself more firmly on the ground and bent forward slightly, flicking his eyes across the three deadpan, ebony faces, trying to make out what they might be thinking.

There was no making out. Those were three of the deadest pans he had ever seen.

It was all familiar. It made him feel at home. He was in his element.

And in the three across from him, he felt somehow subconsciously, he had the best dickering opposition he had ever met. And that made him feel good too.

"Tell them," he said, "that I'm not quite sure. I may have spoken up too hastily. Paint, after all, is a mighty valuable idea."

"They say, just as a favour to them, not that they're really interested, would you tell them a little more."

Got them hooked, Taine told himself. If he could only play it right —

He settled down to dickering in earnest.

*　　*　　*

245

Hours later Henry Horton showed up. He was accompanied by a very urbane gentleman, who was faultlessly turned out and who carried beneath his arm an impressive attaché case.

Henry and the man stopped on the steps in sheer astonishment.

Taine was squatted on the ground with a length of board and he was daubing paint on it while the aliens watched. From the daubs here and there upon their anatomies, it was plain to see the aliens had been doing some daubing of their own. Spread all over the ground were other lengths of half-painted boards and a couple of dozen old cans of paint.

Taine looked up and saw Henry and the man.

"I was hoping," he said, "that someone would show up."

"Hiram," said Henry, with more importance than usual, "may I present Mr Lancaster. He is special representative of the United Nations."

"I'm glad to meet you, sir," said Taine. "I wonder if you would —"

"Mr Lancaster," Henry explained grandly, "was having some slight difficulty getting through the lines outside, so I volunteered my services. I've already explained to him our joint interest in this matter."

"It was very kind of Mr Horton," Lancaster said. "There was this stupid sergeant —"

"It's all in knowing," Henry said, "how to handle people."

The remark, Taine noticed, was not appreciated by the man from the UN.

"May I inquire, Mr Taine," asked Lancaster, "exactly what you're doing?"

"I'm dickering," said Taine.

"Dickering. What a quaint way of expressing —"

"An old Yankee word," said Henry quickly, "with certain connotations of its own. When you trade with someone you are exchanging goods, but if you're dickering with him you're out to get his hide."

"Interesting," said Lancaster. "And I suppose you're out to skin these gentlemen in the sky-blue vests —"

246

"Hiram," said Henry, proudly, "is the sharpest dickerer in these parts. He runs an antique business and he has to dicker hard —"

"And may I ask," said Lancaster, ignoring Henry finally, "what you might be doing with these cans of paint? Are these gentlemen potential customers for paint or —"

Taine threw down the board and rose angrily to his feet.

"If you'd both shut up!" he shouted. "I've been trying to say something ever since you got here and I can't get in a word. And I tell you, it's important —"

"Hiram!" Henry exclaimed in horror.

"It's quite all right," said the UN man. "We *have* been jabbering. And now, Mr Taine?"

"I'm backed into a corner," Taine told him, "and I need some help. I've sold these fellows on the idea of paint, but I don't know a thing about it – the principle back of it or how it's made or what goes into it or —"

"But, Mr Taine, if you're selling them the paint, what difference does it make —"

"I'm not selling them the paint," yelled Taine. "Can't you understand that? They don't want the paint. They want the *idea* of paint, the principle of paint. It's something that they never thought of and they're interested. I offered them the paint idea for the idea of their saddles and I've almost got it —"

"Saddles? You mean those things over there, hanging in the air?"

"That is right. Beasly. Would you ask one of our friends to demonstrate a saddle?"

"You bet I will," said Beasly.

"What," demanded Henry, "has Beasly got to do with this?"

"Beasly is an interpreter. I guess you'd call him a telepath. You remember how he always claimed he could talk with Towser?"

"Beasly was always claiming things."

"But this time he was right. He tells Chuck, that funny-looking monster, what I want to say and Chuck tells these aliens. And these aliens tell Chuck and Chuck tells Beasly and Beasly tells me."

"Ridiculous!" snorted Henry. "Beasly hasn't got the sense to be . . . what did you say he was?"

"A telepath," said Taine.

One of the aliens had gotten up and climbed into a saddle. He rode it forth and back. Then he swung out of it and sat down again.

"Remarkable," said the UN man. "Some sort of anti-gravity unit, with complete control. We could make use of that, indeed."

He scraped his hand across his chin.

"And you're going to exchange the idea of paint for the idea of that saddle?"

"That's exactly it," said Taine, "but I need some help. I need a chemist or a paint manufacturer or someone to explain how paint is made. And I need some professor or other who'll understand what they're talking about when they tell me the idea of the saddle."

"I see," said Lancaster. "Yes, indeed, you have a problem. Mr Taine, you seem to me a man of some discernment."

"Oh, he's all of that," interrupted Henry. "Hiram's quite astute."

"So I suppose you'll understand," said the UN man, "that this whole procedure is quite irregular —"

"But it's not," exploded Taine. "That's the way they operate. They open up a planet and then they exchange ideas. They've been doing that with other planets for a long, long, time. And ideas are all they want, just the new ideas, because that is the way to keep on building a technology and culture. And they have a lot of ideas, sir, that the human race can use."

"That is just the point," said Lancaster. "This is perhaps the most important thing that has ever happened to us humans. In just a short year's time we can obtain data and ideas that will put us ahead – theoretically, at least – by a thousand years. And in a thing that is so important, we should have experts on the job —"

"But," protested Henry, "you can't find a man who'll do a better dickering job than Hiram. When you dicker with him

248

your back teeth aren't safe. Why don't you leave him be? He'll do a job for you. You can get your experts and your planning groups together and let Hiram front for you. These folks have accepted him and have proved they'll do business with him and what more do you want? All he needs is a little help."

Beasly came over and faced the UN man.

"I won't work with no one else," he said. "If you kick Hiram out of here, then I go with him. Hiram's the only person who ever treated me like a human —"

"There, you see," Henry said, triumphantly.

"Now, wait a second, Beasly," said the UN man. "We could make it worth your while. I should imagine that an interpreter in a situation such as this could command a handsome salary."

"Money don't mean a thing to me," said Beasly. "It won't buy me friends. People still will laugh at me."

"He means it, mister," Henry warned. "There isn't anyone who can be stubborn as Beasly. I know; he used to work for us."

The UN man looked flabbergasted and not a little desperate.

"It will take you quite some time," Henry pointed out, "to find another telepath – leastwise one who can talk to these people here."

The UN man looked as if he were strangling. "I doubt," he said, "there's another one on Earth."

"Well, all right," said Beasly, brutally, "let's make up our minds. I ain't standing here all day."

"All right," cried the UN man. "You two go ahead. Please, will you go ahead? This is a chance we can't let slip through our fingers. Is there anything you want? Anything I can do for you?"

"Yes, there is," said Taine. "There'll be the boys from Washington and bigwigs from other countries. Just keep them off my back."

"I'll explain most carefully to everyone. There'll be no interference."

"And I need that chemist and someone who'll know about the saddle. And I need them quick. I can stall these boys a little longer, but not for too much longer."

"Anyone you need," said the UN man. "Anyone at all. I'll have them here in hours. And in a day or two there'll be a pool of experts waiting for whenever you may need them – on a moment's notice."

"Sir," said Henry, unctuously, "that's most co-operative. Both Hiram and I appreciate it greatly. And now, since this is settled, I understand that there are reporters waiting. They'll be interested in your statement."

The UN man, it seemed, didn't have it in him to protest. He and Henry went tramping up the stairs.

Taine turned around and looked out across the desert.

"It's a big front yard," he said.